Feb 2009
Concord MA

Denton Welch was born on 29 March 1915 in Shanghai, where his father was a businessman. He was the youngest of three brothers and particularly close to his American mother, an enthusiastic Christian Scientist who was to die when he was eleven. Welch was sent back to England to attend St Michael's prep school in Uckfield, and then Repton School, where his main achievements were in art. Soon after his sixteenth birthday he ran away from school, an episode later described in his first autobiographical book, *Maiden Voyage* (Routledge, 1943). With his family's approval he enrolled at the Goldsmiths' School of Art in April 1933 to study painting. He showed great promise as an artist but in June 1935, while still a student, he was knocked off his bicycle by a motorist, severely damaging his spine and kidneys; for the rest of his life he was a semi-invalid. The accident and his long convalescence, minutely detailed, form the basis of *A Voice Through a Cloud*, which was unfinished at his death and first published in 1950 by John Lehmann.

Welch settled in Kent, in a succession of rented flats and cottages. His final home was Middle Orchard in the village of Crouch, where his faithful friend Eric Oliver – eventually his literary executor – cared for him until his premature death on 30 December 1948. In the last five years of his life Welch received much encouragement from other writers, notably Edith Sitwell, E. M. Forster and Herbert Read, and the majority of his work dates from this period. After *Maiden Voyage* was given enthusiastic reviews, his reputation as a writer increased rapidly and was further enhanced by *In Youth is Pleasure* (Routledge, 1945). His remaining stories were published in *Brave and Cruel* (Hamish Hamilton, 1949) and *A Last Sheaf* (John Lehmann, 1951), which also included poems and reproductions of paintings. Other posthumous publications were *The Denton Welch Journals*, edited by Jocelyn Brooke (Hamish Hamilton, 1952) and a collection of poems, *Dumb Instrument* (Enitharmon Press, 1976). The main biographies have been Michael De-la-Noy's *Denton Welch: the Making of a Writer* (Viking, 1984) and James Methuen-Campbell's *Denton Welch: Writer and Artist* (Tartarus Press, 2002).

Denton Welch is one of those mysterious writers who are always interesting. The more his world is reduced to a hospital room and a handful of human contacts, the more fascinating he becomes. Is it the precision of his observations, the fierce but gentle strangeness of his personality or his love of nature that captivates the reader? Like Colette and Jean Rhys, Welch has the power to generate interest out of even the most meagre materials. He had this gift from the beginning but suffering and illness refined it into a white-hot flame.

EDMUND WHITE

DENTON WELCH

A Voice Through a Cloud

ENITHARMON PRESS

Published in 2004
by the Enitharmon Press
26B Caversham Road
London NW5 2DU

www.enitharmon.co.uk

Distributed in the UK by
Central Books
99 Wallis Road
London E9 5LN

Distributed in the USA and Canada
by Dufour Editions Inc.
PO Box 7, Chester Springs
PA 19425, USA

ISBN 1 904634 06 0

British Library Cataloguing-in-Publication Data.
A catalogue record for this book is available
from the British Library.

Typeset in Bembo by Servis Filmsetting Ltd
and printed in England by
Antony Rowe Ltd

ACKNOWLEDGEMENTS

In preparing this new edition of *A Voice Through a Cloud*, Enitharmon Press gratefully acknowledges the advice and encouragement of Ronald Blythe, the late Alan Clodd, Richard Hutchings, James Methuen-Campbell, Jeremy Reed and Edmund White. Thanks are also due to David Higham Associates and the Harry Ransom Humanities Research Center, University of Texas at Austin.

FOREWORD

THE MANUSCRIPT of this nearly completed novel by Denton Welch was at his bedside when he died at the age of thirty-three. He had suffered thirteen years of chronic and painful illness caused by a road accident in which he sustained a serious fracture of the spine. At the time of our first meeting in the autumn of 1943 he was in bed at the tiny cottage on the outskirts of Tonbridge in which he was then living. His conversation was so animated and yet so profound, and so altogether detached from his precarious state of health, that it was only afterwards that I discovered he had been gravely ill, with a high temperature. Shortly after my first visit he moved to a bigger house in the Wrotham district, which I shared with him, and it was there that he made his great final effort to finish this novel. He had started it two years before, but had left it to write *Brave and Cruel* and other short stories. But now he felt, and told me, that there was not very much time. As late as the summer of 1948, long after most people in his condition would have adopted the life of a permanent invalid, his tremendous will-power enabled him to live normally and even strenuously during the increasingly short intervals between the crises of his illness. Then his condition became too grave for even him to continue physical activity, and in the last few months of his life he was being given morphia to alleviate the constant pain. Still he worked on, though the effort to do so gave him a high temperature and he would have to lie on his bed blindfolded without moving. Towards the end he could only work for three or four minutes at a time and then he would get a raging headache and his eyes would more or less give out. Complication after complication set in, and the left side of his heart started failing. Even then, he made colossal and nearly successful attempts to finish the book. He died on the afternoon of December 30th, 1948, still upheld in his last hours by the high courage which seemed somehow the fruit of his rare intelligence.

ERIC OLIVER

7

I

ONE WHITSUN holiday, when I was an art student in London, I got on my bicycle and left my room on Croom's Hill for my uncle's vicarage in Surrey. I took very little with me, only pyjamas, toothbrush, shaving things, and the creamy-white ivory comb which I had bought with my grandfather's present to me. I was very fond of this comb, so I wrapped it up carefully in the pyjamas and stowed it with the other things in the shiny black bag that was fastened on the back of the seat.

I had not told my aunt that I was coming, but I knew that she would find room for me somewhere.

As I walked up the hill to Blackheath, I looked at all the charming rather squalid old houses again, at the little rubbed brick gazebo with the late seventeenth-century date and the harsh new roof, and at the row of houses, now turned into flats, which had carved Medusa heads above the doors. Then I turned to the other side where Greenwich Park, with its ancient squat Spanish chestnuts, rose up in a hump, on which stood the Observatory. Below me was Inigo Jones's Queen's House and the winding river with the Isle of Dogs on the farther bank.

The wind was blowing on Blackheath, flattening the shiny colourless grass to the earth. There were no lovers under the trees in Chesterfield Walk at this time of day. I jumped on my bicycle and pedalled quickly across the heath until I dipped down into Lewisham. I passed the clock tower and came to the campanile of the Roman Catholic church. Feeling inquisitive, I got off here and went inside. I had been in twice before; once with another student, when we had tentatively added two candles to the bright mass round the Virgin Mary and had then been frightened away by a keen, glittering-eyed youngish priest in buckled shoes. He came up to us, smiling, and asking where we lived. As we stood in front of him I was filled with the fear of having done something wrong. I thought that perhaps only expectant mothers or women desiring to have children were supposed to light candles to the Virgin. The other time I had gone in on some saint's day and found pretty girls with wreaths in their hair, carrying on their shoulders a little enshrined image smothered in flowers. Very slowly they moved round the church to the sound of organ music. I was at the end of a pew and the procession stopped close to me. The girls stood almost touching me, breathing deeply, wriggling their shoulders a little to ease them under the weight of the holy shrine. On their faces they wore nervous expressions which were nearly smiles. I thought the procession so beautiful that I wanted it to go out of the church doors into the street where all the people gathered round the market stalls.

Now, as I entered, I found two nuns in wide starched caps kneeling in a curious, thrown-forward position, as if they had been naughty boys ordered to 'bend over'. Their lips were moving, and I heard the bony rattle of their rosaries. Again I was overcome with a feeling of trespass and ignorance. I left without daring to dip my fingers in the holy water.

I bicycled on under the railway bridge with the blackened Queen Anne house beside it, past the delightful little alms-houses lost and dwarfed amid hoardings and tall new buildings, until I came to the corner at Catford, where little painted pleasure-boats bump together and drift on a round pond under bald-looking weeping-willows. Here I turned to the right and rode towards Beckenham.

I was not used to traffic, usually only riding my bicycle on country roads in the holidays, so I felt pleased when I saw how well I managed the lights and the cars. When the lights were against me I remembered what I had seen other people do and threaded in and out between huge lorries and waiting buses until I reached the front line.

Near Beckenham I saw teas and light refreshments advertised on a newly painted board next to some old gates. The gates made me wonder what the house would be like. I decided to turn in and order some coffee. I rode down a long drive through parkland laid out as a golf course. Figures, made to look very small by the wide expanse of smooth green, moved about alone or in groups of two and three. Behind them were soft clumps of trees turned feathery and blue by the light heat haze.

The drive led me at last to the front of a small eighteenth-century house with a portico of Ionic columns rising to the height of two storeys. Under the portico there were niches for statues on either side of the front door. It was a beautiful little house, and I stood in the drive looking up at it for some moments before mounting the shallow stone steps and entering the dark hall. Above my head, half lost in the shadows, was a gallery, with the doors of the bedrooms opening onto it. I passed through the hall and found myself in what must once have been the drawing-room. It was oval, with three huge sash windows reaching from floor to ceiling. Panelled shutters folded into the thickness of the wall on each side of the windows, and the double door by which I had entered was of deep rich mahogany set in a framework of plain white-painted wood.

This noble room was spoilt by a counter with sizzling tea-urns, and by the wicker tables and chairs, the Japanese crape tablecloths, and the glossy plaques advertising Schweppes's soda water and Players' cigarettes. Except for the two waitresses behind the counter, the room was empty. I sat down at one of the little tables and ordered coffee and biscuits. As I waited, I looked out of the windows at the little figures moving against the bright green and the pale pink of the bunkers. Looking at the sides of the windows, I saw that some of the beautiful little brass handles on the shutters were broken or missing. I was given a vague uneasy feeling of universal damage and loss. The waitress brought my coffee then retired behind the counter again and began to laugh and talk quietly with her companion. I wondered if she was laughing at me, but her voice was so low I could hear nothing.

I drank my coffee and ate my biscuits. I did not want anything more for lunch. Long after I had finished them I was content to sit in the oval drawing-room, taking in its details with my eyes, at the same time thinking happily about my life and this Whitsun holiday. I thought of the picture I was painting of a Corinthian capital with strange plants and weeds growing in the crevices. Some of the plants were imaginary, but others I had copied from things I had found in the playing field behind the art school. I had rooted them up and brought them back to the still-life room, where I stuffed them between the twists and volutes of the plaster capital. I thought that this was going to be my best picture so far, and it made me feel warm.

At last I got up to go. I gave the room a final look, then recrossed the galleried hall and passed out beneath the portico. My head was full of plans for restoring the house. I was ruthlessly sweeping away the waitresses, the laced parchment lamp-shades, the wicker furniture and the food counter.

My bicycle had been left leaning against one of the garden urns. I wheeled it over the gravel, looking back once or twice; then I jumped on and rode down another arm of the drive until I reached the main road again.

It was now only early afternoon and the heat haze seemed to be drawing nearer, to be shimmering on the grass as well as on the distant trees. I passed through the gates and pedalled on towards Bromley. I hoped that I might arrive at the vicarage in time for tea. Once I had to look at my map, and then ask the way. As cars and lorries sped past me, I remembered how my father used to call me Safety First when I was a small child, because of my fear of traffic and my great caution in crossing roads. I thought that the ride had been very easy and pleasant so far. I felt I had wasted many opportunities by leaving my bicycle in the country and not bringing it to London before.

I was going along a straight wide road, keeping close to the kerb, not looking behind or bothering about the traffic at all . . .

I heard a voice through a great cloud of agony and sickness. The voice was asking questions. It seemed to be opening and closing like a concertina. The words were loud, as the swelling notes of an organ, then they melted to the tiniest wiry tinkle of water in a glass.

I knew that I was lying on my back on the grass; I could feel the shiny blades on my neck. I was staring at the sky and I could not move. Everything about me seemed to be reeling and breaking up. My whole body was screaming with pain, filling my head with its roaring, and my eyes were swimming in a sort of gum mucilage. Rich clouds of what seemed to be a combination of ink and velvet soot kept belching over me, soaking into me, then melting away. Bright little points glittered all down the front of the liquid man kneeling beside me. I knew at once that he was a police-man, and I thought that, in his official capacity, he was performing some ritual operation on me. There was a confusion in my mind between being brought to life – forceps, navel-cords, midwives – and being put to death – ropes, axes and black masks; but whatever it was that was happening, I felt that all men came to this at last. I was caught and could never escape the terrible natural law.

'What is your name? Where do you live? Where were you going?' the policeman kept asking. I could hear the fright in his voice. The fright made the voice more cruel and hard and impatient. I realized that he had been asking me these questions for a long time, and I told myself that I must give him the right answers at once, that I could think quite clear bloodless sentences, if I tried.

The words came out of my mouth. Some of them were slightly incorrect, others a little fantastic. I knew this, but felt that I had no real control over the words, and if I tried to repeat them again soberly they would arrange themselves in a still more grotesque pattern.

And as the shaken policeman bent over me, trying to take down my words, I felt the boiling and seething rise in me. It was drowning my brain, beating on it, plunging over it, shattering it. The earth swung, hovered, leaving my feet in the air and my head far below. I was overcome and drowned in waves of sickness and blackness . . .

It was night now and there seemed to be walls round me. A ball of light shone through a screen of coarse green twill. I was exquisitely conscious of the textures of things. There was torture in the smooth sheets, in the hair of the mattress and the weight of the blankets. My eyes darted about, consuming the smoothness of the paint on the cupboard beside me, then fixing voraciously on the tiny balls of cotton woven into the twill of the screen.

There was a noise. The walls round me seemed to be shaking and moving, then a gap appeared and two nurses came towards me, carrying something which I took to be a papier mâché tunnel for a child's toy railway. It seemed rather large, but I had no real doubts as to what it was. They pulled back the bedclothes and put this toy tunnel over my legs. As they did so a memory suddenly leapt up in my mind . . . I was walking with my mother and her friend, and I was eight years old. The friend was saying to my mother, 'Rosalind, I was so comfortable in the nursing home this time, because they put a hoop-like object over me to keep the bedclothes off . . .'

Now, as the nurses settled the cradle firmly on the mattress, I cried out, 'But I don't want that! You only put those things over people to keep the bedclothes from pressing on their stomachs when they are going to have babies.'

I saw the nurses exchange superior and knowing smiles. I was aware of having said something silly. I even felt slightly ashamed, so I said again in a louder voice, defiantly, 'I'm not going to have a baby.'

This time the nurses both gave short hard laughs. They spread the bed-clothes over the cradle, tucked them in, then turned to leave. As she pushed back the screens, one of them said to me, 'Now just you keep quiet and still. We don't want any more of that talking.'

I was left alone, wondering at the coldness in their voices and their laughs. It was bewildering; I seemed to be in disgrace, and my thoughts were trapped in my body. They turned and twisted in a terrible maze of pain and heat. I saw myself running for ever down a heated metal passage, banging my head on the walls, never able to escape.

I tried to tell myself that the agony was not real, that I would wake up to find it a dream. It seemed too violent and extraordinary to be real; but then I knew that it was real and that the comforting thought was the lie.

The next time I regained consciousness I saw the screens moving again. No nurse appeared, but a white rounded hand reached towards me. At the same moment I heard the voice of one of my aunts. I was surprised, and told myself immediately that I must behave normally, brightly, intelligently. The idea of proper behaviour obsessed me.

'Is that you, Aunt Edith?' I asked, for I still could not see her face; it seemed to be too far above me.

'Don't talk,' she said softly, coming nearer and grasping one of my hands. I wanted to shake her hand, but she did not let mine go; it rested under hers and I felt all her mournfulness and helplessness beneath the soothing words. I hated her sadness; I wished she would talk.

'How did you get here? Did someone drive you up?' I asked, still filled with my mad determination to make ordinary conversation.

'Don't talk now,' she said again. 'Lie quite still and try not to think of anything at all.'

She turned her head and I heard her murmuring something to the nurse; then she left me and I saw for a moment the alarmed interested eyes of my cousin as he stared through the gap in the screens. I heard them walking away.

One pain inside me began to conquer all the others. I did not know what was happening. When I could bear it no longer, I cried out to the nurses, but they were as stern and unbending as Roman matrons. They told me not to be silly and not to make a fuss.

At last one of them must have realized what was wrong with me, for she went to call a male nurse from a far wing of the hospital.

When, after a long time, this man appeared in his white coat, I took him for a doctor.

I screamed at him for help.

'I'm not a doctor, son,' he said quietly; he put down his tray on top of the cupboard and pulled back the bedclothes.

I remember being filled with a sense of surprise and wonder as I watched him pushing the soft little rubber tube down the urethra. It seemed to me an extraordinary thing to be doing, and I felt that I ought perhaps to resent his taking such strange liberties with my body when I was defenceless. I wondered, too, why I did not feel alarm as the little tube sank deeper and deeper into me. But I had neither of these feelings. I watched him with a peculiar interest. It seemed marvellous that anything could be pushed down such a tiny and delicate passage.

The relief, when it came, was so enormous that I forgot for a moment all my other pains; and in that moment I loved the man better than anyone else on earth and felt that I could never thank him enough for what he had done.

He sat down on the edge of the bed with his hands on his knees, waiting till all the water should have drained into the kidney-dish. He felt in one of the pockets of his overall and brought out a stub of cigarette; he lighted it and began to smoke with extreme caution, shielding the glowing end with his hand and only letting minute puffs of smoke out of his mouth.

I realized suddenly that it was not right for a nurse to smoke on duty, and that this one was taking advantage of the screens round my bed. I disliked him for it violently. I felt tricked and cheated; for he was no longer perfect and I could no longer feel whole-heartedly grateful to him.

After a few more furtive puffs, the man stubbed out the cigarette and put it back in his pocket; then he withdrew the catheter with a careless swiftness which startled me. He collected everything on the tray again, spread a cloth over the top and stood up to go.

'Good-night, son; you'll feel better now,' he said.

I looked up at his face. He had a little coarse moustache, rather light-brown, with peppery white hairs in it. He wasn't young and he wasn't middle-aged. His face was brownish-red. He looked sweet-tempered and lazy; unbelievably lazy, I thought.

When he left me, I lay still, trying to make myself think clearly. But nothing came, except the frightening vignette of myself lying on the grass and the policeman bending over me. After leaving the old house at Beckenham, I could recapture nothing but this one little picture.

As I looked at the green glow of the lamp, heard the hissingly quiet voices of the nurses, felt the drumming, thundering tingle in the legs which I could not move, it seemed to me that something had happened which I had expected all my life. The nurses appeared to take my situation quite calmly, to show no surprise at the terrible change in me. I began to believe that I ought not to feel bewildered and lost myself, that I ought to accept the horror as something quite ordinary.

The nurses came back to tidy my bed after the male nurse's visit. They talked across me brightly.

'Nurse,' I said suddenly, addressing one of them and breaking in on their conversation, 'I have been run over, haven't I?' It all seemed clear to me in a moment.

She looked at me sharply, then she nodded her head, shaped her lips into 'yes', but said nothing aloud. She seemed uneasy, as if she expected a whole string of embarrassing questions from me.

'Now you try to go to sleep,' the other one said briskly, to stop my talking.

'But, Nurse, I can't go to sleep!' I said, suddenly terrified of being left alone for the night.

'You must try.'

It was horrible; they were going to abandon me, and my legs were bristling and burning and I could not move them, and my head was throwing out waves of black sickness which seemed about to drown me. I began to talk to the nurses wildly. I asked them questions; I told them things; I laughed and smiled. And all the time I knew that they were watching me and judging me. They were not taking anything I said seriously.

Then the pain, like some huge grizzly bear, seemed to take me between its paws. I screamed from sheer shock at its sudden increased violence.

'Stop it,' the nurses said together. 'You'll wake the others.' They seemed about to stifle me if I dared to make another sound.

I must have screamed again, for all I can remember is a shriek and a pain invading my whole body. The shriek seemed to be following the pain into every limb. I was nothing but a shriek and a pain. I was sweating. Everything was wet. I was crying. Saliva dribbled out of my mouth.

In the middle of the furnace inside me there was a clear thought like a text in cross-stitch. I wanted to warn the nurses, to tell them that nothing was real but torture. Nobody seemed to realize that this was the only thing on earth. People didn't know that it was waiting for them quietly, patiently.

I felt that if I bore the agony a moment longer it would split my skin. It was such a growing and powerful thing; it would burst out of the tightness of my body.

I heard footsteps hurrying away; then silence. One of the nurses was still holding me, trying to stop me from moving.

At last the other one came back and she had a dainty dish and a little gun or model road-drill with her. It struck me that these articles were so small and finical that they could only be drawing-room tea-toys, and I thought that they should have been made of silver and not chromium.

The nurse lifted up my arm, swabbed a little place with cotton wool. I realized that she was trying to help me. I knew what the gun was for now, but I did not believe in its power. It was still associated in my mind with sugar-tongs and tea-strainers.

But the moment she pricked me so heartlessly, pushing the needle right in with vicious pleasure, I had faith; I knew that it was magic. It was like the Sleeping Beauty magic. Exactly the same, I thought, amazed at the similarity. Everything was there, the sudden prick, the venomous influence wishing me evil; then there would be the hundred years' sleep. I knew it in spite of the pain. The pain did not abate at all. It was still there, eating me up; but in the hundred years' sleep it would die. It couldn't live for a hundred years. And brambles would grow and everything turn marble-grey. The dust would be as thick and as exquisite to the touch as moleskin; and there would be moonlight always.

II

EARLY IN the morning someone was washing me. The top part of my body was naked, and I saw all the cuts on my chest and hip and side. There were some, too, in the tender delicate hollow of my groin. The biggest ones were covered over with dressings and the rest were painted with some bright yellow liquid, which turned the redness of the gashes to a peculiar dead-meat orange.

The nurse who was pretending to wash me dabbed round these wounds, then ran the flannel carefully along my jaw.

I lifted my hand quickly and touched all my teeth, one by one. They were all there and I could find nothing wrong with them, except for a tiny chip which I imagined I felt at one corner.

When the nurse had dried me, I saw that she pulled up an extraordinary flannel nightdress, all darns and patches. She tied the tapes at the back of my neck; there was no other fastening. The garment remained open at the back from top to bottom.

'This is queer,' I said. 'Where are my pyjamas? I had some in my bicycle bag.'

'You don't wear your own pyjamas here,' was her only answer.

She left me, and nothing more happened till a nurse with a different shaped cap pushed the screens apart and wheeled in a glistening glass and chromium trolley.

After giving me one preoccupied witch-like glance, she undid the tapes at the back of my neck and the nightshirt was pulled down again. She stared at my cut body, then, without any warning, stretched out her hand and ripped off one of the dressings.

My mouth jerked open and I heard my own shuddering intake of breath. The shock made me feel sick.

'Don't!' I implored, when I saw her stretching for the next dressing. 'You can't, Nurse!'

'Can't what?' she asked, affronted. 'This is the right way to do it. I've got too much to do to waste my time playing about. Just you show me what you're made of instead of creating.'

I suddenly had an idea.

'Nurse, I will loosen them for you while you are getting the new dressings ready.' I began desperately to ease the corner of one of the pieces of sticking-plaster.

'You leave it alone,' she said, slapping my hand; then she caught hold of the corner I had lifted and tore the dressing off.

After this I waited, helpless and defeated. Sometimes she ripped off the dressings almost painlessly. There was the swish of her arm and then the coolness of the air on the exposed cut; but at other times there was the delicate crackle of tiny hairs being torn out of the flesh round the wound. Then I cried out and she took no notice. She coolly and efficiently made new dressings and fitted them. I saw how proud she was of her duties and her position. She knew that whatever she did was right.

When she had finished the cuts, she pulled the bedclothes down further, and I saw for the first time that one of my legs was in a splint which reached from ankle to knee. The nurse began to unwind the many layers of bandage. I watched, growing more and more amazed as the leg emerged. It was all of the deepest plum colour, with a sort of cerulean blue and a mustard yellow in it, too.

'Nurse, isn't it extraordinary!' I said in wonder.

She bent her head and I saw that she was paying special attention to the ankle, which was swollen to the size of a young tree trunk.

I could not move either of my legs, but they were both filled with a biting, bristling tingle which never left them, and the pain in the broken ankle was like fire.

When the nurse touched the flesh of the bruised leg, it yielded in just the way that a wine jelly yields to the pressure of a spoon.

The ordeal of refitting the splint began. It was in vain that I told the nurse that I could not bear so tight a bandage on my terribly bruised leg. She said that the splint had to be tied tightly and that I was not to try to teach her her own business.

She swirled away with her trolley, leaving me without another word.

I lay with my head right back and my chin in the air, exhausted from the pain, wondering what new terrible thing was in store for me.

Someone brought me some milk in a pap-bowl and I winced, thinking that he was a new torturer. The curiously shaped drinking-cup alarmed me. But realizing that I was everybody's victim now, I let this man, who must have been another patient, hold it to my lips. I hated drinking from the pap-bowl; I hated to be fed. It seemed the final degradation. But I couldn't fight or use my will any more.

Later in the morning I opened my eyes to find a thing like a bier by my side. I realized at once that I was going to be moved, and the idea was so horrible that I called out urgently to the sister. I told her that I felt I could not stand being jolted or lifted.

'You'll be all right,' she said firmly and soothingly. 'You're only going to the X-ray room; you'll be back in a few minutes.'

I shut my eyes and took a deep breath; then I surrendered myself to the porters. There was nothing left for me to do but yell if the pain became too strong.

As the porters lifted me they said things to quieten me, for they saw that I was as raw as a piece of butcher's meat.

I said nothing, but I gasped and lifted my lip. They laid me on the high trolley. As they wheeled me along I stared up at the ceiling. The ward seemed never ending; there were two glass partitions dividing its gigantic length.

We were in a lift now; then I was wheeled into a little room with one large window. After moving me on to a table over which hung large lights and other apparatus, the porters went out of the door, talking together.

I was alone.

I moved myself on my elbows, trying to ease the pain at the bottom of my spine, trying to make the hardness of the table a little more bearable.

When I looked down, after the great effort of moving myself a few inches, I saw a neat little lump lying on the table. It reminded me of the little sausages dogs leave tidily at the side of the pavement. I was amazed and interested, realizing that for the moment I had lost control of everything below the waist. With a sort of resigned amusement I picked up the little pellet at once and threw it out of the open window. I watched it drop, feeling a childish pleasure in my own adroitness.

The next moment the door opened and a sober-looking man came in. He began quietly to X-ray me. He spoke hardly at all, and his hands were cold, but he gave me no feeling of hardness or indifference; I even gained a little strength from his cool remoteness.

The porters came back and wheeled me away. I entered the harassed, bustling life of the huge ward again. I saw that some of the patients were out of bed, helping the nurses by passing bottles or carrying water. I saw one man whose heavily bandaged leg was fixed to a pulley and stretched out above his head. His whole attitude, and the rope and pulley, made me imagine, for a moment, that he was being tortured for some misdeed. The picture was so entire that I could not disbelieve; then I told myself sharply that such imaginings were ridiculous.

Another man with a bandaged ear looked up from his book and fixed me with a condemning stare. His expression was a blank of hopelessness, deadness. Other people seemed to show interest; their expressions seemed to ask, 'What's your story? What's happened to you?'

When I was put back into bed I sighed many times. The mattress, which had been so torturingly hard, was soft and kind in comparison with the trolley and the X-ray table. I lay, trying to recover from my journey. The noise in the ward stupefied me. I tried to think of someone who could help me. All my thoughts fixed on a friend who had known me all my life. They fixed on her because she was a Christian Scientist and I longed to be told to get up and walk.

When Sister came and stood by my bed I was filled with an unnecessary wiliness.

'Sister,' I said, 'would you telephone a friend for me and tell her what has happened? I was going to tea with her today and she will worry.' This was a lie, but I felt that I had to make up some story, if I wanted Sister to take any notice of my wish.

She looked at me and then memorized the message and the number. I was surprised that she did not question me or raise objections. I had imagined the communication with the outside world would be forbidden, that telephone calls would be thought preposterous.

Sister went away, and I waited. I felt happier, not so abandoned and lost. I knew that Clare was the right person to call.

Sister came back, looking slightly bewildered.

'Are you getting muddled?' she asked, speaking kindly but frowning at the same time. 'I gave your message, but your friend said you weren't going there to tea this afternoon.'

'Oh, I thought I was,' I said as convincingly as possible. I was bitterly disappointed, afraid that Clare had not understood and so would not come. I looked miserably at Sister; then she said, 'When I told her what had happened, your friend said she would come here as soon as possible. I've told them to let her in, although visitors aren't really allowed till this afternoon.'

Sister wanted me to realize how good she had been. I was filled with so much pleasure at the thought of Clare's visit that I was able to give her all the gratitude she expected.

I tried to lull myself to sleep, to forget everything and wait for Clare, but all the pleasant things that only yesterday I liked so much rose up to haunt me. I thought of eating delicious food, wearing good clothes, feeling proud and gay, going for walks, singing and dancing alone, fencing and swimming and painting pictures with other people, reading books. And everything seemed horrible and thin and nasty as soiled paper. I wondered how I could ever have believed in these things, how I could even for a moment have thought they were real. Now I know nothing was real but pain, heat, blood, tingling, loneliness and sweat. I began almost to gloat on the horror of my situation and surroundings. I felt paid out, dragged down, punished finally. Never again would my own good fortune make me feel guilty. I could look any beggars, blind people in the face now. Everything I had loved was disgusting; and I was disgusting, too.

As this terrible gloating unhappiness flooded over me, my head began to swim; the pain sucked me under and I wanted to die and not be tortured any more.

Then someone in brown was standing beside my bed. Sister had brought her. I saw Sister going away. I could see on the brown person the satin-lined tie of her coat glistening richly, like wet mud. I suddenly thought the skin-like reflecting surface exceedingly pretty. I put out my hand to feel it. I knew that it was Clare who was standing there, but it was the satin tie that I wanted to touch. Because Clare stood so close to my bed, her face seemed too far away to be seen properly.

As she stood over me, I felt a strong emotion flowing from her to me. It was startlingly unlike the nurses' slick indifference and my aunt's unhappy helplessness. Clare's feeling seemed to arise from a stern purposeful marshalling of forces; she was gathering up her love, her fierce denial of the evidence of the senses, all the obstinate fight in her body.

She said little or nothing to me, because she was so busy denying the power of evil; but it was delightful to have her there – even the tingle in my legs seemed to be less biting. I began to be frightened of losing this deep calm when Clare should leave me. I started to talk rapidly, in an effort to keep her. The brown satin tie of the coat still held my attention. 'What is it?' I asked. 'It's like a little silk animal.'

I patted and stroked it again, then I asked Clare if she understood the made-up message given to her by Sister.

'It wasn't true,' I said.

'I understood,' answered Clare; 'that's why I've come.'

Words began to pour out of my mouth in a continuous stream. I asked Clare questions, but did not wait for the answers. I laughed; and my voice must have grown louder and louder, for Sister came up and told Clare that she must go.

I saw her taking Clare away. It was terrible. Clare's promise to come the next day meant nothing to me. It was nothing but so many words. I wanted her now.

The tingling increased in my legs; I became more and more aware of the brutal tightness of the splint. As the day wore on this pain became so unbearable that I felt down my leg and came to the knot of the bandage at the knee. I touched it and played with it again and again, wondering if I dared to undo it. I knew how furious the nurses would be; I even condemned myself for wanting to do anything so destructive; but at last I could stand no more. I pulled at the knot and had it undone in a moment. I was delighted to see how quick and nimble my fingers were. All the rest of my body seemed spoilt, but these and my arms still acted perfectly.

Rapidly I unrolled the bandage. Soon the bed was full of bandage and cotton wool. The padded splint fell away and I breathed with a glorious relief. The torturing tingle was still in my legs, but the relentless iron pressing of the splint on the bruised flesh had gone.

I lay very still, hoping that no one would discover what I had done.

A little while later Sister came up to me with a pap-bowl of tea. She told me that I must drink it and that I would like it; then she held my head up and gave it to me carefully. I wanted to drink it for her, to make up for my behaviour over the splint.

When I had finished the tea, Sister bent down to tidy the bed. She saw something stiff lying at a curious angle in the bed. She felt through the clothes; I watched her in fear.

'Maurice, what is this?' she asked ominously.

To be called Maurice was an added shock for me. It was my first name, which had never been used, and I wondered how Sister knew it, until I realized that I myself must have given it when being questioned in only a half-conscious state.

'Sister, I had to take it off. I couldn't bear the pain any more,' I explained.

She pulled back the clothes and saw the bed full of tangled bandages and cotton wool.

'Maurice, you are a very naughty boy.' She spoke with the threatening sternness one uses to a child or a dog. 'I didn't expect this sort of thing from you. It's not good enough. We do all that work for you and this is your return!'

Under her grief she seemed violently angry.

'I'm very sorry, Sister, but I couldn't stand it pressing on my leg. You know my leg is just black jelly. It doesn't look like a leg at all. *Please* don't put the splint back just yet; I don't know what I'd do.'

I watched Sister's face to see if my words made any impression; but she showed no sign. She turned away, saying grimly that she was going to fetch another nurse.

I was left to wait with my fear.

When Sister reappeared with the nurse she said nothing; they set about their work coldly. Sister held the splint against my leg while the nurse bound it on again. I was past imploring. I bit my tongue hard, to give myself another pain to think of.

The nurse finished her binding and turned to me; she said that it was too bad to make all that extra work, and I couldn't be trusted.

I turned away, feeling the shame she wanted me to feel. Why couldn't I fight their petty bullying? I longed to, but I had no power left.

'It will be plaster of Paris tomorrow for you, my lad, and you won't be able to do anything about *that*,' said Sister with a mock sternness that suddenly showed her real good nature.

After putting me further in disgrace with a few more remarks, they left. I waited until they were out of the ward, then started deliberately to undo the bandage again. I seemed to have no compunction left, nor did the thought of the consequences trouble me. My present pain was the only important thing.

The knots were tighter this time, but again I delighted in the agility of my fingers. All the quickness in my body seemed to have gone into them.

The scene at night, when my second disobedience was discovered, shook me. In my weak state I was made to cry. The matron herself was brought to stand over me and intimidate me. The nurse who readjusted the splint fixed it so that the knots were at the ankle, out of my reach; for I could not sit up or move my legs. She pulled fiercely on the knots, making them into balls as hard as oakapples.

Then she pricked my arm; and after a little while I began to float away, and the pain began to float away, too. I imagined the pain as diamond dew evaporating in the morning sun. This time my mind was filled with the thought of dew; its jewel-like wetness, its faint ghostly steam as it rose and disappeared in the air . . .

I could only have slept for a few hours, for when I woke it was still dark. All I could see was the green-shaded lamp on the night nurse's table.

For some reason I was terrified. I knew nothing. Everything had been forgotten. I was lost and obliterated. I seemed to be hovering in the air, looking down on the row of beds. I suddenly saw myself lying in one of the beds. I could tell myself perfectly, by the nose, the throat, and the tight-curled matted hair. I sailed through the air, so that I hovered directly above myself in the bed. Then began an extraordinary sort of elastic play between myself in the air and myself on the bed. It was like nothing so much as the bouncing and springing of a tennis ball fixed to a long piece of rubber. The see-sawings, the magnetic drawing downward and then the springing away were exciting, like a ride on the scenic railway. But, like the scenic railway, they were followed by a sickening after-effect; and mixed with this sickness was a black terror which seemed to be swelling and growing. I was so over-come with nightmare and bewilderment that I cried out. I heard steps coming towards me quickly, then I saw the very young face, of the night nurse. It seemed to wake me out of my horrible trance; I felt inside me a great leap of gratitude towards her. I caught hold of her hand and held on to it tightly. I held on so fiercely that I must have hurt her. In the darkness her face glimmered palely above me. She bent closer and I saw her worried frown. She tried to withdraw her hand, but I clung to it desperately. She said, 'Don't,' and left her mouth half open after the words. She was uneasy.

Suddenly she pulled away her hand, whispering at the same time, 'I'll bring you some hot milk.'

While she was away I thought she must be a very new nurse; she had not yet become inhuman, but was trying to learn the trick.

She brought the milk, not in a drinking-cup, but in a tall glass. She held it to my lips, but my head was thrown back too far and so some of the milk dribbled over my chin, burning it. The rest went into my mouth in painful gulps.

I wished she would take the milk away and just stay with me until I felt safer; but when I tried to hold her hand again, she had become perfectly hard and professional. She put my hands under the bedclothes, then tucked the bedclothes in tightly, as if she would imprison them.

'Try to go to sleep now, and don't make any more noise; you've got to think of the others, you know,' she said mechanically. I waited, wondering how to make her more human and real.

The next moment she had slipped away from me into the dark. I was left to face the blackness alone. I could trust no one and no one would help me. My fears and bewilderment came flooding back. I cried out many times. I cried out madly again and again.

III

AFTER THE terrible night the sunrise came as a wonder. I looked out of the window and saw wild streaks of rose, lemon, emerald and violet. Below were countless mauve-grey roofs and crooked chimney-pots. I knew for certain that I was back in London.

I wondered dimly why I had been brought all the way back, when the accident must have happened in the outer suburbs, or even in the country. I tried again to force a memory of something that happened after my leaving the colonnaded house, but no spark glowed.

I gazed at the beautiful fantastic sky and thought of the night that had gone before, its stifling blackness, seemingly everlasting, the pain and fear which had magnified themselves in the darkness until they were monstrous scarecrows, bearing down to smother me in their horrible rags.

Now the darkness was gone, and I was so lightened and relieved that I forgot my helplessness for a moment. I was not resentful when the nurse washed me, or when one of the convalescent patients held the pap-bowl to my lips.

Later Sister appeared with the nurse who had done my dressings. They both looked grim and purposeful. They pulled down the bedclothes, and after taking the splint off began to wrap my legs in bandages soaked in plaster of Paris. They did their work carefully and beautifully. As I felt the plaster hardening, I became filled with a sort of panic. I would never be able to get at the leg again, never be able to ease the pain and tingle by undoing the bandages.

Sister and nurse seemed pleased with their work. As if echoing my thoughts, Sister said: 'You won't be able to do anything about *that*.' She went on to tell me that I must keep myself tidy, because the doctor was coming to see me. I rebelled against her solemn tone, her assumption that a visit from the doctor was rather like a visit from a god.

He came in the middle of the moming. He had a little circle of students round him. He asked me several questions, but did not seem to show much interest in the answers. He kept the students in the background; I saw them staring at me over his shoulder. I resented their apathy, their curiosity, their dull loutish faces, their keen bright-eyed ones. Some of them scribbled notes on little pads, some of them picked their noses; others blew theirs, or scratched the spots on their chins. I told myself that they were more like animals than human beings. They were stupid bullocks following a dispirited bull. As the sorry little group moved from bed to bed, my intolerance grew. Would they never have done with their pawing and prodding and catechizing? Was this the indignity in store for each patient each day?

I realized that I was prejudiced, that all my feelings were humourless and excessive, but this knowledge had no effect on my mood.

In the afternoon the ward began to fill up with visitors. I lay there watching, trying to forget myself and my pain by looking at the people. As each bed came gradually to have a visitor standing or sitting beside it, and I had none, I felt that I would probably be left quite alone in the hospital until I died. By this time I thought that even Clare had forgotten about me.

I idly watched two girls who were looking from side to side in rather a bewildered way, as though they were searching for someone. Suddenly I realized that they were Cora and Betsy from the art school. Cora was wearing a little yellow hat and holding a small red book against her bosom, while Betsy wore no hat but carried a bunch of roses wrapped in blue tissue paper.

'Cora! Betsy!' I shouted excitedly.

Their heads jerked round; they came walking quickly towards me. As they approached, I saw the dismay spreading over their faces. Cora tried to wipe the expression off, but Betsy's mouth fell into an 'O'; she almost ran up to my bed.

'Sonny Boy!' she exclaimed. They had once given me this distressing nickname. Mixed with the horror in her voice was a peculiar sort of amusement.

I said, 'What's it like, Betsy? What's wrong? Show me quickly in your mirror.'

I was all agog to see the damage to my face. I wasn't afraid, but interested and amused.

Betsy opened her bag, then turned suddenly to Cora and said, 'Do you think I ought to?' She spoke as if I wasn't there.

While she turned to Cora, with the worried frown on her face, I put up my hand and snatched the little mirror from its slot.

I looked at my face and saw that I was unrecognizable. My eyes, tiny and slit-like, were sunk in two bulging purple velvet cushions. A forked cut, like red lightning, spread right across my forehead and down my nose. On my head were cuts, surrounded by large bald patches where the hair had been snipped away. The rest of the hair stood up in isolated curls and jagged tufts. The parts of my face that were not purple or red were dyed brilliant sulphur-yellow.

Betsy's absurd 'Sonny Boy' kept ringing in my ears. Could anything be more grotesque than such a name for such a face?

After the first shock, I was quick to see that the damage was not really serious. Black eyes would pass away, my hair would grow, the cuts were not deep. The yellow colour was due to some antiseptic. I felt made up for some stage performance, disguised as a frightening bogey.

'No wonder you were looking all over the ward for me!' I laughed.

Cora and Betsy began to shower me with questions. They could hardly believe that I knew no more than themselves.

'Try to remember,' they insisted.

I tried and felt hopeless. To stop them from questioning me, I asked how they had found out that I was in the hospital.

'We went to your rooms to see you,' Betsy said. 'Miss Hellier opened the door and told us at once about the accident; she had just received a message from your aunt. So we came here as quickly as we could. It's the strangest old hospital, Sonny Boy. The porter told me it used to be an infirmary or workhouse or something. It's got an ancient barbaric saint's name that suits it exactly.'

'Horrible!' said Cora, making herself shiver. 'Makes me think of faggots and flames and martyrdom and the gospel.'

I felt very gay with Cora and Betsy. They brought back my active life so vividly that it seemed all wrong for me to be lying in bed, unable to move my legs. I refused to believe that I should be in this condition for long. I told myself with only the slightest hint of defiance that I would be up and about in a week or a fortnight.

The bell was ringing to clear the visitors from the ward. Cora and Betsy left their presents on my bed and stood up to go. They looked sad.

'Get well quickly,' said Cora.

'I do hope they get you out of this place soon,' murmured Betsy.

I watched them until they passed behind one of the glass partitions at the far end of the ward; Cora's little yellow hat bobbed and twinkled to the last. I felt like a child whose newest toy has floated down the river out of sight.

I turned to the roses, trying to bury my thoughts in them. I breathed in their scent and stared at the bright beads of water which nested between the petals. The colour and the shape of the roses seemed to mean nothing to me. I had lost delight even in touching their creamy smoothness. They were uneatable brussels sprouts, doll's cabbages. Alone and forlorn in that hideous ward they only looked gruesome, pathetic, wasted.

Next I opened the little red book that Cora had brought. It was *The Rose and the Ring*. I turned the pages until I came to the delicate picture of the Princess Angelica giving the plum bun to the little dirty wretch.

Holding the book above my head, I tried to begin to read; but my arm and my eyes and my mind ached. The book dropped from my hand. I stared up blankly at the ceiling.

After some time I stretched out my hands behind my head and caught hold of the iron bed-rails. I enjoyed the feeling of hanging on to something; I felt steadier, more secure. It was a moment or two before I realized that, by clutching on to these bars, I could move myself from one side of the bed to the other without hurting my back and legs so much.

I hated to think of my legs; I concentrated on my quick-moving still strong arms. I turned my stiff body from side to side, delighted with my discovery; then I lay flat, exhausted.

I seemed to be swimming now, and I wasn't certain whether it was night or day. I saw all the other faces in the beds and I wondered why there were no women's faces there. I could not understand this exclusively male line of faces. I saw the female nurses running about and I thought that there should also have been female faces mixed with the male ones in the beds. That there were none seemed curious, not quite natural.

Clare came again that evening when it was quite dark, long after visiting time.

In my clouded state I felt certain that she had been sent to rescue me under cover of darkness.

The words which she chose from the Bible and *Science and Health* seemed wonderful, deep, true, like poetry and music. She denied the reality of all physical ills with such pugnacious determination, such violence of feeling, that I might have been alarmed if I had not been exalted. Why wasn't I healed at once? Surely only my own laziness and disbelief held me back now! I embraced this added weight of blame.

After this wild exaltation and hope, I was appalled to find that Clare was about to leave; I could neither follow nor keep her with me. I was powerless, as useless as ever, unchanged – a dupe, a fool.

I called out her name. She looked over her shoulder and waved; then I was left to face what I dreaded most, the long parched hours of the night.

I looked about me desperately and saw that Betsy or Cora or some other visitor had left a ball of knitting wool on the green-tiled top of the locker. I snatched this ball up and began to unwind it under the bedclothes. As I unwound the wool I rewound it on my fingers. I did this time and time again, sometimes varying the rhythm by looping the wool into a long lanyard, crocheting with my fingers in the way my mother had shown me when I was four or five.

Once the night nurse came up to my bed. She stood eyeing me curiously and suspiciously; then she asked what I was doing under the bedclothes.

I was ready to fight for my ball of wool, to bite her hand if she tried to take it away; but after satisfying herself that my game with the wool was harmless, if foolish, she left me with the impossible, inevitable command, 'Go to sleep.'

When the pain intensified, I unwound and rewound with increased speed, so that the whole night is left in my memory as a time of mad racing movement. My fingers twirl and twiddle again like mad mice, and my teeth are set on edge by the oily, dusty, harsh and soft touch of the wool.

I waited, greedy for the first streak of daylight. When the sky was again lit up magnificently, although I was very much aware of the cruelty of the shining colours, I became flooded with a relief which made me sing out loud.

Someone told me to shut up, but I took no notice.

My eldest brother came to see me that morning. He had only just returned from a week-end in the country; he had known nothing of the accident until he found a message waiting for him at his flat. He explained all this rapidly, while looking about him with a sort of expressionless distaste.

He wanted to move me at once from the noisy great ward of this old infirmary.

'We'll get you out of this, we'll get you out of this,' he kept insisting, as if he had found me in all the uproar and squalor of eighteenth-century Bedlam. He wanted to take me to the nursing-home in Hanover Square where he himself had once spent a comfortable fortnight.

But the doctors would not allow me to be moved. However much I hated the ward, I agreed with the doctors. I could not think calmly of the torture of being carried and jolted. The short journey to the X-ray room had been enough of an ordeal.

My brother began to tell me what the police had told him. A private car, driven by a woman, had run into me from behind. The road had been straight and wide, with little traffic on it. It had, of course, been broad day-light. There appeared to be no reason for the accident, except the gross carelessness of the driver. There were several witnesses, and there would be a court case.

These bald details half interested me, half repelled me. I did not want to hate the disgusting little woman too much. (I thought of her thus, but for all I knew she might have been tall and appetizing.) Since I could not remember the accident, I wanted to feel outside it and beyond it, free, at least in thought, from its grim sordidness.

I wished my brother would not dwell on this side of the affair; it was for me the least important. His talk of solicitors and barristers seemed dull and irrelevant. My only wish was to be well and free again.

Before he left, he told me that a little bone in my spine had probably been bruised or fractured and that a specialist would soon be coming to examine me. He spoke lightly and hurriedly, as if my trouble were no more than a cold in the head. I knew that he was trying not to alarm me, doing all in his power to help.

After my brother, Miss Hellier, my landlady, appeared. She wore her tight black turban, her short shaggy black jacket made of astrakhan cloth. But she didn't look hot; her face was calm and pale. Her deep-brown eyes looked from side to side with unconcern; she might have been at a fruit and vegetable show, glancing at the marrows and the pears as she passed.

She brought me chicken essence, Ovaltine and chocolates. She seemed to take it for granted that I was hungry, and that I would be up and about again in a few days' time.

Later in the day a convalescent patient stopped at the foot of my bed and stared at the glass jar on my locker. He had the face of an old sponger – eager darting eyes and lips, the stupid grin of the cunning.

'What's that, mate?' he asked.

'Chicken,' I said.

'Chicken!' he echoed.

'Yes.' I was not encouraging.

'Well, that's the first time I've seen chicken in a little glass bottle.' He seemed to look on the Brand's Essence as a sort of magic conjuring trick. I was amused, irritated, too weak to bother to repulse his cadging.

I asked if he'd like to taste the chicken. He reached forward eagerly and dug the spoon deep into the jar. I watched the scrubby white hairs on his adam's-apple rise and fall as he swallowed. He smacked his lips in extravagant and unappealing dumb-show.

'That's all right, that is! That'll do!' he said, still continuing to lick his old cracked lips.

After this he came over to me at every meal-time, begging for some titbit. He seemed to imagine that my locker was stuffed with delicious things. I would give him a chocolate, or a spoonful of jelly; but when these were finished, there was nothing to give; then I began to hate his wheedling importunity, his stupid slyness, his nasty old body. For him to be near was an insult, a degradation; I hated to think that he also was a human being. When I looked at him, the outrageous words of the Negro song leapt into my mind: 'Common people I avoid; I would have them all destroyed.' How I agreed with the words in his case! He had outraged me by paying court to me for the things in my locker. I understood how heiresses must feel when they discover that they have been wooed for their money. My contempt for all fawners, toad-eaters, sycophants, parasites, grew and grew until even I, in my strange fanatical state of mind, told myself not to waste so much feeling over the man.

Although I could still eat hardly anything, I allowed him to think that I had suddenly become gluttonous; for it freed me from his constant begging. He had not believed me when I told him that I had nothing more to give.

Now, when he passed the bottom of my bed, he did not speak. He would glance sorrowfully at my locker, then pass on.

IV

ONE DAY someone of about my own age was wheeled up to the bed next to mine. As the porters put him between the sheets, I saw that he wore his own striped pyjamas; this caught my attention, since everyone else in the ward was forced to wear the curious hospital nightdress, split from top to bottom at the back. I looked at his face. It was of an even bread colour and shiny; his hair seemed almost to match his skin, both in colour and texture. Because of this lack of contrast, his appearance just missed being pleasant and became rather disquieting. I had an uncomfortable picture of him caged in one of those large earthenware covers under which celery is blanched. In spite of this colourless quality, he made a great show of being lively and gay. It was easy to tell that he was trying to fight his own uneasiness and the noisy, inhuman deadness of the ward.

He began to talk to me at once, explaining that he had come into hospital to be operated on for appendicitis. He kept laughing and joking and saying that he didn't care. He told me that his Christian name was Dick and that his girl would be coming to see him after the operation. Soon he became tired of talking quietly only to me; he wanted the whole ward for audience. He began to shout remarks to the people in the beds on the other side of the room. Some joke-telling, argument, and sharp repartee followed; then one of the older men snarled, 'Shut up and don't be so full of yourself.'

For the moment Dick was silenced; a dull flush spread upwards. It was as if a frivolous baker had suddenly decided to add a pink colour to the face which he had modelled in dough.

But soon Dick was talking to me again. He told me that he had been in hospital once before, with a slight rupture. 'And after the operation, d'you know what the doctor says?' he asked. ''E says, "Never sit on the pan in the ordinary way; always squat on yer 'aunches."'

35

It was difficult to know what to reply, so I said at random, 'I hope you're good at balancing.'

This seemed to amuse him excessively; he let out peals of laughter; then subsided into a monotonous chuckling. Between the bursts he told me that he had nearly fallen off the seat several times at first.

'Better to fall off than to fall in,' I said dryly.

Again the excessive mirth.

'Yes, say if I'd fallen in after pulling the plug! I'd 'ave gone down the drain,' he wailed, dashing the back of his hand across his brimming eyes.

He continued to elaborate this old and widespread fantasy of disappearing down the drain. Soon he had spun out a long facetious story of adventures with rats in the town sewers.

The more Dick talked, the more apparent were his signs of nervousness. The laughing and joking increased until their hollow sound was painful.

I wondered why the thought of the operation should upset him so much. Or was there some other deeper cause for all this false heartiness? I decided to tell him that there was nothing to worry about; his operation was a simple one, and he would be quite well again in a fortnight. Perhaps I spoke callously, disregarding his case because my thoughts were centred on my own.

Immediately I saw that it would have been better not to have talked about the operation. His eyes became really troubled and he began to be even more boisterous than before.

In the morning the nurses began to prepare him for the operation. Through the cracks in the screens round his bed I saw one of them bending over his bare stomach and cutting some hairs away with bright scissors; then I saw her swabbing the grey-white flesh with some orange liquid which I took to be iodine.

When the porters moved the screens away and started to wheel him out of the ward, he sat up on the trolley, so that the red blankets fell off him, and shouted out in a loud voice, 'Now I'm going for a nice ride. Don't you wish you were coming too, boys! I'll be back in time for dinner.'

There was a lot more about being tough and being able to 'take it'; and he laughed so much that the man with the bandaged ear became exasperated and said, 'Why do you make so much noise? That shows you're windy. If you didn't care, you wouldn't say anything.'

Such austere biting words at that moment were too cruel. Again I saw the immediate flush under Dick's thick pale skin; I didn't like the man for bringing it to his face.

As Dick disappeared out of the door, he raised his hand in a mock military salute, then dropped it rigidly to his side.

I thought about him for most of the morning. I tried to imagine the scene in the operating theatre.

I put myself in Dick's place, under the anaesthetic. I invented dreams for him, and tried to see him dreaming these strange dreams while the surgeon cut into him. There was something so arresting about this picture of the dreaming patient and the busy surgeon cutting and sewing with blood-stained fingers that I dwelt on it until it became bitingly clear and tiny, like the jewelled diminished picture reflected in a dewdrop.

And suddenly I realized how delightful it was to have these mental images, to forget the dead weight of my legs, the high fever which clapped down on me, and the pain all over my body. I thought that I must be getting better if I could identify myself with someone else and let my mind wander and invent in this way.

When they brought Dick back on the trolley, he looked dead. For one silly moment I thought he was; then I realized that a corpse would never be brought back from the operating theatre and put to bed solemnly in the ward.

Dick was still unconscious, that was why his face had the marble smoothness and repulsive death beauty. The pale drained quality of his face and hair was increased, so that he seemed to be spun out of white sugar.

For some time he did not stir; then I heard low moaning and retching. As I listened to the distressing noises, I thought that he had been right to dread this operation. Now it seemed as bad as he had expected it to be. The change from even false heartiness to this misery was hateful.

Towards evening the fumes began to wear off and he grew better. He no longer asked the nurses strange questions, or swore at them filthily, or cried out like a tiny baby.

When it was quite dark I turned over carefully to his side and whispered, 'You're all right now, aren't you?'

'Yes, chum,' was all he said in a voice so scrubbed and stripped and sober that I could hardly recognize it.

As usual I watched the faces of the visitors eagerly as they flooded into the ward on the next afternoon. But when no one appeared for me at once I turned to see if Dick had anyone by his bedside.

He had been talking to me most of the morning about his operation. Now that it was over he loved to discuss it. The whole business of surgery had fascinated and impressed him. He had regained most of his liveliness, but I was disconcerted to hear a forced note in it still. I had to accept the fact that this was his habitual manner and that it had been only slightly exaggerated by fear of the operation.

I was beginning to imagine that he, too, was to be left without a visitor, when two girls detached themselves from the crowd and came towards his bed. One was tall and rather pretty with hot brown hair. The other was much shorter. She limped because her two legs were not the same length. On one foot she wore a gruesome black boot with sole and heel several inches thick. Her hair was soft mole colour, and on her face was the strangest mixture of brooding sadness, dulled sensibility, timidity, and matter-of-fact acceptance.

I took it that she was Dick's sister and that the other unexceptionable girl was his sweetheart.

But when the lame one bent down to kiss him, I knew that I was wrong.

They clung together; Dick's lips seemed to be trying to move, even while they were pressed flat and hard against the girl's. There was an ecstasy of sleepy, greedy enjoyment in the curve of his closed eyelids. The girl bent over him with a sort of weary humility, as if she would bear anything, do anything he asked of her.

When at last she lifted her face, she put her hands on his shoulders and looked down on him. She seemed to be searching for something without much hope, even with a pale indifference.

After this long, piercing, sad gaze, she let her hands fall to her sides. No one spoke for a moment; then the other girl filled the gap with some provocative remark and they all began to talk at once.

There was so much chattering in the ward that I could not hear their words clearly, but I heard enough to know that the two girls were telling him of the happenings at home and he was describing the life in the ward and the wonders of the operating theatre.

Suddenly, as she talked, the lame girl lifted the hair at the side of her face, combing it back impulsively with her fingers.

With a shock of horror I saw that she had no ear under the hair, only a frightening hole in the side of her head.

For her sake and for my own I turned away abruptly. I could not look at her again without a kind of fear. I thought of all the terrible cases of legal mutilation: ears cropped, tongues slit, eyes gouged; she was linked in my mind with these atrocities. She appeared to me as the victim of some horrible medieval brutality.

When the bell rang for the visitors to leave, both girls bent down to say good-bye. The lame one waited till last; then she kissed Dick with such a resigned, suffering, deadened look on her face that she appeared to be indifferent to all human beings and only waiting for her life to end.

She linked arms, with the other girl leaning on her a little; they moved towards the door. Before they disappeared, they both gave jerky little waves of the hand. After the visitors were gone there was silence in the ward. People felt lonely and deserted. When talk began again, a man turned to Dick and asked, 'Which is your girl?'

Dick called out gaily, 'The one with the game leg.'

This naked statement seemed to outrage the man's sensibilities. 'You didn't ought to talk about her like that,' he said very severely; and immediately several others joined with him in condemning Dick. They turned on him fiercely; their voices were shocked and hard.

For a moment Dick looked nonplussed.

'Why shouldn't I say that?' he asked confusedly; then some of his jauntiness came back and he shouted out: 'She's got no ear, too; she was born like it.'

He looked round the ward as if challenging other patients to silence him. He still seemed a little bewildered. Since he took his sweetheart's misfortunes so lightly, why couldn't these strangers do the same? What was the fuss about?

After a moment of uneasy silence, the older men all began to talk at once.

'That's not the way for a chap to talk about his girl.'

'You didn't ought to say it.'

'What would she think?'

'It's not fair.'

'It's bloody mean.'

'He's a bloody mean little bastard.'

39

They did their best to hurt him and make him ashamed of his words. Something in his baldness had flouted their sense of decency.

He turned to me and began to talk quickly to shut out the ill-will of the older men. He told me about his marriage plans, the council flat and the increased pay he hoped for. I tried to look under his words for something hidden, something more; but each plain statement refused to be given more depth or colouring. His girl was his girl. She had no ear. She had a game leg. They had no house or flat yet. He hadn't enough money yet. Still, they would be married. No more thought need be wasted on the matter.

V

WHEN I grew a little better, and the cuts on my body healed, and the plaster was taken off my leg, I began to be massaged by a tall man with very large arms. His body and face were flat and broad. The great arms hung down loosely. When he set to work, he rolled up the sleeves of his starched white coat with a sort of lazy bullying pride. He put lavender talcum powder on his hands before he began to knead me.

He would start with my arms, but since these were unharmed he spent little time on them, passing quickly to my back and legs. He would turn me over and rub and press and stroke my spine, my ribs, my shoulder-blades; then he would pommel me until my flesh shook.

When he reached my still bruised and tingling legs, I held my breath. Sometimes he dealt roughly with them and I would be ready to cry out as he pressed down hard on the bone under the hurt flesh; but the next moment I would be soothed by the rhythm of his movements. The pain itself became almost a sharp pleasure.

As he massaged, he would talk to me. He told me about people dying of consumption, the thinness of their faces, the colour in their cheeks, their sensual imaginings. He described them lying all day in the open air, winter and summer. But if, to add to this conversation, I should mention Switzerland, a sanatorium in the mountains, or children playing naked in the snow, he would treat my remark as an irrelevant interruption.

'Most people can't go off to Switzerland just because they have T.B.,' he scoffed.

He would rub and roll my muscles in contemptuous silence before beginning another monologue on a different subject.

I soon found that nearly all suggestions and opinions were either disregarded or contradicted, so I lapsed into silence and let him get on with his work. I think he looked on me as his punch-ball, his rag-doll and plaything; therefore it was natural for him to pay no attention to anything I said.

One morning, just as he had reached the end of his routine and was revolving the balls of my feet, two trolleys were wheeled into the ward.

I looked away, because I was anxious not to see fearful sights; my mind was pleasantly drugged by the masseur's rubbing and his monotonous conversation.

But later in the day, long after the masseur had gone, I could no longer ignore the new arrivals; for one of them began to breathe in a terrible way. The noise bellowed through the ward, until I felt that my iron bed would vibrate.

I saw Sister hurriedly leading two women in dusty black clothes up to one of the beds behind the screens. They seemed to stay there a long time. When they appeared again, one of them was bowed down. She looked like a shapeless old bolster propped upright. The bolster shook. She lifted her yellow-grey face made hideous with crying. The tears were like oil on her cheeks.

I longed for something to stop the noise; my heart seemed deafened by it. If only the stertorous breathing would stop! then I could think and feel again. I would see more than an old black bolster with a horrible face; my blind hatred would melt away and I could rest.

Hour after hour until far into the night the noise continued; then, suddenly, it stopped.

It was as if the great engines in a ship had been turned off. I waited for the noise to begin again, hardly believing that the silence could last; but when it did, I turned myself over with infinite relief, then, letting go of the bars of the bed, I sank down into a heavy sleep, free at last of the terrible human foghorn.

In the morning I looked across the ward and saw that one of the beds was empty. 'He really is dead,' I thought gladly. Death seemed the tidy answer, the only good to expect. The green screens had also been taken away from the other bed, where a young man sat up stifly. His face was pale and drawn, his forehead wrinkled, as if a difficult problem kept teasing his tired brain.

Someone spoke to him. I was just able to hear his low, flat answer.

'Me and my mate was goin' along on the motor-bike; then something 'appened. We must've 'it a telegraph pole —' The words slurred together and he stopped talking for a moment; then a wave of excitement roused him.

'You should have seen the bike! Coo!' He smiled broadly and made an amazed whistling noise.

'I was all right; I was riding pillion,' he mused. 'I 'ad a good shake up; got a few cuts.' He pulled up the sleeves of the hospital nightgown and seemed to be studying his arms intently. He smiled again, then let his mouth drop open in a chuckle.

Suddenly he looked at the empty bed beside him.

'Joe's dead!' he said, staring blankly, as if he had not missed his friend until that moment. He began to cry.

He cried quietly. The man in the next bed tried to comfort him by saying that it was better for his friend to die, since he had been so badly injured.

After a little time the man began to dry his eyes on the sheet. He still repeated the name Joe and some other words which I could not hear. As he mumbled, he gazed into space, wrapt in a kind of daydream.

A nurse rustled by busily. 'You mustn't carry on like that, you know,' she said; 'we're all very sorry about your friend; but you can't upset the other patients. Just take a hold on yourself. Men mustn't cry.'

There was a silence; then the man burst out, 'Bloody well sod off! Bloody well sod off!'

His voice mounted to a plaintive, outraged howl, as if he had been baited beyond endurance. Tears rained down his face again.

The nurse stood at the foot of his bed, too dumbfounded to speak. All at once she turned on her heel and hurried away.

She returned with Sister. Both women bore down on the man with the set, grim faces of executioners.

Sister insisted on the man apologizing; she stood over him until he said, 'I beg your pardon, nurse.'

His crushed, humbled tone stung me. I longed for him to burst out against the women, to swear again. To forget the scene I turned angrily to my drawing book. Clare had brought it for me. Sometimes I tried to draw the other patients; but usually I did things out of my head: bent tubes with tulips and daisies growing out of them; butterballs on a dish; a strangely shaped vessel, like an alchemist's retort, or the lower and more sinuous part of a lavatory basin; a stone lion on a column; and a boat with high pointed prow and veils floating in the water behind.

With the drawings were mixed some lines of writing. They were usually built round some imperfectly remembered and therefore mysterious word; a classical name perhaps. For days and nights this half-remembered name would drum through my head; and I would ask, 'Who was she? What did she do? Was she a traitress or a heroine?' A jingle would form and I would write it down, devising a sort of secret sense out of the jumbled phrases.

My mind would wander from my drawing or my writing and I would see things in a reverie. The Medusa head often appeared to me, with its hair of snakes coiling and writhing exactly like the eels I had once seen on zinc trays in a little shop near the Marquis of Granby at New Cross.

As I lay there, I wondered about the life in the huge city round me. I would think of the people under the roofs of the little houses surrounding this high hospital ward. In imagination I lifted the mauve slate lids and saw them there, in their underclothes, ironing, or washing, or making love on the beds. I saw them bending over frying-pans; brushing the hair away from their eyes as they peered at the spiritualistic blue vapour hovering above the spitting fat. I saw them beating their children with slippers, and, afterwards, kissing and cuddling them voluptuously. I saw the dark-grey socks, unchanged for a month, stiff with sweat, lying beside the sleeping man – tobacco-coloured hairs sprouted from his ears. His collar-stud had marked the whiteness of his neck with a cruel red spot.

Always my mind turned to the food smell behind the wallpaper in passages, to the bugs that lived there, to gurgling cisterns in the roof, and the harsh feel of London smuts on window-sills, where the withered paint came off in flakes as delicate as flies' wings.

At this period I nearly always imagined scenes that would be called sordid. Did I enjoy their squalor for its own sake? Or was I afraid to think of pleasant things because the return to the reality of the ward would have been too painful? My flight to a world that seemed beautiful or romantic to me was to come later, when I had almost completely lost touch with the life of everyday.

But perhaps I am right in thinking that even this lifting of the lids of the grim little houses around me was also an escape to pleasure. I know that I often wanted to be the fat blowzy woman with her falling hair and frying-pan; the tired man who didn't change his socks; or one of the perverse secretive children who never behaved as children are expected to behave, but were candid, deceitful, trusting, cruel, kind, malicious or loving at the most unexpected moments.

I envied everything which moved on its own legs freely. To be able to walk and run with ease seemed the chief delight of life. Without this foundation, nothing else seemed worth very much.

Clare, who came to see me so often, and who insisted with such force that nothing but good had any real existence, filled me with some of her own fire, so that I found myself saying over and over again, 'Today I shall walk. Nothing can stop me. I shall get up and amaze them all.'

I would imagine the strength and sensation returning to my legs; a sort of desperate excitement would overcome me, making me tremble.

But I still lay there and still could not walk when, after a month in this old infirmary, the specialist said that I was well enough to be moved.

My brother came to tell me that I was to go first to another hospital in an old square in Bloomsbury, where the specialist could visit me regularly; later he would have me moved to a nursing home in the country.

In spite of my longing to be gone, I hated the thought of entering another and a strange hospital; at least I knew the grimmer aspects of the one which held me. I would be nothing but a prisoner escaping from one gaol to another.

The ambulance came for me on a soft warm day in early July.

Now that I was to leave the ward for ever, a strange disembodied, unearthly feeling swept over me. I was light; I was nothing. Why did they bother to move an empty shell? The fact that someone in the ward had renamed me Ted added to my sense of lost identity. As the trolley bore me away through the glass partitions, voices called out, 'Good-bye, Ted'; 'So long, Ted.' I waved, but they might have been talking to a stranger. I was not Ted. I was no one.

I gazed out of the windows at the roof-tops for the last time; I thought of the terrible nights and extraordinary dawns I had known in that place. I tasted hot milk in tall glasses, sweet strong tea in squat pap-bowls. Jars of flowers glowed, then faded, on the green-tiled top of my bedside locker. I saw the man with his leg slung up in the air, and the other bad-tempered one with the bandaged ear. I heard Dick's forced chuckles and the elephant trumpeting of the man who died.

I felt the efficient nurse tearing off my dressings – the tiny hairs crackled as if on fire.

I had strayed into a nightmare land where I had no part or place. Like Alice I had burrowed down a rabbit-hole to find myself in a world of twisted sight, sound, taste and touch.

As I was wheeled into the lift, something sprang to life inside me. The smell of the shaft, the momentary glimpses of faces, fire-extinguishers, frosted windows, as we sank through each floor, seemed to intoxicate me. Then there was the open door of the hospital.

After more than a month under a roof, I had the air and the sun on my face again.

The direct air and sun were the strangest things of all. In the ambulance I reached up to look out of the window and take notice of the transformed world.

Everything was different. The sound of the car's engine was muted; it was no more than a soft purring. When a tram passed, it did not clang and lurch as I had expected, it glided noiselessly like a skater on ice, or a swan on silky water. And the people inside – they had dark staring liquid eyes, like the eyes in portraits on the lids of late Egyptian mummy cases; their hair seemed dusty and still, unblown. They grasped their shopping bags unfeelingly, as children hold their dolls. With deep thoughtful faces they went about their almost sacred household tasks, keeping strict silence.

The tram conductor with his bell, his clipping machine and his peaked cap reminded me of some bird; a crow perhaps. I took it that he had the sly evil eyes of a bird.

Close to a pink-grey wall, where every brick seemed to jump out at me separately, I heard music from a wireless or barrel-organ. We were travelling slowly, and for a moment the music wrapped me round. It must have been loud music, but it came to me as a spidery tinkle, filtered through a thousand cobwebs, or the sound of some mermaid blowing on her comb in a cave under the sea. It seemed as beautiful and far away as that.

I saw a girl throwing up a scarlet rubber ball; as she lifted her bare twig-like arms in the air she shut her eyes and bent back her head, so that her throat swelled out. It was clear that she observed a secret rite; every gesture held some meaning. She must have played this game day after day for months and years. I saw the long unbroken chain of movements stretching out behind her.

The girl and her scarlet ball were with me long after she was lost to view. Her intense preoccupation, the stinging point of colour, glancing through the air, snatched, flung away, and lovingly caught again, seemed to complete my awakening.

I suddenly became greedy for the life in the streets. If only the ambulance would go slower!

But all too soon we came to the square where the hospital stood. Most of the old houses had been destroyed, but here and there a few still cowered between the gross modern blocks. Their sashes were bleary, hopeless eyes; their brickwork sagged in despair.

On the shallow steps of the hospital stood a little group of people. Two of the girls wore white jackets with stethoscopes hanging out of their pockets. The third looked about her expectantly. She was beautiful. Behind the protection of my black glass window I studied her cold face. It was difficult to believe that she could not see me. Suddenly I recognized her as one of my brother's greatest friends. All three girls were his friends; he must have asked them to see me settled in this new hospital. The fact that I hardly knew them, that they had come to please him, made the situation false for me. As the stretcher was carried out of the ambulance, the girls all smiled and called out gaily. I felt bound to respond, although I could only think of myself as a loaf of bread being lifted out of the back of a baker's van on a wire tray.

The porters took me into the dark hall. It was a relief to lie back there, not to smile or seem jolly just because I was helpless on a stretcher. The girls' determined gaiety made me conscious of my face. Had it shocked them in the strong sunlight? Did it look ghastly, yellow-white and drawn?

We waited for a little time in the hall. The two girl students stood nearest to me; they explained how they had run across from their own hospital on the other side of the square. The other girl still gazed about her. In one hand she held something lightly wrapped in tissue-paper. Her thoughts seemed to be far away.

Soon two porters came to wheel me into a high old-fashioned ward. They put me in a bed near the door. My brother's friends gathered round and laughed and chattered; but I was only conscious of the ancient, down-pressing melancholy brooding in the space between the shadowed ceiling and the window-frames. It was as if a dark spirit hovered there, spreading its wings over every bed. How much quieter it was in this ward than at the old infirmary! The freakish notion came to me that the patients were all gagged with face flannels. I pictured the nurses stuffing the hard balls of Turkish towelling into each mouth.

The musing, beautiful girl brought her eyes back to her fragile parcel; she unpinned the roof of tissue-paper, then balanced a basket of wonderful strawberries on my chest. A violent pink label hung from the beautifully made little trug. FIRST PRIZE it declared in bold black letters. I was in the marquee of some fruit and flower show. There in the sick green light my little trug reigned over all the other strawberries. My gaze fixed on the sugar-pink label and the fresh blood colour of the fruit, until a vibration was set up in my eyes. The strawberries were too beautiful to eat. I likened them to some wonderful Victorian upholstery – crimson satin, caught down with small varnished wooden buttons.

Long after my brother's friends had gone, I left the strawberries on my chest and watched them rising and falling gently.

No one had been near me since I was first put into the bed. I began to feel restless and alone and forgotten. Perhaps the move had shaken me more than I knew. I plucked at the bedrails above my head and sang some Shakespeare songs under my breath – 'Where the bee sucks', 'Hark, hark! the lark', 'Who is Sylvia?' I twisted the words about to make incongruous, ridiculous sentences. Often my singing tailed off into exaggerated gruntings and sighings. I remembered making noises this way as a child of five or six. That time came back to me vividly; scenes formed and melted like great wax pears. For a moment I lived in them again; I wore my red-striped socks; I felt my nurse's comb tearing through my matted hair.

The tingling grew worse in my legs and I began to drum wildly on my chest; for this distracted my mind a little from the pain.

The nurse who had come into the ward to take temperatures found me beating a mad tattoo and humming.

'Well, and what's wrong with you?' She spoke disdainfully, as if she suspected all men of trying to take 'liberties' with her.

The bustling noise of her shoe heels, the stiff rustle of her apron, broke the stagnant calm in the ward. I was more than ever conscious of the apathy of the other patients. The ones with open eyes looked even deader than the ones who slept; these at least appeared to be living inside their own heads. But the ones with open eyes had nothing within or without; their very eyeballs were as unmysterious and hard as uncooked bullaces.

The last of the sun was striking through the green flesh of some leaves close to one of the courtyard windows. On the other side there were subdued noises from the square – the tinkle of a bicycle bell, a boy shouting, an animal squeak of brakes, dove-wing rush of passing cars.

And again I found that I could not understand the meaning of anything, could explain nothing that I heard or saw. I felt myself beginning to tremble; so I said to the nurse in that steady rather uninterested voice always kept for catastrophes, 'I don't know what anything is about. Do you?'

She gave me one more look, decided that I was not worth answering, then went to fetch a bowl of water and washing things.

VI

THE NEXT morning I was moved right across the ward to a bed between the chimney-piece and the door to the lavatories. Behind the bed was a tall window looking on to a little blind well, where soot, collecting on the brickwork layer on layer, had come at last to resemble a cushiony growth, a sort of black velvet moss.

Hard wooden boards had been put under my new mattress, and the mattress itself was of cool springy rubber sponge. These changes added so much to my comfort that I looked on them as the purest luxury; I found it difficult to believe that the sister really meant them for me.

I watched her as she moved about the ward. She looked calm and good and busy; but once or twice I caught a glance which pleased me even more – a slight wavering, an uncertainty, as if she could not feel pleased with herself. I knew then that Sister was not smug.

I soon found that there was also a good Irish nurse in this ward. She was plump and comely, but with rather too many freckles on her face and arms. My attention would be caught by these little brown spots, so that I could not see her as a whole. I liked her for her boisterous, easy-going efficiency. When she came near, this spirit flowed about me and I thought, 'She is strong enough for anything. Nothing troubles her.' But I was soon to be surprised by a strange twist in her nature.

She had put the screens round my bed and had begun to wash me, when someone called her to the other end of the ward.

While she was away, I decided to try and help by going on with the washing myself. I threw back the towel in which she had draped me and started to rub myself all over with the soapy flannel.

In the middle of my washing she returned and saw me lying on the bed quite naked. This did not perturb me, I had long ago grown used to living in public; but the face of the Irish nurse stiffened. She seemed to bristle.

She, who had always seemed so broad and lively and careless, now startled me by exclaiming: 'Maurice! What is this? What do you mean by it? You must never appear like that before me again.' She quickly threw the towel across and started to scrub me punishingly.

'But, Nurse,' I began, bewildered, 'you see such awful sights all day. Nothing's new to you –'

She cut me short by saying fiercely, 'That's nothing to do with it. Just you remember what I said, Maurice, and don't let it ever occur again. The very idea!'

When she left me, I brooded on her anger for a long time. At first I had taken it for a game – she was only pretending to be outraged – but she had soon made it clear that this was no game. All the squalors and horrors of a hospital could not do what I had done; I had shocked her. Why was it so? Could she possibly suppose that I had thrown the towel off for her benefit? I gulped, turned hot and jerked my head to rid it of this notion, so obviously the true one. She really believed that I enjoyed being washed, that I took pleasure in lying naked on a bed before her. If she could but know how, deep down, I hated to be touched.

Perhaps I should have retaliated by insisting on her coughing discreetly another time before pushing through the screens so freely; but I had no energy left for playing games. I allowed her to bully me.

Soon after this teasing little upset I was taken to be X-rayed again. They wrapped me in scarlet blankets and wheeled me down wide stone-floored corridors filled with an old uneasy atmosphere all their own. The bare walls seemed to be waiting for just another human sight or sound or smell to be swallowed up in them. They had sucked in so much hope and fear and boredom; but nothing showed. Their blank faces stared back and sinister little draughts struck against my face and ears and hair. I heard hurrying feet and strange voices, and saw through half-open doors into other wards, where the patients looked even more grotesque than the ones in my own, since I was given no time to grow used to them.

A woman was in charge of the X-ray room in this hospital. She was examining something at the window; without turning round she told the porters to put me on the table.

I was beginning to wonder if I could bear the hardness of the table any longer, when she at last left the window and came towards me purposefully, her eyes taking no notice of me except as part of her day's work.

She stood beside me with a frown on her face. She seemed to be considering some problem.

Suddenly, without any warning, she gave my body a sharp little jerk which sent such agony through me that I screamed out in distraction. Sweat broke out all over me; I lay there, wondering what the woman would do to me next. She had me there alone, I could do nothing but beg her not to jerk me again.

The woman, after the first shock of my scream, said: 'Oh, I never pinched you! Fancy making all that fuss! I never pinched you.'

Again she tweaked my body more into the position she desired and again I yelled out uncontrollably.

This time she said nothing aloud, but muttered under her breath as she went about her business. Her movements were fierce and flapping. I guessed that she was taunting me for my weakness, blaming me for adding to the difficulty of her day.

Through my pain I remember wondering why she denied pinching me when I had made no mention of pinching. Had she set out with the idea of pinching me? Was she like one of those little girls who have a taste for this method of giving pain? In my present state I could believe anything of her. I saw her as a woman who lived only to hate and inflict pain. Her life spread out before me, day after day – the dreary work, the strain, then the gradual vicious treatment of each patient, until she had become so aware of her cruelty that she felt bound to defend herself before any accusation had been made.

Since she had me at her mercy, quite alone there, I wondered dimly why she stopped at jerking my injured back; could she think of nothing else to do? She had not even tried to twist one of my tingling legs. How strange to miss such a chance! But she was back at the window again, examining something there, no longer taking any notice of me. She still had her back turned when the porters came to take me away. She did not trouble to look round; I was relieved, for my little stock of strength had drained away and I found my fingers slipping even as one of the porters tried to lift me. He had told me to cling round his neck, but hand and arm seemed useless, my fingers scrabbled wildly at the button. Blood was all flowing out of me into the air. I thought of rosy sunset mists, of pink froth at a horse's mouth.

Back in bed once more I was content just to be still, to lie there in a void; but soon I found myself trying to count all the different signs of cruelty; the darting eye, the spitting tongue, the snarling lips, the bristling hair, the heart as dried and shrivelled as a dead frog. I thought that I would always be watching for feet shot out to trip, and sly twisting fingers which, even as they moved, invented new pains . . .

Then I began to gulp and retch and be sick. Everything was swallowed up in my sickness. The X-ray woman melted away and all the thoughts I had built round her. I was only just conscious of the male nurse who came to look after me. I saw his stiff dark hair springing up from his forehead, his eyes fixed on me, the meaty lips no longer smiling. He was Hardy, the male nurse I liked best. How strangely the strong black bristles swept behind his ears! They were like thousands of tiny birds' legs tucked up for flight.

I watched him walk away, then come back with a basin of steaming water. He began to wash me vigorously, trying, I think, to cheer me up with so much briskness. Assuming his most frolicsome mood, he put the soapy flannel over my heart, cupped it with his hand, then bounced it up and down lovingly, as if it had been a fine full breast.

'That's what the girls like, isn't it, Maurice!' he exclaimed with mock relish, his eyes turning up in idiotic ecstasy.

And instead of being angry, I began to giggle at his absurdity, at the X-ray sister's cruelty, and at my own helplessness. The three conditions moved together to make a fantastic picture in my mind. It was as if some gigantic buffoonery had descended upon the whole earth.

I laughed for all the horrors I could imagine existing at that moment; for all the terrors and despairs and tortures and madnesses. I laughed to think of the strange things that were happening to human bodies all over the world. Some were feasting, some were locked in dungeon cells, some were copulating, some were singing, some were having babies, some were starving, some were weeping, some were having Turkish baths, and some were being torn to bits. I thought of the infinite number of postures, expressions, gestures and functions of the body; and these were the funniest thoughts of all.

Hardy, seeing me laugh so much, said, 'Oh, you are ticklish, Maurice, aren't you!'

Then he began to scratch like a little mouse under my arm and to splash the water about gaily in the basin.

Late that night I woke up and saw the night nurse sitting at her table, her head bent low under the lamp with its shade of milky green glass. She seemed to be working at something; the fingers of one hand were taut and angular and the other hand kept rising and falling.

For some time I watched her, lulled by her plucking movements; then the rhythm broke and I saw that she was coming towards me.

'Why aren't you asleep?' she asked in a low voice.

'Oh, I woke up and have been watching you, Nurse. I've been trying to see what you are making,' I said.

After a moment's pause, she replied, 'I've been making my lace.'

She turned and walked away; I had grown used to the abruptness of nurses and imagined that she had left me for the night, but soon she was back with a broad white band hanging from one arm. She shone her torch on it and I saw that it was a beautiful lace of birds and flowers. The torch shining through the holes made an arresting shadow-play on the wall and bed.

It was plain to see that the nurse was proud of her work; she lifted the folds and let them fall, so that the shadow flowers and birds danced. She did not ask for praise – she simply expected it.

'I do a lot of this,' she said carelessly; her voice was the comfortable, dreamy, well-fed voice of the craftsman who is working.

The lace was fit to trim an altar cloth, or the table at a royal banquet; it suddenly delighted me to think that the nurse could work at it so happily in that grim place, where everyone else lay idle, all their energies rotting away in the long blank nights and days.

She stayed by me, talking without expecting answers, until some thought called her back to the table. I saw her writing on a little pad, then the delicate pecking movements began again, and this time I was swept away on them. A white porpoise, dipping and rising, dipping and rising, carried me on its back through the waves.

In the morning the Canadian House Physician came to look at me. He smiled his cosy smile, which made him look too warm, like a young bear on a hot day. Was it his sandy, bushy eyebrows that reminded me of a bear?

The face itself was more like a pink crab . . . but he was talking to me, saying in his pleasant burr, 'Were you sick to your stomach, then, yesterday, Maurice?'

I smiled back; but I told him nothing about my time in the X-ray room. It seemed too far away to be real. The woman herself was only a fairy-tale witch who had tried unsuccessfully to tweak and prod me into her oven.

VII

ALL DAY I lay now in a sort of reverie. The dreaming fit clapped down on me a few days after my visit to the X-ray room. One of the nurses would wash me in the very early morning, sometimes before it was light, then I would lie on my back, cross my arms and float away to an old brick house set in damp green fields in the depths of the country.

Usually I found myself in a narrow, lofty room panelled from floor to ceiling in pine. Corinthian pilasters divided up the walls, and three tall thick-barred sash-windows stood opposite a fireplace framed in a plain bold moulding of green and white marble. Silver snipe with coral beaks ornamented the ceiling. They were in high plaster relief; they made me think of the dugs on a sow.

I realize now that this room was reconstructed from my memories of the old panelled rooms in the Victoria and Albert Museum. As a child I had delighted to look in at the windows of these rooms; they were a sort of giant dolls' house to me. I could imagine people from the past lurking in the cupboards and dark places, waiting to come out until the museum should be closed and the peering eyes gone.

In this daydream room, to which I was always returning, the wide floor-boards were so fanatically waxed and polished that even the old nail-heads glistened like silver. Over these floors played a very small blue Persian kitten. It danced and frolicked, jerking itself this way and that, leaving its hind-legs in the air, pretending that they were paralysed and that it would have to play 'wheelbarrows' for the rest of its life. Sometimes it would almost turn somersaults, or walk sideways, like a crab.

I never picked this kitten up or touched it. I just watched its antics and felt happy to have it with me.

A fire usually burnt in the grate, illuminating a wide semicircle on the floor. The rest of the room was only lit by silver sconces fixed to the pilasters. I remember that there were fat silver fire-dogs, too.

Close to the fire was a winged arm-chair covered in old needlework. Red and white feathery carnations tied with bows were worked on a mustard-yellow ground, and there were little scenes with men and women and trees and animals.

On a round table, in front of the chair, a delicious meal was spread: a large speckled brown egg, some thin golden toast, curls of fresh butter sprinkled with dewdrops and resting on ice, translucent jam made from white cherries, and a squat silver pot filled with a foaming mixture of milk and coffee.

I would sit down in front of this meal and begin to eat slowly, savouring each morsel, sometimes reading a line from the book I had opened. The kitten would be playing on the floor, making light thuds and scratching noises with its claws. The wood hissed and crackled in the grate; but there were no other noises. Outside, in the night, there was perfect silence.

Between the windows, on an old lacquered side-table, stood a cracked blue K'ang Hsi jar filled with a most extraordinary pot-pourri. I never tired of pondering on its ancientness: how many summers' flowers had gone to make it, layer on layer, year after year? – how many spices and salts and essences lay hidden between the petals?

After my meal, I used to go up to this jar, take off the china lid and put my face down to the dark opening. I would breathe deep into my lungs the smell of mildew and of dust, then the scents of all the embalmed flowers and the smells from the century-old cinnamon, clove, orris roots and bay leaves. There would seem to be a hundred other smells, too. I believed that even the porcelain jar had a sweetish rank scent of its own.

When my nose could take in no more smells, I would leave this room and go out into a black-and-white marble-floored hall, and so through the front door into the open air.

The scene in the room was candle-lit and fire-lit, but outside it was always day.

Above the front door, worked in rubbed brick, two cherubs with ugly crying faces held a wreath over the crumbling date. Keeping close to the walls, I would walk right round the house, always glancing over my shoulder when I turned a corner.

I seemed to be expecting dangerous people or ghosts to spring out from the dark shiny-leaved bushes.

Across the fields the tops of carts and coaches and people on horseback could be seen passing along the deep-cut lanes. Once I imagined a postillion who blew a silver trumpet as he jogged along, and then showed his teeth in a snarling doggish laugh.

In one part of the garden, behind powdery orange walls, a dirty old gardener in leather clothes worked, turning up the damp earth in soft chocolate chunks, or picking dew-sprinkled cabbage leaves, which glinted and changed from purple to grey-green as if made of shot silk.

Out of doors my nostrils were always filled with the smell of humid earth and dank grass, and my heart with the pleasure-fear of seeing ghosts and apparitions. I would be led to explore other disused wings of the house, where dry-rot was turning the wainscot to dust, and where bird- and mouse-droppings broke the smoothness of the floor, making miniature mountains on a vast plain. In the corners of the rooms velvet bats hung upside-down, and whispering little gusts of wind, which were really evil powers and emanations, swept through the openings where doors had been brutally torn from their hinges. Spikes of wood still clung to the mangled brass. Smashed panels grinned hideously.

While I was sunk in these never-ending, constantly repeated daydreams, I felt almost entirely cut off from life in the ward. I would hear the banging of enamel basins, the slopping of water, the calling out of patients, and the loud laughs of the male nurses; but it was as if all these sounds were filtered through a thick fluffy blanket.

The peace in my heart was something quite new to me. I was utterly content to lie there and dream, to burrow backwards forever. I sometimes felt that I had never been so happy or so satisfied before in my life, and I knew dimly that this feeling was dangerous, for it made me turn away from every 'reality' with dislike, or alarm. I wanted to make no effort. I only wanted to be left alone.

When at lunchtime I was given the plate of boiled chicken which I had every day, I would look at the sinews and tendons of the drumstick, or at the strange little pieces of tubular entrail which always seemed to get into the pot with the edible flesh, and I would think, 'Those are the remains of a bird that was once alive, that walked on those legs and had blood pumping through those curious veins and tubes.'

And when I thought of the feathers and the beak and the darting needle eye, I became so disgusted that I felt I could not eat. But I did eat, hardly tasting, and then fell back into my dream state.

If the nurse roused me or the masseur came to give his treatment, I would submit to them; but all the time I would be saying to myself, 'Let me get back. Don't keep me here in this dead, grey, disgusting world. I want to go back to the world of pleasure.'

For I realized, even then, that everything in my daydreams had been invented for my pleasure. Even the ghosts and the mouse-droppings were for my pleasure. And everything was beautiful in my eyes, too. Everything was made in my image, and I was a sort of small god, keeping carefully within his own territory.

It is good that I was so often dead to the sights and sounds around me, for the patients in this hospital were suffering from nervous diseases, and many of them behaved in a startling way.

Even the ward maids were epileptics. Sometimes, in the middle of their sweeping and dusting, a glazed, far-away, epileptic stare would come into their eyes; and their hands would shake and the broom and the dustpan would fall to the ground with a clatter. The next moment, if Sister or one of the nurses had not been able to hurry them out of the ward, they would make wolfish noises in their throats and then throw themselves down on the ground in a seeming ecstasy. There was something religious and sexual about their horrible bouncings and tremors; I felt that I was being allowed to see some ancient rite, and I watched with an amazed fascination.

I thought I should never forget the shock of horror that plunged through me when I first saw one of these fits; but I soon learnt that other people at least could take them calmly.

One day a specialist was in the ward, examining a patient, when the patient fell down in front of him in a fit. The patient was a fat middle-aged man; he shrieked and trembled and rolled on the floor, as if he were wallowing in hot mud. It was a terrifying and grotesque sight, but the specialist watched it with a smile on his face. He neither raised the patient up nor prevented him from cutting his head on the corner of the bedside locker.

When at last the convulsions had subsided and the patient, with blood on his face, looked up bewildered, the specialist's smile grew even more Buddhistic and bland and he said in a fluting voice, so that other people should hear, 'Well, I must say there's one improvement this week – you're falling so much more gracefully!'

He gave a light little well-bred laugh, which at once raised up in my mind a picture of some woman with enormous bust measurement, swathed in strainingly tight red velvet. He seemed delighted with his own urbane, unsentimental wit, and I felt that at that moment he would have used the words 'heartless elegance' about himself. He seemed really to be living for a moment his conception of an eighteenth-century French marquise in her brilliant salon.

I suddenly began to hate the specialist for his clownish show of vanity and facetiousness. I hated him so much that my face began to burn. I felt insulted and outraged; I wanted to have the specialist publicly beaten in front of all the staring patients. I imagined his black pin-striped trousers being taken down, and his squeals of shame and pain ringing through the ward.

My extravagant hatred of this specialist continued and even grew, so that whenever he came into the ward I would listen and watch intently for any signs of cruelty or conceit or stupidity. I made him the symbol of all I hated in doctors.

He was nothing to do with me, so of course he never spoke to me or even noticed me; but my eyes followed him round the ward, hating him intently and quietly.

VIII

SINCE MY bed was on one side of the door to the lavatories, many people used to pass the foot of it every day.

On their way back to the common-room or to their beds some of them would stop and talk for a few minutes. There was one person, perhaps a year or two younger than myself, who, after darting looks at me for several days, suddenly said, 'Good morn,' and then stood quite still, holding on to the bottom rail of my bed.

I smiled at him, and he tried to smile back, but it was painful to watch; for one side of his mouth leapt up in a startling, hollow animation, while the other side remained drawn and rigid and dead.

He had had some operation on his head, so he wore an enormous white turban of elaborate bandaging. This, together with his liquid animal brown eyes and delicately shaped nose gave him an arresting, Hindu appearance. Only the neat truculently jutting chin was out of harmony with this smooth Eastern effect. It was a schoolboy's chin, cocky, even bullying.

I had seen him at the far end of the ward, and had noticed that he gesticulated and sometimes showed great exasperation with the nurses. But I had also heard him joking with them and laughing in a strange way, making a deep rasping croak in his throat, then shooting up to a gleeful titter.

I wondered why he said 'Good morn' instead of 'Good morning'. I was just about to decide that it was just a little archaic and affected, when he added, 'How you to –?'

I saw him trying yet unable to finish the word. A look of frustration came into his eyes and he said, 'Damn! Flame!' and the halves of other swear words under his breath. His eyes seemed to search mine for some information; I found myself suggesting, 'Today?'

'That's it,' he said, without any difficulty. My correct prompting seemed to delight him and stimulate him to further efforts. One part of his face was beaming. It was clear that he wanted to tell me the whole of his story. He began, and in spite of the serious interference with his powers of speech I was able to piece the bits together. He had been coming back from Worcester in a lorry with some friends. They had been playing football, and all felt gloriously tired and yet still full of a sort of exuberance. They linked arms and swayed about drunkenly in the back of the lorry, laughing, singing, shouting.

Suddenly the lorry stopped and Ray, for that was his name, struck his head violently on a metal spar just above him. He was knocked out, but his friends laid him on the floor of the lorry and looked after him, and in a little time he felt quite well again.

It was soon after this that he began to have the terrible pains in his head. Then he became partially paralysed and they brought him to the hospital to have the operation on his head. He said that his head didn't hurt at all now. When the wound was dressed, he felt nothing.

He asked if I believed that hitting his head on the beam could possibly have caused the tumour on the brain. He seemed very contemptuous of the idea.

He told me how fine it was to have someone to talk to. He couldn't talk to most of the patients because they were common and ignorant and half daft. As he said this, he lifted one side of his lip in an attempted sneer, and the effect was very sad and ludicrous.

The corner of his lip dropped, the sneer was wiped away. He burrowed deep into my eyes and suddenly jerked out:

'Will you teach me my alphabet again?'

Then in a rush of shame and pride and defiance he added, 'I've only forgotten *some* of the letters.'

His face had taken on a noble bird-like look, as if he were insisting on his own unharmed essence.

I was so taken up with noting this expression that I could only nod my head and say 'Umm' as enthusiastically as possible.

He hurried away at once, dragging one foot slightly. When he came back he held a child's brightly coloured picture alphabet. He told me that he had asked his mother for it. He pointed to one of the letters he had forgotten and said, 'What is that?' When I told him, he mouthed it in an agonized way, wrinkling up one eye. His jaw seemed to become locked, leaving his mouth gaping. I saw his tongue waving about powerlessly; tears sparkled in his eyes. At last he spat the letter out and gave a great grunt of joy.

For some reason he found the letter 'B' difficult. He pointed to it several times, I said it very clearly and he repeated it without any mistake, but he kept asking, 'B, B, what is B?'

I said many words beginning with 'B', but got no response until I tried to shock him into remembrance by snapping out an obscene one.

A smile of recognition came into his eyes and he began to laugh his croaking gasping laugh. He wanted to get a book at once, to discover if I could help him to read simple sentences. I pulled out of my locker *The Rose and the Ring* which Cora had given me.

When he saw the pictures in it he seemed to dislike it for being a 'child's book'. I imagine he wanted some smooth novel, or tough crime story. But soon he was so absorbed in deciphering the sentences that he forgot their innocent content and kept showering me with questions, or crowing when he discovered anything for himself.

'What's this?' 'How do you pronounce that?' 'What does it mean?' The questions poured over me, until I felt submerged and drowned. I lay back against the pillows, half-closed my eyes and made a would-be humorous face to show that I was defeated.

Ray screwed up one eye, looked at me piercingly and said, 'You feel ill.'

I nodded, and he remained silent for a moment, looking down at his feet. But he could not sustain it; he began to tell me that he was allowed to wander about aimlessly in the ward or the common-room, but he wasn't allowed into the sunshine in the square or to visit his father's friend who lived near. What were the matron and the doctor thinking of? How could he ever get well if they wouldn't allow him to return to normal life?

'But I shall be going home soon,' he said fiercely; 'my mother is coming to fetch me.'

At this point I was really delighted to see a nurse approaching. She told Ray Anderson that he was not to stand by my bed any longer. He was to go to the common-room and wait there for the dressing on his head to be changed.

Ray made snarling, whining, dog-like noises in his throat and said that he didn't want to go. The nurse took him by the arm and tried to lead him away; he became furious and shook her off roughly.

He turned and gave me one more look, as if to say, 'See how I am treated!' His expression reminded me of a Chinese pottery Kylin lion – eyes slanting upward to heaven, and full of fierceness and longing and pain.

I watched his flat back receding. The dragging rise and fall of his walk with its broken rhythm now reminded me of a dancing doll, and I wondered why awkwardness in movement always made me conscious of underlying grace. Gawky people expressed a hidden grace every time they moved.

I shut my eyes and took in deep breaths.

The next morning Ray came to me for talking and spelling and reading, and although he was never allowed to stay by my bed for long, he contrived to spend a little time there every day, until he had established it as a custom.

Then at last it was decided that he should go home.

The bandage on his head was much smaller now. He came over to me in his raincoat to say good-bye. I could see how delighted he was to be dressed in his clothes again. He kept patting the lapels of the raincoat, straightening his tie, even trying to sleek his hair, until he remembered his turban of bandages.

He shook my hand with jerky violence, thanking me again and again for my lessons in reading and spelling. He gave me a large envelope with his address already on it and asked me to be sure to write to him.

As he went down the ward, he shouted to me and to the other patients, then waved his hand with so much vigour that he almost upset his balance. He lurched his way through the door with angry determination. I was left with a feeling of blankness and envy and gladness.

I wrote to him in a few days' time, but had no answer. I took it that he still found it too difficult to write, and did not wish to dictate to anyone. I knew how resentful he could be when he did not want to be helped. My mind began to close over him. He was almost forgotten, when one day one of the male nurses spoke of him as he washed me.

'You remember Ray,' he said; 'did you know he died last week?'

The nurse went on washing my chest and arms; I could feel the slithery movements of his soapy hand; but my thoughts had all flown to Ray. I saw him, so eager to learn to read again, so amused at remembering swear words. His jerky imperfect movements and extraordinary facial expressions made him appear more alive than any healthy person – violently, extravagantly alive. How confounding now to be told that he was dead!

I thought again of the ride in the lorry which his bald description had made so clear to me. The boys singing and shouting and fooling, then the sudden stop and the thud of Ray's head against the beam.

The futile ending of Ray's life dismayed me. We both had felt the savage change from fair to dark; now he could feel no more; but what was left to me? I kept saying, 'Knocked on the head, struck down, out, done for, dead,' until all the ordinary expressions lost their meaning, turned into a string of glass beads, rippling through my brain. I chanted them as if they had been charms.

Although I began by thinking only of Ray struck down and dead, my mind soon began to play round all the trappings of death. I saw the quiet workmanlike obsceneness of a coffin. There was a faint smell in the coffin, of camphor perhaps; and round the coffin, as if to mask its shape and cover the faint smell, branch upon branch of white lilac had been massed. I watched tiny creatures crawling in and out of the flowers, falling into the coffin, trying to climb out again with a terrible patience. The breath from the flowers was so sweet that it seemed to coat the inside of my nostrils.

I could not rid my mind of these white flowers, so melodramatic, so obvious, waving falsely over the corruption, trying to hide the sight and the smell of it.

Under the lilac plumes were the utterly still features. They looked like some rather timid wax sculpture. Somehow the skull was beginning to smile its way through the drawn flesh, which had grown almost as clear as a sheet of carpenter's glue.

I saw all this, and Ray's jaw fallen open, as the jaws of all corpses in schoolboys' books are fallen open. I could see his white teeth and the darker patches of silver stopping in the back ones. His mouth gaped, so that I could even see to the place where his wisdom teeth had begun to sprout. Like the tips of snowy cob nuts or cold fresh buds pushing up through the earth, they appeared to me. And his dead tongue was stiff as the metal clapper of a bell and the purple-brown colour of burnt iron.

'Everything spoilt and wasted,' I thought; 'the new teeth, the strong bones, the fresh scarlet blood and smooth skin, springing hair, shining eye.'

My thoughts were all for the body, over which I saw now the exquisitely jointed little wood-lice crawling. I felt their tiny tickling feet, wading through the hairs on Ray's leg, mounting the creamy smoothness of his belly, skirting the navel's volcano crater, and continuing up to the tougher still sunburnt skin on his chest, reaching at last the little well at the base of his throat where they would nestle close together.

Was it Charlemagne who was found with inch-long nails sticking through the jewelled gloves on his dead hands? I wondered if Ray's nails would grow after death. Perhaps they would grow as long and thin and curved as those razor shells which I used to find on the seashore when I was a child. And would his hair grow, too, until the operation wound was covered over, thatched with a matted roof?

I saw Ray's coloured alphabet gruesomely transformed. Instead of the bright picture of an apple after 'A', I saw printed the agonized, extraordinary noises Ray sometimes made when he tried to say this vowel. And after 'B' was no charming picture of a bee sucking the nectar from a Morning Glory flower, but the threatening question, 'What is "B"?' repeated several times in print that enlarged itself hysterically with each repetition.

I wondered what had happened to my letter to him. I thought that to see a dead person's name on an envelope would give me a strange uneasiness – a feeling that I ought to try to forward the letter in some way to the spirit world.

I was reminded of the letters I had written to my mother when she died and I was eleven years old. I used to take these letters out with me into the fields; there I would post them in rabbit-holes, under the overhanging cornices of streams, amongst the tangle of roots and stones and earth, in empty birds' nests, in old tins and bottles and the pockets of ragged clothes on rubbish dumps, down waterfalls and millraces and a deep forgotten well in the garden of a ruined cottage.

Once I posted a tiny note in a fat bunch of grass which I gave to a cow. As I watched her munch my message and take it down into her huge body, I pretended to believe that this note at least would reach its destination; it would live in her blood, be emptied on the ground, where it would make leaves and flowers grow. It would open like a fan, shooting out calls in all directions.

All day I thought of Ray and hugged the dread and fear which my thoughts bred.

I looked across to his bed and saw an old man lying there; an old man staring at the ceiling, his hands outside the sheets, plucking aimlessly.

I thought of the many people who had said to me, 'You're young; you've got plenty of time to recover.' This seemed the coldest comfort, the grimmest fact of all.

IX

B UT BY the next day I had almost forgotten Ray's death. Life seemed now nothing but a long reverie, made up of imaginings and memories of childhood. Over this sunken, buried life, the facts of every day rippled and tinkled like a shallow stream; and they seemed to move so rapidly that I had no time for reflection. I was only able to note them with a flickering interest; then they were gone, hidden and submerged by new happenings.

In this way the grey-skinned man with several weeks' grey beard on his face crowded out the memory of Ray.

I saw him leap from his bed and walk towards the lavatory door, muttering words and holding out his hands prophetically. He wore no trousers, only his short pyjama jacket, and his awkward, muscular legs and the twisted position of his hands reminded me of Rodin's John the Baptist.

When the epileptic ward-maid saw that his genitals showed below the short jacket, she stopped in her sweeping, leant on her broom and tittered showily. 'Just look at that!' she said, turning to me. Her voice was so full of silliness, derision, pretended modesty, that I could only stare at her, willing her violently to feel something, to come alive. But she still gazed and tittered, ridiculing his age, his nakedness, his sickness.

I watched anxiously as he drew nearer. I saw that there were no nurses at hand to lead him back to bed, and I felt that the maid would do nothing to help.

When he was within a few yards of me his stiff, dignified movements dropped from him, he ran past the foot of my bed, flung himself at one of the closet doors, slammed it after him, bolted it, then began to batter against the panels, shouting and screaming as he did so.

The noise was so sudden and so alarming that it startled the whole ward.

Even the maid seemed to realize that something must be done. She ran to fetch a male nurse, returning with him in a state of high excitement. It would cap all, I felt, if she fell down in a fit at that moment.

It was clear that the male nurse had been rather frightened by her story. He stood outside the closet door and called the patient by name. He masked his nervousness with a truculent, matter-of-fact air. The man responded with a shattering rain of blows on the door, and with obscenities and despairing words screamed at the top of his voice.

The male nurse's hands joined together convulsively.

'Just come out and be sensible,' he implored; for what he dreaded most was that the patient *should* come out *without* being sensible. He was afraid of being seized on by a maniac. I understood his fear, and, being so near the door, caught some of it myself. I looked about me, trying to think of some way of protecting myself; but there was nothing for me to do; I could only lie there, waiting.

Suddenly the male nurse seemed to realize that he could shift the responsibility and also leave the danger area. 'I'm going to fetch the doctor,' he called out in a loud voice, so that all could hear. He ran down the ward, looking quite happy and relieved.

There was silence in the ward, and a still more threatening silence in the lavatory. Everyone who was able to use his mind was waiting for some catastrophe.

When the doctor appeared, the chief expression on his face was exasperation. His manner implied contempt for the male nurse's alarm. He walked into the lavatory boldly.

'Unbolt that door and don't make any more fuss,' he ordered; then, since there was no answer to this testiness, he grew more coaxing. Still no answer, not even a movement.

I saw the male nurse and the doctor murmuring together; I wondered if they were going to try to force the door open.

As suddenly as the noise had ceased, it began again, with increased violence. First came a string of demoniac blows on the door, then the grey man flung it open and, with an unearthly scream, ran straight at the doctor and the nurse. For a moment they grappled with him, but he quickly threw them off and dashed across the ward to the door exactly opposite, which led into the bathroom.

I caught sight of the hairy grey legs and buttocks flashing past; there was the noise of a sash-window being thrown up and the soft thud of someone jumping down.

'He's out of the window!' the male nurse shouted.

I thought for a moment that the man had jumped down into the deep area and been killed or injured; but I soon realized that there was no area outside the bathroom window, for the male nurse, whose courage had increased marvellously with the excitement, himself jumped out and began to give chase.

The patients near the windows which looked on to the square all sat up and turned round to watch the spectacle. They clapped their hands and whooped like children or men at a football match. I heard their wild descriptions, but could see nothing myself.

The doctor had not jumped out of the window; he had hurried to the front door and was now also in the square. Doctor and nurse both chased the half-naked man round the square, catching him at last as he tried to climb the railings to hide in the bushes.

His eyes were rolling when they brought him back. His face streamed with sweat and the grey hair stuck to his forehead. His jacket had been torn in the struggle; a hank of darker hair showed through the rent. He lay back in the arms of the doctor and the nurse, looking like the tortured and exhausted victim of some human sacrifice. The bed to which they were leading him might have been the gruesome altar stone.

Two male nurses sat by him until well into the night; but he was still now, not even uttering a word, only plucking fitfully sometimes at the hem of his sheet.

This incident, like the last, lived in my mind for a little, then was wiped out by the night nurse, who did pictures in pen and ink, and who was going to leave the nursing profession to become a Roman Catholic priest.

When he found out that I was an art student, he brought some of his pictures to show me. I particularly remember one of praying hands, elaborately modelled and built up with cross-hatching. On one forefinger was a huge pontifical ring, and the veins and the nails, even the cuticles, were shown with grisly care.

The male nurse's face was the colour of newspaper that has been spread on a shelf in an attic. His eyes were very dark and soft and his hand movements flowing. Perhaps these details of appearance and manner, together with his drawings, prejudiced me against him; for, in spite of his pleasant smiles and willingness to talk, I felt that there was a core of something much darker and less friendly within him.

On one of his nights on duty I fell into a doze soon after he appeared. For a long time I was in that troubled half-conscious state when the reasoning faculty is extraordinarily active but utterly awry. Everything that is heard or seen or thought is turned into a terrifying threat. You are not asleep, and yet you are not awake; you hang between the two states feeling mad.

I lay there in the darkness, consumed by some fire. Each thought was a leap of flame. I had no hope, did not expect any help, but I longed for it, and this longing made me call out and talk aloud.

The night nurse, when he heard me, came across the ward. Although his footsteps sounded forbidding, I welcomed them as something real and concrete.

The pale moon of his face glimmered above me; I saw two black holes for the eyes and one for the mouth.

Pleased even to have this sinister mask above me, I put out my hand to touch the sleeve of his coat, and was just about to grip his arm when he thrust his face close to mine and spat 'Shut that bloody row, do you hear!'

This sudden violence, instead of waking me properly, threw me into an even greater state of confusion. I must have called out again, for the next thing I knew was that the nurse had caught hold of my shoulders and shaken me, knocking me from one side of the bed to the other. He ended by slapping my face. In a still moment of realization, he stared down at me, savouring what he had done. There seemed to be guiltiness and delight in his face. I stared back at it blankly, until I was swamped in rushes of pain and could see nothing. Even then I felt that he was still there, above me in the darkness, gloating.

Later, when I had recovered a little from the shock, I looked carefully from side to side, but he had disappeared. I could think of no one else; my mind was overflowing with the most grotesque fancies. He appeared to me as a great black tarantula in cassock and biretta, with hairy spider ankles and wrists just visible. I smelt his breath, and saw again the discoloured celluloid disc of his face hanging above me in the dark; it was like a shaving mirror. Or, it was a cat's smirk of satisfaction. He had worn such a look when he showed me his black drawings. The drawings themselves were grim enough to have been done with a corpse's dirty finger-nail split down the middle and dipped in the excrement of cockroaches.

Once more I told myself always to expect evil. I had imagined human hearts as dried and shrivelled frogs before; now I thought of them as daffodil bulbs treacherously plump, full of black rottenness. When I put out my hand, the nurse had squirted his black rottenness over me; I had it on my fingers now. I hated as he did.

In the morning, in the very earliest dawn, the night nurse came to wash me and to give me some tea.

He had stolen a pinch of Sister's china tea for me; as he told me this, he thrust the cup under my nose, so that I should smell its fragrance.

I looked at him with a sort of wonder at first, even drew my hands away from the cup; then something relaxed in me and I took it quite gladly. Still looking at the nurse, I thought that words and actions would never hold the same meanings again. I would take what came along, never questioning; for questioning brought on a feeling of craziness. Was this man hateful to me? Or was I grateful to him for his little attention? Could I ever trust that old newspaper face again? Why was I smiling at him? Why was I trying to make myself believe that he wished me well? No use to ask, just take your cup, smile, think, 'How kind of him to bring me this special tea!'

So all my feelings seemed to pass into this calm indifference; and when, a few nights later, I heard nurses hurrying, and screens dragged up, the soft plash of water, oxygen pumping, tang of metal instruments on glass, the low urgent voices murmuring together, and hideous gurgling, strangling sounds, I knew at once that someone was dying; but the knowledge had no power to move me any more, except to awaken a faint spark of my old curiosity.

'How does a man die?' I asked myself; then, 'Who is dying?'

Raising myself up slightly, I saw that the screens were round the bed of the grey-haired man, and only then did some human feeling pass through me. I was glad for him that he should no longer have to lock himself in closets and batter on the doors. Epileptic maids would never ridicule him again and where he was going neither the tops nor bottoms of pyjamas were needed to cover nakedness.

There was more escape for him now than the escape through a bathroom window into a caged square.

Dying itself appeared as such a perfect and serene resolving of all difficulties that I was filled with satisfaction. I saw that it was best to die at night – more beautiful in the darkness, with only the lamps; the traffic stiller in the city, and most people asleep, or cut off by the meltingly soft black veil.

I found that my fear of the night had turned back into the love I used to have for it when I was well and free and could walk over the wind-bitten grass or bicycle for miles down lanes that were almost tunnels.

As I watched the screens round the death-bed, I noted idly how much glowing green colour there was: green cloth screens with the light behind, the translucent green shade of the night nurse's lamp. I had had green all round me when first I found myself in hospital; so this unsubtle, luminous grass green has become associated in my mind with death and disaster.

When at last the grey-haired man died, the atmosphere suddenly lightened. Voices and movements had been freed from some clogging constraint. The relaxation of tension surged towards me in a wave. It was as if the nurses and doctors were all saying, 'Well, that's that. Now we can get on with our routine jobs.'

In a moment everything seemed ordered, arranged and tidily under control. There was no more tingling in the air, no more fighting against some unaccountable thing.

The low trolley on its cushiony rubber tyres luxuriously bore the corpse away down the middle of the ward. There was speed and secretiveness and deftness in its movement. Over the dead man's face was a blanket, so that age, torture, ugliness and fear, all were hidden.

Instead of looking on this covering, this careful manipulation as an hypocrisy and cheat, I saw it for what it really was, a desperate effort to make life bearable and sane.

I admired the doctors and the nurses. I admired every human being in the world who, on top of a million, million horrors, yet built a nest, a haven and calm place.

X

As the days passed into weeks, and the weeks passed into months, I began to wonder why Mark Lynch did not come to see me.

To begin with, I had not thought anything of it, but now his neglect seemed strange; for I realized suddenly that I had seen more of him than of anyone else at the art school.

When I had first gone there I had known nobody; and my evenings in my room on Croom's Hill were spent all alone. I used to come back and climb the stairs and throw myself down on the bed, sprawling out my legs and burying my face in the pillow. I would be thinking of the pleasures and the pain in the day that had just passed. Then, turning over, I would stare at the uneven ceiling and wonder how much longer my life would lack direction, how much longer I would be cut off yet searching for my true place in the world. I thought of the hours wasted at the art school, with the drawing-board in front of me and the pencil in my hand, the feeling of uselessness that came upon me as I sat there, staring into space.

It was always a relief and a pleasure to reach the end of the day, when I would go down to the refectory, buy an enormous shortbread biscuit wrapped in silver paper, and sit eating it alone at the far end of one of the long tables. I would have beside me a glass of very hot milky coffee from which I took sips now and then.

But there was sadness, too, in coming to this point in the day, for it brought with it the realization that another precious piece of my life had melted away; and I had done nothing to catch it, to hold it, to *know* it.

A wave of shame and guilt at my own indolence would flood over me. I felt that somewhere inside me was so much power – if only I could dig a channel down which it could pour.

And when at last I had been lashed by my longings and made too restless to lie still any longer, I would jump up and go out on to the heath. I would climb the hill, then pass down Chesterfield walk, behind the seats where all the lovers gathered. There were often so many there that some men and girls had to lean up against the hard corrugated bark of the ancient tree-trunks.

As I gazed at the scene, I always wanted to make a picture of it. I saw in my mind's eye the strange grouping of the lovers – the darkness fusing them into pyramids, two-headed ghosts and fantastic pagodas – but the problem of the night setting never ceased to tease me. How was the darkness, the exciting brooding of the great arms of the trees above, to be suggested? I wondered.

Near the locked gates of Greenwich Park I would stand under a weeping-willow at the edge of the pond, where the ruffled water seemed to be curling its black lips at me.

Sometimes I grew happier and more satisfied with the life inside me, but at other times my sense of desolation grew in the emptiness of the heath; then I would be ready to talk to anyone, to do anything to shut myself away from the blankness of my own heart.

In this way I made contacts with people who often filled me with dislike or fear, so that I suddenly dashed away in the middle of a conversation, leaving the man or woman in complete bewilderment.

Once I found a drunk man lying on his back in the grass. His breathing had turned to an alarming bellow, and I knew that I ought to do something. I knelt down and undid the stud of his collarless shirt. As I did so, the sweet smell of strawberries met me. It clung all round his mouth, even obscuring and confusing the beer smell.

He opened his eyes and stared up at me; all I could find to say was, 'You've been eating strawberries.'

A curious, sly, animal grin came into his face. He turned a little to one side; then, when he thought I was not looking, his hands shot out as if to grab me round the waist. I sprang back, laughing nervously. Because he had startled me, I began to curse him as he lay there in the grass, so repulsively helpless. He shouted some clouded, smeared words after me, but I left him to his fate.

After wandering in this way, sometimes till late into the night, I would suddenly be overcome with tiredness and would want nothing more than my bed and the silence of my room.

As I paused at the top of the hill, I thought of the nuns and their pupils sleeping close to me in their convent. Far below me on the river sirens would be hooting, expressing amazingly some universal sadness. Trains clanged down to Woolwich, sparkling like giant tinder-boxes on wheels.

I would shut my mind to it all, and while tramping down the hill I would be seeing and hearing nothing, only longing for bed.

Many nights I spent like this, alone; until one evening at the art school a senior student, who was setting up a still-life group, turned and spoke to me.

Having persuaded myself that I had finished my drawing of the Clapping Faun, I was sitting side-saddle on my wooden donkey, reading a very old and cheap blue-backed edition of *De Profundis* which someone had left on the floor.

When I looked up from it I found Lynch staring at me, his hands still fiddling with a cone and ball which he was arranging on a pedestal.

'Is that interesting?' he asked, smiling.

For so young a man he had hollow cheeks, and I described his eyes to myself as 'fever bright', because they were small, quick-moving, and the flesh all round them was crinkled up from the smile.

'There's a lot about Jesus and Christianity,' I said in a flat non-committal voice. I was really very disappointed in *De Profundis*. I think I had expected a revelation of prison horrors and a passionate protest against the system of locking people up.

Lynch smiled at me even more broadly and continued to talk about books. While he talked, I noticed the round shape of his head and the swarthy roughness of his upper lip and jowl. His strong beard was remarkable, since he could be no more than twenty, and his hands and wrists, in contrast, were unusually smooth and white. His nails, unlike those of most art students, were unstained and clean and carefully filed. There was no pencil dust under them, or gruesome Crimson.

'What do you do in the evenings?' he asked me suddenly, cutting through my contemplation of him.

'Oh, walk on the heath or read,' I said.

'Don't you get rather dismal, all alone?'

'Sometimes a little, perhaps; but then I like being alone, too,' I said as vaguely and lightly as possible.

There was a slight pause in which Lynch seemed to be arranging the words in his next sentence. At last he brought it out.

'I spend most of my evenings going round to my various friends, cheering them up.'

He looked at me very gaily and brightly, and I saw at once that he wanted to come and cheer me up, too. Therefore his next question was not at all unexpected.

'Whereabouts do you live?'

I told him, but I did not suggest that he should come and see me, not altogether caring for the idea of being cheered up.

However, a few nights later the door-bell rang after supper, and, looking down over the banisters, I saw Lynch being ushered into the hall. After the first moment of reluctance, I came down and greeted him, and we sat in the dining-room by the fire and drank coffee.

In spite of my misgivings, this first evening was a success. We talked and kept each other interested and amused till well after midnight. The fire died down in its frame of old scratched grey marble, and Lynch began to tell me a ghost story of his own invention.

At last he got up to go; I followed him down the steps and into the almost deserted road. We parted at the street lamp on the corner of the Circus.

As I walked back alone to the house, I thought that Lynch was a delightful companion, and I wondered why I had not felt in sympathy with him when he first spoke to me in the Antique and Still-Life room.

A few nights later Lynch came again, and again we talked till after midnight.

We met very little at the art school, only passing each other sometimes in the corridors on the way to our different classes; so all our communication was saved up for the end of the day.

Soon Lynch, or Mark as I now called him, was appearing at Croom's Hill almost every evening; and at the week-ends we would often take a bus and then walk in the country near Farningham and Eynsford. We would pick sour sorrel by the side of the road to quench our thirst; and once we climbed a great oak in the grounds of Lullingstone Castle, and hid in the branches, because it had begun to rain and the stags were grunting lustfully and dangerously. In the autumn we walked through endless orchards where the scarlet and yellow apples were left to rot into a brown pulp on the ground. We would fill our pockets and our satchels with the still unrotten fruit, wishing for something much larger, a packing-case or a laundry basket, so that a little more could be saved from the waste.

At the end of these long days together we would sometimes quarrel, even hitting each other in a half-hearted way; and I wondered, now that Mark did not come to see me, if some taunt or criticism of mine had offended him more deeply than I had intended.

I remembered in particular one evening, not long before the accident cut short all that old life. I had wanted to be entirely alone. I knew that Mark would come to see me, so quickly after supper I flung out of the house in a black mood.

'Now if he comes,' I thought, 'he'll find an empty room and he'll have to amuse himself.'

Instead of climbing up to the heath, I went down the hill to the church, then past the pawnbroker's shop and the covered market.

The dirt, the darkness, and the secrecy excited me. Under the decay and the squalor was a secret – something enduring and still and living, like a foxglove in the silence of a wood. Beyond was the mysterious promise of the river, unseen but heard, and smelt with every breath.

I threaded my way down until I could see it, black and vast, glimmering like oily mercury where lights caught its ripples. I was by the domed mouth of the tunnel which led under the river to the Isle of Dogs. Surely a magic spot – the name, the Isle of Dogs, and the procession of people coming up the spiral staircase from under the water!

I stood by the door of the tunnel and watched them – sailors with kit-bags on their shoulders; the strangely Assyrian looking girls with black pom-poms on their eyeveils; old scavenging men and women with thin wisps of hair and very prim toothless mouths; surly lads of my own age, half-garrotted by their own scarves, looking as if they'd like to knock me or anyone else down.

I stared at all the types, and a terrible feeling of loneliness swept over me; this in spite of my special wish to be alone that night. I felt that everyone was cut off from me, that it would always be so, and that nothing I could do would ever make any difference. I turned away from the people, hating them passionately, yet longing to be taken to their bosoms.

And at the thought of being taken to so many and such strange bosoms,

I thankfully burst out laughing and dashed through the passage under the Ship Inn, feeling altogether lighter. I tried to imagine a 'Ministerial Whitebait Dinner' being held in one of the rooms above me. I had no clear idea of the banquet and could only see it as a succession of tiny fishes on dolls' plates set before enormous politicians in wigs.

I was by the pier now, the gates were fastened with a huge chain and padlock. It was a symbol to me and I hated the sight. The frustration of the lock and chain had power over me. I turned away and followed the balustraded walk in front of the hospital, where the colonnades, like birds' wings, touched with light, spread out from the black body of the building. I imagined a procession, with naked torches, threading in and out of the columns.

Stopping in my rapid walk, I leant on the balustrade and thought of Mark, lying on the bed at home, waiting for me patiently; and the thought was so enraging that I found myself turning utterly against him. Would he never leave me alone? Would nothing break his persistence?

Down below me on the muddy river beach I heard noises and, bending farther over the parapet, I was just able to make out two children playing on the brink of that forbidding water. They were intent, shut off from all the rest of the world.

'When I say, "Bum, bum, bum, bum, bum," you must answer, "Yes, your Majesty,"' the older one dictated. She was delving in the mud with two sticks, scuffling out some mystic circle and cross, with other magic signs.

The smaller child first nodded gravely, then some irrepressible impulse made it say, 'Yes your Bumship.'

I waited, realizing that punishment would be meted out for this frivolity and impudence. There was the harsh sound of a slap and the smaller child set up a terrible wailing.

'If you won't do it properly, it's no good,' I heard the older one say; 'and if you don't stop your row I'll take you home and we won't have no communication tonight after all.'

I knew then that they were playing some spiritualistic ghost game.

I turned away and left them leading their thrilling life there, close to the horrible black water. The river sights and sounds were overwhelming me with their insistence, their never-ending story of time passing, longing, death.

To ease my ache I started to run. I ran until I sweated and panted. I ran through side streets and alleys and came out at last on Croom's Hill again. I looked up at the window of my room, saw that it was lighted and knew that Mark was waiting for me there. Stamping up the stairs noisily, I threw open my door and found him lying on the bed full length, reading one of my books. He raised his eyes, but did not get up.

'Where *have* you been?' he asked with studied laziness. 'I've been waiting here hours; it's nearly midnight.' Underneath the laziness there was an accusation in his voice.

'Well, if it's so late, why didn't you go home?' I snapped.

I turned abruptly from him and started to slap back my hair viciously with the stiff brushes on my dressing-table; then I picked up my towel and flannel and said, 'I'm going to turn on my bath.'

I left the room, but in a moment or two Mark came to the half-open bathroom door and stood there diffidently.

'I'd better go,' he said in a flat voice.

'Good-night,' I said and shut the door. I heard him going down the stairs, then the click of the latch.

I sighed and lay back in the hot water, exaggerating my relief, delighting in the thought that it would be some time before I had another visit from Mark. Then a realization of my own meanness came to me; I remembered the times when I had enjoyed his company.

Now, as I lay in bed in the hospital, I thought of all these past incidents. I began to wonder if I should ever see Mark again. When Cora and Betsy next came to see me I asked them about him; but, as neither of them knew him well, they were able to tell me very little. They saw him every day but hardly ever exchanged words.

Then, one visiting day, as I lay waiting, watching the door eagerly, hoping for Clare or some other friend, I saw Mark's round head bobbing about at the far end of the ward. He was looking in all directions and his hands were held rigidly to his sides. As he came nearer, I saw the tenseness of his expression and the lizard-like darting of his eyes. There was a sort of fluttering alarm in them which I had never seen before. I had remembered them only as bright and rather penetrating.

He was upon me, almost, before he had recognized me. I called his name, and he started; then he came straight up to the bed, caught hold of my hand rather desperately and began to pump it up and down.

'I've been looking for someone with no face or only half a face, and all the time you've been lying here looking more or less the same!' he exclaimed, stringing all his words together.

Mark was still holding my hand, shaking it up and down mechanically; and although I was genuinely pleased to see him, I found that his perturbation had upset my thoughts and that I had nothing to say.

'I've been walking round the square since one o'clock,' he told me suddenly.

'But why, Mark?' I asked in amazement.

'Because I didn't know what you'd look like, and, anyhow, hospitals always fill me with horror. I can't bear the special smell they have. It isn't disinfectant; everybody makes that mistake. I think it's just plain floor polish made horrible by association.'

I laughed, and Mark's tense expression slackened a little. He began to ask me a great many questions about myself, and when I had answered them all he told me of his elder brother's sudden death the week before. Even as he spoke, Mark seemed to be apologizing for bringing me this sort of news. It was almost as if he were saying, 'I know I am bringing coals to Newcastle, but you mustn't think that I pay you any the less attention because of my brother's death, nor must you think that I feel very deeply about it.'

In his even, light voice he went on to tell me of the consequences to himself of his brother's death. He would now have to support his mother as well as himself on his scholarship money and the little private teaching that he did. The difficult prospect appeared to amuse him. He wore a curious, quirkish smile which seemed to ask me to treat the whole subject as extravagant melodrama.

I was at a loss to know how to behave, or what to show on my face. I wanted to show gravity and a concern for his new responsibility; but these expressions would have made him feel that he had burdened me with his troubles. It was one of those absurd painful little situations when each step leads farther into the bog, until one doubts if one will ever be natural again.

I was glad when I heard the bell ringing to clear the visitors from the ward; but this reminder of hospital routine brought back the guilty look to Mark's eyes. Once more he grabbed my hand and jerked it up and down; he muttered something about coming to see me again; then he was away, hurrying down the ward as if the police were after him.

XI

THERE WAS that other time, soon after Mark's visit, when the long-haired man was wheeled up to the empty bed on the opposite side of the fireplace.

His face was peaked and narrowed, the moonstone-coloured flesh stretched tight across humped cheekbones – a beggar's face in a romantic picture. On either side long tassels of goldish hair lay tangled on the pillow. In spiky contrast to this softness a young beard sprouted on his chin.

By his side walked a girl in pill-box hat and soft rich-coloured woollen clothes, tight-fitting and wrinkled to the shape of her body. The little mustard jacket, caught in at the waist by one silver button, flared out behind like a Toby ruff or the petals of a large daisy. She, too, had long fair hair. It swayed from side to side with every movement, reminding me of the hand-loops in underground trains. She was holding the man's hand, and on her face was an expression of exasperation and despair which told me at once that the handclasp must be anything but comforting.

As the trolley was wheeled down the ward, the man murmured things to her, but she could hardly look at him. Her eyes kept darting from side to side, as if to escape from the sight which they knew they ought to face.

When the porters raised up the man to put him in the bed there was such a screaming that the air seemed broken to bits; nothing was important but the silencing of these screams.

Gradually they subsided into groans and whimpers and things said imploringly to the nurses and the young woman.

As soon as I saw this man's strange face, I associated it with a face I had seen in the Youth Hostel at Taunton a year ago. That face, too, had been pointed and framed in dangling fair hair. But the man at the hostel had arrived on a tandem with a much plumper girl than the one who walked by this ill one's side.

I remembered that he wore corduroy shorts, and thonged sandals, on hairy feet, turned floury grey by the dust on the road. He kept pushing his hair back from his face; as he did so, I caught sight of a little coral stud in one of his ears. This immediately interested me and I began to watch him.

He and the plump girl started to unpack their evening meal on the common-room table. First garlic sausage appeared, then radishes and a long roll of twisted bread. They ate with one knife between them, and with their fingers. I heard the man say 'Ma chère' to the girl; and after he had cut some sausage, I saw him wipe his fingers in his long hair.

They spoke to no one while they were rather greedily eating, but when they had finished, the man looked round the room, as if to find something to hold his attention. His eyes finally lighted on me, perhaps because he had noticed me taking in the details of his appearance and behaviour. He gave me a sharp look, then showed all his teeth in a smile. I smiled back rather apprehensively, not altogether liking that first shrewd glance.

'And where have you come from?' he asked, still smiling. I told him that I had only walked a little way that day because I had sat down under a bridge and tried to draw a stream and rushes.

'But I'm a painter, too!' he said with extravagant surprise, thrusting out his hand to grasp mine. I took hold of it with embarrassment and explained hurriedly that I was only a student.

The man began to tell me all about his studio over a shop in Shepherd's Bush. He lived there with the fat girl; and when they felt hungry after a hard morning's work they would run across the road and get meat pasties and ham roll from the little restaurant on the corner. At other times they would stay at home and cook kippers and sausages and bacon over the gas-ring.

After all the talk about food, he added, in the simplest way imaginable, 'If we want money, I just sell a picture.'

'But can you always do that?' I asked, amazed at his cool assurance.

'Oh yes,' he said, 'someone always wants one. I have no difficulty at all.'

'No one's ever said that to me before,' I replied, perhaps too decisively; for the man's purring accent changed.

'What's all this moaning and groaning about?' he asked angrily. 'People either won't sell reasonably or they won't take the trouble to find the right market. I work and then I sell. Nothing could be easier.'

After this outbreak, the man returned to his soft gentle tones and to his smiles; the plump girl complained that the shape of her legs was being spoilt by bicycling, and I looked round me for some means of escape. I was afraid that the man was going to ask to see my drawing of the stream and the rushes. I was very curious to know the name of this artist who sold everything he painted, but I dared not linger.

I said good-night and left him rubbing 'Ma chère's' legs and pinching the calves to see if the muscles ached.

As I went out, I heard other people in the common-room criticizing the painter and his friend. They were drawing attention to the strange clothes, the dirt, the archaic table manners and the affectation. The leg-rubbing was being judged particularly severely.

Even while I listened to these remarks, I could feel my own mild opposition turning into a quite different feeling. It was almost as if I was in league with the man and woman against these dreary fault-finders. The scene at Taunton had been made vividly alive again by the arrival of this new patient.

I had now almost convinced myself that he was the man of the youth hostel; and this growing conviction was strengthened when the young woman, who had turned slightly away from the man while the nurses were attending to him, now looked in my direction and, after wavering a moment or two, walked straight up to my bed.

Her eyes were fixed on the ceiling. I imagined she might be coming with a message from the man; but when she reached the foot of my bed her eyes suddenly came down to mine and she said in a fierce, dramatic undertone, 'I can't stand it any longer; it's driving me mad.'

It was evening, with the light fading, and this sentence, thrown at me at that time of day and after the screams of the man, was in some way horribly startling and shocking. I just waited, wondering what would happen next, gazing at her sleeked, rolled-under hair and at the saucy pill-box on top. The fear came to me that she might break into violent lamentations for all the ward to hear, so at last I forced myself to say, 'It must be awful, but you'll feel better now he's here.'

'I couldn't have stood it another moment at home – not another moment!' Her voice shrilled on the repeated phrase. 'If I left his side for an instant I was called back and kept chained, unable to move. I'm so tired that my nerves are all to pieces and I can't sleep. His everlasting demands were tearing the life out of me. And I could do nothing right! I had to do everything, and yet I was always wrong.'

Here, the lids half-closed over her eyes as she cast a glance down to me on the bed, and her lips tremblingly formed themselves into a pout so sullen and aggrieved as to make her appear almost negroid.

'He says I'm a traitress for arranging to have him moved here behind his back, but I had to do it; I've *got* to be left alone to sleep.'

The woman tossed back her hair and stared out of the window, away across the square and into the unthinkable future. My heart had gone stiff, and my tongue; I could only say again, 'What a terrible time! but I'm sure they'll do all they can for him here.'

She seemed not to be listening, but still to be following her own train of thought.

'I had to do it all in secret. You can't imagine the strain of concealing it all from him; but I managed it somehow, and I've got him here at last.'

After these words she became aware of me again, for she looked down and said, 'Oh, are you like it, too?'

Without asking her what she meant, I replied at once, 'Oh no, I've been in an accident.' I had no wish to hear a naked description of her husband's paralysis or other disease, and I knew that she would treat me to one if I did not stop her.

She sighed, jerked her head suddenly, so that her hair switched from side to side like a horse's tail; then she began plucking at the glove and spotted navvy's handkerchief in her hand.

I was trying to decide what to do if she should sit down on the bed and begin to cry, when she burst out with the words, 'Life's a nightmare, isn't it? Each phase is worse than the last.' Then she added perfunctorily, 'And I don't suppose you're enjoying it much, either.'

Again the curious self-centred prisoner's look came into her eyes. They flitted from point to point, never resting. It was as if her soul darted out to grab and to find, only to withdraw into itself once more with no food, no help, no hope.

She stood by me, telling me more of her trials and troubles, throwing down now and again the sort of glance she might give to a strange-looking fungus growing on a tree-trunk at her feet.

When at last she left, she raised her eyebrows so that they, pencilled and black, almost reached the dried-up blonde ends of her fringe; then she went back to her husband, the nurses withdrew a little, and she stood there, making some long-suffering reply to his complaints.

Suddenly she said good-bye, turned from him abruptly, and began to walk down the ward without once looking round. Her hair was swinging and the points of the red navvy's handkerchief cascaded masculinely and dashingly from her coat-cuff. She looked free and relieved and determined.

The man called out and implored her to come back. She stopped, uncertain, then fluttered her hand faintly and walked on, still without turning to look at him.

The man, when he saw that she would not come back, seemed to go mad. He screamed her name, her pet name, and 'Darling'. He shouted that he'd been betrayed and left to die alone.

He was still shouting and moaning when the pleasant Canadian doctor came to see him. The doctor began at once to ask him questions about himself. I was amazed to see how quickly he responded to this treatment. Soon he was telling the doctor all about his journey on foot across Europe and into Africa. The wife seemed quite forgotten. By listening carefully, I was able to hear almost everything. He was boasting to the doctor, reeling off a string of place names with rapid and facetious descriptions of scenes and peoples. His talk reminded me of comedian's or conjurer's patter. There were pauses for laughter or amazement, and whenever some particular adventure was reached it was always described with a heavy elaborate under-statement, very irritating to hear.

There was so much to tell, so many names had to be dragged into the conversation, that at last the Canadian doctor began to edge away with a cast-iron smile on his face.

The man was engrossed in his story and noticed nothing until the doctor was several paces from the bed; then he started to call out again in his old desperate way. The doctor walked on, a sly uncomfortable smile taking the place of the rigid one. He seemed to be wishing that the other patients wouldn't look at him; but, like the wife, he refused to turn back.

The man's cries grew louder. 'Doctor, doctor, come here! I've got something more to tell you.'

No answer, only the uncomfortable wriggle of the doctor's shoulders.

As soon as the doctor was out of the ward, someone called out, 'Shut up, for Christ's sake!' This encouraged others to raise a murmur against the man. For a moment the ward was full of angry voices. The man tried to defend himself by appealing to their pity. 'You can't attack a man who's helpless,' he said. He went on to explain his pains and fears; but no one allowed any glimmer of sympathy to show, so he was forced into silence.

Soon afterwards the nurses came back to prepare him for the night, and then all the noises that had gone before were as nothing.

Between his piercing screams the man shouted, 'Ah! Ah! Don't touch my legs, Nurse. Please don't touch my legs. Please!'

I listened to the hissing intakes of breath, so like the 'Ah' sound of excited pleasure. I heard his accents, mad with supplication, and I thought of that picture of Prince Arthur pleading with Hubert for his eyes. Without forgetting the horror of the man's screams, I began to wonder why this picture was so often pointed out to children as something likely to appeal to them. I remembered my own sudden and terrible realization of what grown-ups were capable when it was first shown to me.

The screams continued and I found myself going hard and numbed and dead, as if I had been physically battered. Then I think the nurses must have done something to him, for soon he was asleep, snoring deeply. I heard no more till the morning.

By this time I was being carried once or twice a week to the bath by one of the male nurses; and as we passed the foot of the long-haired man's bed that morning he looked up and saw that I had on a black-and-white cotton kimono, the sort that Japanese men wear after their steam baths. He said, 'Hullo, Nangki-poo,' or some such thing; then the male nurse put me down on one of the seats near his bed and abandoned me, because the bathroom door was locked.

The man must have seen how reluctant I was to be left there, for the malicious grin broadened on his face and he began to say other teasing things. His pain and illness seemed quite forgotten for the moment; he was only intent on finding me amusing.

I looked at him, at the beard growing on his chin, fringing his lips, at the long dark hair, at the sole-shaped staring eyes and at the sharp points of his teeth. I distrusted him, not liking anything I saw.

He began to tell me about his school near the Wrekin; then he reverted to his travels and I had to hear all that the doctor had heard and more. I was powerless to move. I had to listen to descriptions of the strange African diseases which may have been the cause of all his later sufferings.

It should have been clear to me now that he was not the man of the Taunton Youth Hostel – this one was a journalist – but a part of my mind still clung to the idea that here was the painter of the year before, met again in very different circumstances. Even as I listened to him talking, I could not quite decide against the strange coincidence. I wanted to believe in it; therefore I was careful not to ask if he had ever been to Taunton.

When the nurse came back to lift me up and carry me into the bathroom, I spoke to the man for the last time; for very soon afterwards he died. There were no screams then. He was unconscious. No wife was to be seen either. I wondered what had happened. Perhaps she was sleeping. Perhaps she had gone away; had decided not to come; had been told not to come; or perhaps Sister had not been able to get in touch with her in time.

The next morning I suddenly caught sight of her pushing through the glass doors at the end of the ward. No one was with her, her hair lay blown about on her shoulders. She had evidently come in straight from the road.

She hurried forward, then stopped when she saw that his bed was empty. From my corner I was staring at her and saying, without opening my mouth, 'Died, not there; no sight or sound again.'

But I don't think she got my message or even noticed that my eyes were full on her. She just turned on her heel with a gym instructress's neatness and walked briskly out of the ward.

XII

SOMEONE HAD put a dahlia in a pencil-thin vase on the table in the middle of the room, and as I saw the sun glint on its tongue petals, flashing them into scarlet spears, and on its smaller spoon petals, making them brim over as with molten sealing-wax, I was filled with an extraordinary upsurge of delight, a fierce renewal of pleasure. For a moment my whole body was concentrated on the flower; its perfection and pungent colour, and the wonder of its paper-smooth flesh – the face it had on it, somehow all innocence and guile together. I was in the state to make it human: that vibrating scarlet ball set me thinking of everything beautiful away from the ward.

It was autumn now, with the plane leaves falling in the square. I thought of the iron railings, just waiting for the orange winter rust; and I longed to get away.

If I could be lying in a field of spongy grass, close to the fiery wood where the light under the leaves was yellow, like lamplight! If I could hear the cold grass-snake slithering close to me, polishing a tunnel through the razor grasses. If I could see again the grim hut in a field near my grandfather's, where a wild beast man lived with his goat, his beehive and the skeleton of a child's perambulator. He swore at passers-by and made horrible faces, showing his jagged fangs.

If I could go to the bottom of Spring Hill and drink water so bitingly clear that it had almost the 'black' look of old glass. I would cup my hands, or sink my face in, wetting my forelock.

I thought of all these things. And then they came to get me up and into a wheel-chair, with a red blanket over my knees.

At first, when I was stood on my feet, the blood roared into them. They were bursting. My head turned. Black shutters slid over my eyes.

The male nurse Scott tucked me into the chair and wheeled me down the ward. I gazed at the other patients, so much closer to me now, and I could hardly believe in them or in the movement of the chair. Nothing was real. I was wrapped in a dream of warped images. Nurse Scott seemed hairier and swarthier than a monkey, and his starched coat seemed to be made of harsh plaster.

'I can't sit up any more,' I said, suddenly desperate to get back to bed, to lie flat and shut my eyes.

'Nonsense,' Scott said, 'of course you can sit up; and whether you can or not, you're going to. You've got to begin sometime.'

'Take me back!' I called out hopelessly, with futile anger.

'Don't be silly now, Maurice. We don't want any fuss, so just make up your mind.'

I began to cry with rage. I longed to be able to get up, hit Scott, smash the chair to pieces and walk out forever; but I was helpless and in his hands – he could play with me as he liked. The thought was so bitter that it seemed to degrade me in my own eyes. My face stiffened into a dead mask.

He put me by a window in the common-room, so that the sun fell on me, then he left me with a last repressive look.

There was only one other person in the common-room, a sunburnt man studiously making a pen drawing at the end of the long table. He smiled at me, showing large white teeth; then he quickly looked down again because of the tears on my face.

Gradually I was getting used to the pain of the blood in my legs and the strangeness of sitting up. The things I looked at were less distorted.

On my knees the nurse had put my book and the little box which had arrived only that morning from China. A friend had sent me an old Mongolian ring – delicate, minute rosettes fixed to a heavy circlet of silver-gilt. Inside were unknown stamps and characters.

I twisted it on my fantastically thin finger, enjoying the change in my hands – skeleton hands, beautifully bony, and quite strong still. Then I became revolted by their unused colour and the nails, too long and brittle for any work.

I thought of the Mongol who had first worn my ring. I saw him dirty, in a broad hat with tassels, and enormous cloth boots. He was on horse-back, waving a sword, breathing out garlic. I thought of ten thousand miles of ink-blue ocean, huge waves the three-cornered shape of wedges of cheese. I thought of friendship as an egg which never really hatches. Each moment of quarrelling or magic harmony is a pecking away of the shell; but the baby bird's head never emerges.

And when I lifted up my head and saw out of the top panes of the lofty window the sun shining over the jerkily moving trees in the square, the rich feeling of the morning swept back and swallowed me up in happiness. A picture formed of the whole world passing over a curved marble bridge – the people snatching at branches, picking up bright stones, laughing, singing, throwing back their hair, striving after joy through every catastrophe.

I turned the ring on my finger and doted on it, knowing it to be a symbol of all the things I loved most outside my prison life.

I was not ashamed of my tears; they had turned now into an expression of my exaltation. I was only sorry that the other man should be cut off from them; for I felt like a god or an emperor, some being resting on enormous power.

Seeing my transcendent smile, he must have thought that it was safe to talk to me.

'Have you been ill long?' he asked with unexpected solicitude.

'About four months, I think,' I answered.

'As long as that!'

He showed a sort of respectful surprise and asked me other questions about myself. His attention warmed me. I began to tell him my story. It seemed grim and sad and interesting. I felt carried away, as if I had invented it. For the first time I saw the episode as a whole, and I tried to read some shape or meaning into it.

All the time he listened to me quietly, attentively, sometimes making a wry face at a painful description. He looked so well – his face brown, his teeth bright, the whites of his eyes luminous – I unthinkingly accepted him as a healthy man.

It was only after I had finished my story that he told me of *his* accident in South Africa. His horse had rolled on him; for the last two years his legs had been useless. Before coming into the hospital for new treatment, he had been living almost entirely out of doors, wearing only shorts, drinking milk, and eating fruit and cheese and nuts.

I became confused, not liking to remember his attentive expression while I talked about myself. His patience had tricked me. I felt small and was silent.

'When you can't get about, you must do *something*,' he said to me briskly, as if he meant me to take his words to heart. 'The more you do, the happier you are, and so I'm trying to teach myself to draw.'

He pushed the drawing towards me shyly and added, 'What do you think of it?'

He had tried to make a picture out of the fireplace, a chair, and an open book on the end of the table. A blank space had been left, perhaps for a figure, should he summon up courage to attempt one. All was done earnestly, with feathery, minute touches, but his conviction had not yet grown strong enough to make the picture a success.

'Oh, I like it,' I said; 'what fine drawings you'll be able to do soon if you go on at this rate.'

'Does that sound stupid, patronizing?' I thought. 'What is the best, the right thing to say? Each time a picture's shown to me, I wonder.'

I saw him looking at me and guessed what he wanted. 'Shall I sit by the fireplace so that you can try to put me in?' I suggested. 'I'd like that, I'd feel useful.'

I started to wheel the chair, but although my fingers seemed strong, my arms were so unused to work that they soon turned to pleasantly aching jelly. I lay back laughing to cover up my discomfiture.

He saw my trouble and immediately took up his crutches. He balanced himself on them and pushed me into position with one hand. I could feel the power in the top part of his body, and the thought of his useless legs bit down into me.

I sat for some time, keeping as still as a piece of carving, hugging the clumsy ring to me, feeling the warmth of the sun on my neck.

The sun, the industrious man, my new toy the ring, and the importance to me of sitting up in a chair made that a lovely moment in the common-room.

Not even Nurse Scott could spoil it. When he came to wheel me back to bed I was still smiling. I took no notice of his jaunty remarks; I didn't hear them.

I was given the wrong medicine that night – something which fizzed and tasted sour. The nurse said: 'Oh lord! I've made a mistake; but I don't suppose it'll kill you.' She hurried away gaily with the empty glass.

Someone called out in agony after the medicine cupboard had been locked. He called in vain, since no one would go to find Sister.

He was a man who had been wounded in the first war; he had been lying in hospitals ever since.

Once in the bathroom he had said to me in a loud ventriloquist voice: 'My whole life has been ruined!' His eyes were opened wide; it was as if he had had a sudden revelation, as if he had never realized, until that moment, the ruin of his life.

Every evening the pains came on in his head; but tonight he was left to roll about in his bed and call out, because the cupboard had been locked.

By the lamplight I saw an old blind Jew called Mr Abrahams being fed by the tall male nurse who had a curiously feminine, almost pretty face.

The nurse held up a spoonful of whipped raw egg, then pushed it into the eager mouth. He smiled slyly as he did so, seemingly amused by Abrahams' greed, and filled with a sense of power because of the other's blindness.

On his face, too, was a sort of contemptuous affection. He liked to have the fat old Jew for his doll and plaything.

Smiling thoughtfully and looking straight ahead with his blind eyes, Abrahams said, 'That is good, Nurse, very good.'

'You like it, Dad?' The nurse replied archly. He piled up more egg and thrust it into the dark hole. 'Well, you haven't lost your appetite, that's one thing.' He pinched the fat cheek. The blind eyes, so inexpressive, contradicting the knowing mouth, still stared ahead.

How well Dad and the nurse were agreeing together! There was something pitiful and almost gruesome about their food play.

In the grate crackled the first fire of the season. The smoke drifted up in a thin line. Flame and smoke were dwarfed by the huge Gothic-revival stone hood. People rubbed their hands extravagantly and talked about winter. The hot pipes had been turned on, too. I had heard them gently sizzling and singing while Scott was weighing me before putting me back to bed. I had put out my hand to touch them behind me. Hot peppery dust coated them; and then Scott had surprised me by saying that I weighed under five stone. I had parted the red blanket and tried to look at my legs, hardly able to believe what he said.

The gently snapping fire lulled me to sleep early. I remember watching the shadow-play on the high ceiling, then nothing more till I woke, surrounded by something thick that smelt.

I heard feet running and the sound of urgent voices. I decided that it would be unwise to wait for somebody to carry me out, and since I could not walk or even crawl, there was nothing left for me to do but roll. I thought for one moment of trying to climb out of the window behind me, but realized that I would be trapped in the well and perhaps roasted if the fire began to rage.

The idea of rolling down the ward and out of the front door exhilarated me. I was about to wrap myself in a blanket and lower myself over the side of the bed, when the night nurse's voice rang out: 'Everybody stay in bed.' I could just see the white blur of his coat through the smoke. Lights were switched on. Other nurses ran into the ward. Patients called out. Some rummaged in their lockers, or bent down to pull on their slippers.

Clearly it would be better to begin my rolling before too many feet were about, but I hesitated, afraid of being conspicuous. A sort of inertness came over me. I watched the night nurse run back with a bucket and spade to shovel sand or ashes into the grate. Smoke was still belching down the chimney into the room. The night nurse went round the ward, throwing all the windows open, explaining again and again that the ward was not on fire. 'No need to be frightened,' he snapped; 'the chimney hasn't been swept and it's choked with soot; that is all.'

The fright had made him bad-tempered; he poured scorn on the people who had left their beds; and drove other nurses and porters out of the ward, asking them fiercely what they wanted.

I watched the smoke drifting in sheets out of the windows, and wondered why I found the nurse's violent change from wild alarm to scorn so unamusing. 'Surely some people would have split their sides,' I thought.

I ate one of my chocolates and felt glad that the night had been made shorter by the excitement.

The smoke took the swirling forms of the mist in a Chinese mountain picture. Objects, lost to view, suddenly loomed up, then vanished again. The smoke shapes held my eyes and led my thoughts.

XIII

THE FOURTEEN-year-old boy at the foot of my bed had been to the theatre for the operation on his head and had come back. He lay for days, taking no notice of anything, his gun-metal eyes staring unseeingly at the ceiling or at me.

Sometimes the thick eyelids, like white mushroom caps, slid down over his eyes, and then he looked like a statue in bread, discoloured where the lips and the nose had been modelled laboriously, with dirty fingers.

His father and mother came to see him from the country; they brought bananas. But when the mother stood by the bed and held out the yellow sickle fruit to him, he just looked at it, lifted his lip like a dog, then lay still again.

His mother made a despairing face and turned away. The father started to talk in a loud cheerful voice. The boy jerked his head, lolled out his tongue and seemed to be asking them with his eyes to leave.

Slowly their faces turned to wood. They walked away, leaving the bunch of bananas in a position which gave it the likeness of a swollen yellow hand plucking at the bedclothes.

In a week or ten days the boy began to show more signs of life. He smiled dully and said a few words. Soon afterwards he was about in a wheel-chair; and then I saw him dressed in his own clothes and walking in his big farm-labourer's boots.

One afternoon I was put near him in the common-room. There were others there, too, and someone asked the boy if he liked his schoolmaster.

''Tisn't a schoolmaster, it's a woman.' He spoke with a thick deep country accent I could not place.

'A woman for a great lad like you!' the man exclaimed.

'Yeah,' said the boy.

'That's a scandal, isn't it!' said the man, appealing to the others. 'Not to have a man to teach big lads! How can a woman understand them, or keep them in order?'

There were other murmurs.

The boy grinned broadly. He seemed to find the talk thoroughly ridiculous and amusing. What difference could the sex of the teacher make? Everything was the same; nothing mattered.

Looking at his grinning face, I had the fantastic idea that the surgeon had removed most of his brain. I imagined his head as quite hollow, filled with wind.

But in spite of this seeming idiocy his health went on improving, until I thought that he would soon be going back to his father's farm.

Then one morning I looked down at him and saw a curious change in his face. It was whiter; his mouth was open and he breathed uneasily.

Doctors came to look at him and what little food he had was brought in special bowls, kept only for his use. I heard one of the nurses cursing this extra work.

For several days he lay there and I watched him, not knowing what had happened. Then a strange nurse came into the ward and began to change the boy's pyjamas. She was from a fever hospital and she was taking him away. He had diphtheria.

The nurse was a mixture of pity and impatience. 'Come along, son,' she said, 'be a good boy, try to put this on.' She dragged the new fever hospital jacket on to him, then in a moment of irritation snapped, 'Do give a little help, do.'

I watched him being taken away and knew that he was done for. I thought of all the people who had died since I came into hospital – the monotonous line of them in their beds.

That afternoon we were told that we were in quarantine and that nobody would be allowed to visit us. A wave of hopelessness passed over me when I heard this. We were shut in a medieval plague house – prisoners in a dungeon – corpses on marble slabs in a mortuary – skeletons encased in lead in a dripping vault.

Everything that made life bearable was forbidden. We were deserted.

Then something woke up in me and told me to get myself out of the hospital as soon as possible. The voice told me that my brother, the specialist, Clare would not do it; I must do it myself.

I began at once to write to my brother, telling him of the boy so near me in the ward, insisting that I must leave as soon as the quarantine was over. It was a violent letter, not to be ignored, I thought. Or would its very importunity simply make him smile and tear it up? Would it have the power to make him act? As I was sticking down the envelope, another fear came to me: it would never reach him. It would be taken away to be 'fumigated', in other words destroyed.

Already communication with the outside world seemed almost impossible. People in a besieged fortress did not post letters in the ordinary way. I gave mine to the nurse, hardly expecting it to get farther than the entrance hall.

I lay back and wondered if the parents, when they came to see their boy, brought with them not only a fine bunch of bananas and their love, but also the diphtheria.

Visitors came to stare in through the windows looking on to the square; they passed in messages and parcels. The ward seemed like a draughty aviary where mutilated birds huddled together on the ground and allowed themselves to be fed through the bars.

I had two new visitors, a distant cousin, and a friend of my parents', quite unknown to me. The plump cousin brought crystallized fruits; and waved and laughed, as if the whole situation were outrageously droll. My other visitor wore a carnation in his buttonhole, looked sleek and elderly and a little fanatical. He scribbled something on a card, which was passed to me. 'I have been specially sent by your mother,' I read.

What could he mean? My mother had been dead for years. Why should he add to my confusion by dragging in her name so glibly?

Someone in a bed under the windows began to shout that there was never any peace, and if he couldn't have peace he would go mad.

Sister hurried up and said, 'You can't expect the whole ward to be run for your benefit, you know.'

'Take me away! Take me away! Christ take me away!' the man implored in vain.

At last I had a letter from my brother, and with the letter a new book on English China and three bottles of excellent light sherry. I thought the book and the sherry were from him, and my heart sank. I felt that they were offerings to soften the disappointment; then I forced myself to open his letter and discovered that a friend of his, quite unknown to me, had sent the presents.

I stopped reading the letter and thought about my visit from the sleek stranger, and then this present from another stranger. Why had they bothered about me? Why did their kindness make me feel so much more of a victim?

I kept my mind on them, trying to imagine their lives and thoughts. I did this because I was afraid to read further and find that my brother would not have me moved.

I began to look at the glossy pictures in the China book – dishes of apple-green, a Bow cup with raised white hawthorn flowers, two lovers in a flowery bocage – then I forced my eyes back to the letter and saw that, as soon as we were out of quarantine, I was to be moved to a town on the south-east coast where an uncle of ours lived.

With the first shock of pleasure was mixed an uncomfortable fear of new surroundings, and a curious regret for things I did not care about.

There would be no more visits from the dumpy chaplain who once, on a bad day, took my hand in his own parched cracked one, and started to say such lost, bewildered, powerless things that I felt sorry for him. There was desperation in his voice. He seemed to be complaining about the whole order of things – to be murmuring against God. 'Poor boy!' he said, fondling my hand with a sort of panic-stricken pity.

I would never see again the rather mad visitor with her basket of everlasting flowers. In the heart of each posy was a little flag bearing sacred words.

'That's for you,' she had said, handing me one with much satisfaction – I had seldom seen a woman quite so certain of herself. She was gone without another glance or word. No human contacts for her. She was a quite impersonal well-doer. Always bright, birdlike, with darting eyes, her expression never changed. The dried flowers creaked, the little flags waved, the basket swung on her arm. She passed from bed to bed with her presents, then disappeared till the next month.

She made me think of Walt Whitman, although she hadn't the suspicion of a beard.

Now that I knew that I was going, I looked on the ward with different eyes. Everything, even the light and air, seemed changed. Figures suddenly lost their depth and darkness and became harmless marionettes seen only from one angle, watched only for their interest as spectacle.

But in other moods a week seemed longer than a year, and the fear of catching diphtheria and being held prisoner swamped me and sucked me down.

When I looked at the boy's empty bed or heard the sizzle and gurgle of the hot pipes, a snapping, tearing impatience to be away would possess me. All my fantasies were of an amazingly light-footed, springing person – myself transformed, perfected, all illness cast off – diving through windows, swimming downstairs, flying in the air, running hell-for-leather over ground that also moved. The world was turning; I should speed with it.

I began to sort the books in my locker. I gave most of them to one of the male nurses who wanted to become a writer. He turned over the pages greedily, not reading, just showing pleasure in possessing them.

My head swam as I crouched on the floor beside the locker. The noises in the ward seemed far away. The nurses were making my bed and took no notice. I felt that I was no longer part of the hospital.

For several nights now I had been trying to walk. When I was first helped out of bed, I stood up and willed my feet to move. Nothing happened; I just swayed and caught the nurse's hand. But on the second night I felt my slipper slithering over the floor. It soon stopped, but I had forced one foot forward one inch.

I called out, 'It's moving!' and my suppressed excitement was so great that I began to shiver all over.

The nurse said, 'Fine! That's fine, Maurice.' He really seemed pleased in an absent, lazy way; but how could I make him share my joy? How could it seem important to him to move one foot one inch?

The memory of it made me glow. In spite of dizziness I was full of contentment. I decided to give my bottles of sherry to Sister when she came on her round of inspection.

'But, Maurice,' she said, 'you're supposed to have it before meals to give you an appetite.'

'I hate it, Sister; the taste makes me feel sick.'

Sister hesitated; I saw how much she wanted the sherry, so I pressed it on her.

When she had at last accepted, she said, 'If you really can spare it, it would be very nice, because, you see, I am giving a small party in my rooms next week.'

It was delightful that my present had come at just the right moment. I pictured Sister's party to myself. In a small room on the top floor of the hospital, nurses and doctors would be tightly packed together. They sat on tables and the arms of chairs, and some very free-and-easy ones had thrown off all constraint and were sitting on the floor, their legs stretched out in front of them. I heard them remark on my sherry and saw some turn to Sister to compliment her on its quality. Meanwhile she passed amongst them, quick, bright-eyed, full of quiet enjoyment.

XIV

WHEN CLARE came into the ward on the last day and walked towards me triumphantly, her face all happiness and smiles, I felt that something good had happened at last, that the everlasting see-saw had settled for a moment on the right side, and I was blest and fortunate.

The literary male nurse who was to take me to the ambulance said, 'I do hope you get better, Maurice. You're one of the few people I'd like to see really well.'

I laughed at the grotesque good wish. Did he mean that he preferred to see most people ill?

He said angrily, 'I mean it,' but I was too happy to be serious with anyone.

Sister came and walked beside the wheel-chair. Some hands waved, rather grudgingly, I thought; as if the other patients envied me my freedom, felt that it was wasted on me. My first picture of the ward came back with sudden vividness; I felt again the gloom and heaviness brooding in the space between the tops of the windows and the ceiling.

I turned and looked round me for the last time. Someone called out 'Good-bye'; then the ward seemed to settle back into its lethargy.

On the stone steps Sister took my new address, waved and smiled and told me again what a help my sherry would be to her party. The ambulance men put me in, the door was shut; Clare and I were alone.

A sort of deep untalkative gaiety took possession of me. I strained up to look out of the window. Over the rooftops I saw the clear pale sky and the weak sun shining. Watery shadows flickered and shook on the tree-trunks in the square.

Clare smiled and I smiled. The ambulance threaded in and out of squalid streets, crossed the shining river, and drew up at last at the house on Croom's Hill, where we were to collect some of my clothes.

Miss Hellier must have seen us from the window, for the leaf-green door was open and she was standing on the wide step, welcoming us.

The ambulance men put me into a sort of miniature sedan chair and carried me through the hall and up the three steps to the small dining-room.

Surely this early eighteenth-century house could make me forget all the horror and ugliness of hospital? I thought so then, as I gazed once more at the heavy indented cornice, the wavy glass in the thick-barred sashes, the window seat and shutters, the hip-high wainscot, and the mantelpiece painted so many times that all its delicate mouldings were clogged.

Outside, in the park, children played on the rough grass under the huge, decrepit Spanish chestnuts. Leaves floated down.

My eyes came back to the grate, where a fire of little twigs and shining pieces of coal sparkled. Clare had sat down in the arm-chair and was unpacking her basket. She brought out a little grease-proof parcel, a thermos, and a tin of shortbread from Edinburgh. She poured frothy coffee into Miss Hellier's cups and then undid the parcel and offered me a sandwich. I bit into it and found a thick layer of fawn cream dotted with black boot-button eyes. It was foie gras. The luxury seemed to crown my escape. Too delighted to speak, I looked at Clare, then at the black truffles again.

When we had finished the sandwiches, crunched the delicious short-bread and drunk all the coffee, the ambulance men carried me up to my room at the top of the house. I waited for them to leave, then I looked round at the place that had not known me for so many months. I thought of that Whitsun morning, of bathing and dressing and packing my bicycle bag. How I had hummed, thinking of the day in front of me! How springy my feet had been!

Now I was sitting in a carrying-chair; but the change seemed to hold no bitterness for me at that moment. I was too filled with pleasure at the sight of all my things, waiting for me, still, unmoving, beautiful. There stood the early Victorian rosewood work-table, which I had carried across the Heath on my shoulder; and there was the bottom of the Chippendale tallboy with all the handles missing, only the charming key escutcheons left. The oak drawers had had to be scrubbed all one afternoon before the grain showed through the black grease. My great-grandmother's cashmere shawl, all moth holes and lovely colour contrasts, was spread out over the bed. On the back of the door was the crimson and violet alderman's robe which I used as a dressing-gown. Where the ceiling sloped down to meet the wall I saw again my little Rajput miniature of a hunting party between rocks and trees; but over the bed hung my chief prize, the small bottom panel of some early fifteenth-century Italian altar-piece. I had seen it in an old clothes shop one morning when I was hurrying to the art school. In the evening it was no longer in the window. I went into the shop and asked for it anxiously. At first the man said nothing, only looked at me suspiciously; then he grunted, 'I've taken it upstairs to keep it for a dealer. I want ten pounds for it.'

'Could I see it again?' I wheedled, afraid he would think me not worth ten pounds.

After slight murmuring he climbed upstairs heavily and brought it down. It was the Nativity scene, with Mary and Joseph and a cow and a donkey on each side of the baby, who was spiked all over with rays like a golden porcupine. In the gold-leaf sky a tiny angel flourished a scroll on which could still be read, 'Gloria in excelsis'.

I turned it over excitedly and looked closely at the thick panel on which it was painted; then I said firmly, 'I'm afraid I couldn't give ten pounds for it.'

We bargained carefully, until I had brought him down to four pounds. Although I only had ten shillings I stopped there, afraid to press him any more. I left the ten shillings and ran out of the shop to borrow the rest from Miss Hellier . . .

Clare was calling me from the bottom of the house, asking if I had collected all I wanted. Quickly swinging myself out of the chair, I began to move round the room, holding on to pieces of furniture. I took down the Nativity and put three favourite pieces of china into a small suitcase. Clare came in and hurriedly gathered up an armful of clothes. I wanted her to be interested in my room, but she seemed a little impatient with me for losing myself in a reverie, and told me that the men were waiting.

They came to carry me down. I took one last look at the room, wishing I could stay there and go no farther.

I held the picture and the suitcase on my knees. We were out in the road again; then I was waving to Miss Hellier through the ambulance window.

We climbed up to the Heath and dipped down into Lewisham, just as I had done on that early June morning when I set out to visit my aunt. The driver and the porter were smoking and laughing together. I stared out of the window and talked to Clare over my shoulder.

Soon we were past Sidcup and Chislehurst and Swanley. As we skirted Farmingham, I thought again of all the times Mark and I had walked near there; visiting Eynsford church at Harvest Festival, patting the marrows and touching the grapes that hung from the beak of the eagle lectern; eating our sandwiches leaning against an iron fence in earliest spring and going at last to a teashop to warm our frozen fingers round steaming cups of tea. I thought of the sticks and stones we had thrown, and of our teeth biting into white apple flesh. Then I was filled with angry frustration and resentment because that life had been spoilt and made impossible.

I glowered at the plain above Wrotham, hardly seeing it; but the exhilaration of racing down the hill in the sunshine brought back my happiness.

Now we were passing Trottiscliffe where I had often stayed as a child. I strained across the fields to see the white cowls of the converted oasthouse. I imagined I caught a glimpse of them twinkling back to me.

At Charing I remembered going, the year before, on my walking tour, to fetch some milk, and discovering that the farm was built out of the remains of an archbishop's palace. A gothic archway, a lancet window, a broken stone wall, come upon suddenly, in the evening light, had seemed enchanted.

Wherever I looked I saw things to remind me of that tour. The castle at Chilham, perched on its hill in the heart of the trees, brought back my tiredness under the hot sun, my sense of isolation in a world of motor-cars and melting tar.

The ambulance stopped in Canterbury and the men got out to buy cigarettes and run into the courtyard of an inn. While we waited, I thought of the youth hostel, where I had spent the night with forty Dutch boys. Soon after supper they had begun to sing in the paved garden by the canal. They had continued to sing most of the night, rocking the double-decker bunks in the dormitory until the metal joints let out animal squeaks and groans.

The men came back and we started again. Now that we were so near our destination my heart was sinking. I hated the drive to stop and I dreaded the thought of the unknown nursing home, the matron, her nurses.

The ambulance passed down a long road half country, half town, then turned a corner, and almost at once turned again, into a gravel drive. I was just in time to see cement balls on brick gate pillars, a grey rough-cast house, white balconies, and window-frames that had withstood fierce wind and rain.

The door was opened by the fat, short owner-matron herself. She wore no cap and was dressed all in black. She led the way through the dark hall, her heels clapping on the polished wood-block floor. I saw a brass jug gleaming and some late zinnias in a bowl; then I was carried down a narrow passage and found myself in a bedroom with a french-window as big as a garage door. Perhaps the room had once been a garage, for it was at the side of the house, cut off from all the other rooms.

I gazed round me at the high white bed, the beetroot-pink curtains, the new-lit fire just scenting the air with smoke; but what held my attention was the shaggy Indian carpet. It was unexpectedly white, with coarse flowers and leaves twining over it – perhaps the ugliest thing in an ugly room. But it was not ugliness that I was dwelling on as I stared at it; I was hugging to myself the feeling of having a room of my own again. The still-ness fascinated me; no footsteps in the ward, no calling, groaning, crying, swearing, snapping, laughing, joking – only the sound of the wind and the fire and perhaps the distant mumble of the sea.

I smiled at Clare dazedly; the fat matron had me slipped into the bed. She told the ambulance men to eat their lunch in the kitchen, then bustled out of the room herself.

Clare and I hardly had time to talk about the escape from hospital, the happiness of the drive, before she was back with cold meat, floury potatoes and pickle: these were for Clare, not for me. I had to wait till the correct lunchtime for my meal.

I watched Clare eating hurriedly. There was a feeling of urgency in the air – the ambulance men were impatient – the matron would disapprove – there was some threat hanging over us.

Clare jumped up, kissed me and disappeared. I heard her footsteps ringing on the tiled passage, then no sound till the ambulance started. I lis-tened as the faint humming of the wheels faded to nothing.

I was alone in my room, lost, abandoned in a strange place. I gazed into the fire; it moved and rustled as if hands were pushing through the pile of wood and coal. I pictured red-hot fingers groping, and then a glowing face thrust up with flame-blue eyes. Round the head curled orange flames like small snakes. The mouth was open and a forked lizard tongue darted in and out.

The image was broken up by the click of women's heels in the passage again. I hurriedly composed my face and sat up. Now that I was alone, an exaggerated desire to please had taken hold of me. I felt bound to pacify, to allay, to charm if possible.

A rather tall nurse, bearing my lunch tray, pushed open the door. She wore glasses and her eyes behind them looked small and of little value; but they moved sharply, like sparrows' eyes. She swivelled them down to me on the bed and said abruptly, 'I'm looking after you.' Then she put the tray and the bed-table across my knees and stood over me. I smiled, but there was no answering smile. I tried to talk, but my conversation did not soften her. She seemed to be contemplating me as a child or a cow might. There was slight curiosity but almost no other show of feeling. At last she left, still unsmiling, having decided, I thought, that I was harmless and easy to manage.

Her unresponsiveness had chilled me, and I lay looking at my lunch without interest; but when I dug into the mashed potato and creamed chicken and found that they were good, every other feeling was swallowed up in the importance of food. Nothing else mattered for the moment; the pleasantness of life seemed largely to depend on the goodness of the meals. I thought of the evil hospital food and enjoyed my shudders.

The stillness in the room was balm, and yet it frightened me. I wished perversely to be reassured by the noise of the ward. I felt the isolation of my room at the end of the passage with no other door near. Then I hugged the realization to me, loving it, cherishing it, thinking that for days now, weeks and months, I could be still, with no one but the nurse to come near me. I could dream on the pillow all day, watching the fire and the Nativity, which Clare had hung above the mantelpiece for me.

The rain would beat down on the huge glazed doors; but I would be safe in my garage bedroom, my new haven and refuge.

Late that evening the doctor came to see me. He was grey-haired and smiling and he talked about religion, lunch with the Archbishop, and his latest poem on Ethiopia. He smiled to himself, as if the memory of his lines pleased him. I asked if he intended to publish his poem, but he answered, 'Not on your life!' and smiled even more secretly. Then he whipped back the bedclothes, examined me in a flash and was gone.

XV

THE SUN shone down on the bed, dazzling my eyes, telling me clearly that London was left far behind. Outside my window birds danced and bounced on the grass path, which led between borders to a thatched summer-house.

The birds chattered and screeched so violently that I climbed out of bed and moved towards the window with a piece of breakfast toast in my hand. I threw down the crumbs and stood breathing in the autumn morning air, while all round me the birds snapped up the morsels. They were so filled with love of food that they had no room for fear.

I tried to imagine the person who had lived in my room before me; and I saw a woman, tall, tottering, emaciated, who held out her hand for the birds to light upon. She had taught them to expect bread every morning as their right. The wind blew the folds of her long, witch-like dressing-gown; but she stayed outside with the birds.

Nurse Goff interrupted the birds' breakfast and took me up steep stairs to the bathroom. I climbed one at a time and she waited behind, patiently, to catch me if I fell. When we reached the steaming room, she left me. I locked the door thankfully and began to lower myself into the bath. The great effort of climbing the stairs had exhausted me, and I wanted to lie in the hot water for a long time; but first I had to arrange my face-flannel as a cushion between the bottom of my spine and the hard enamel of the bath.

I lay there soaking and dreaming until I was disturbed by feet on the stairs. It was Nurse Goff again; she had come to tell me that my aunt had telephoned and would soon be upon me. As I tried to hurry, I felt secretly pleased that my uncle had been knighted a few years before. It was ignoble, too contemptible even to mention, but I hoped that this fact might awe Nurse Goff, hold her in check just a little. Already I thought I noticed a tamer note in her voice. Then I was afraid that the knowledge might have quite an opposite effect, filling her with a hearty scorn for all such dingy clap-trap so that she behaved with even greater sternness.

I had a vague fond feeling for my aunt, because she had been so good to me as a child, giving me presents and delicious things to eat whenever I went to her house; but I had not seen her lately and felt anxious about our meeting. That she was not my real aunt, but the second wife of the man who had married my mother's sister, gave me an added sense of being separate. I wanted her to be pleased with me and I wanted myself not to be disappointed in her.

She came with her smoke-coloured Chow dog and her invalid Pekinese, Baby. Baby had once nearly broken her back, and so had to be carried everywhere. A large box of chocolates was tucked under my aunt's other arm, while over it hung a brightly patterned dressing-gown. In her gloved hand she held a bunch of garden-wet roses with tough sturdy mahogany-red thorns on the short thick stalks.

I was taken back at once to childhood, to the days when a visit from her meant everything delightful. She sat down on the bed, spreading out my presents and allowing Baby to crawl over the eiderdown. The Chow sat on the floor and showed its black tongue to me, hoping for a chocolate, but my aunt and I took no notice; we were too busy talking.

We had only just settled into this conversation of other days, when my aunt jumped up and said, 'We two must have a long talk soon; we've got *so* much to say to each other!'

Then she was gone, with Baby in her arms and the Chow following reluctantly, its eyes still fixed on the chocolate-box. I lay there bewildered, until I remembered her sudden appearances and disappearances in the past.

My aunt drove away to do her shopping, and the day stretched endlessly before me. I seemed to have no place in the room, the house, or the town. Nothing bound me to my surroundings. I floated.

I even felt pleased when the matron came in, although she asked rather inquisitive questions about my aunt and flapped a duster as she talked. I was beginning to wonder how long she would stay, when there was a knock at the door and a woman with square-cut grey hair looked in. This was the masseuse. Matron introduced her to me as Miss Pierce, then left us together.

Miss Pierce was athletic. She was small and thin. She moved with quick agile jerks, and when she began kneading my legs I could feel the strength in her fingers. Once or twice she became quite painful, but we had quickly begun to talk with ease and so I stifled my grunts.

She was telling me about her early life in London, when she cooked her food on a gas-ring and longed all day to live in the country. At last she had saved up enough money to buy a house and move. She came to the seaside and now she drove in her car to her patients, morning and afternoon. In the evenings she returned and had tea with her friend who kept an arts-and-crafts shop. The rest of the evening was spent in doing housework, cooking the supper, reading, and making toys, embroidered gloves, tea-cosies and painted boxes for the shop.

It sounded a delightfully snug life, and I told her that the early hard work in London had been worth it.

There was something hardy and masculine about Miss Pierce. Perhaps it was her abrupt movement, or her sardonic way of talking about hardship and struggle. Life seemed on a level with sport; it was serious, even dangerous, but never baffling or terrible. Yet she was very feminine, too, when she used old-fashioned school-boys' slang, and when she flicked me lightly on the stomach and said, 'Come on now, my lad, I want to do your back, so turn over.'

I liked Miss Pierce and thought about her after she had left me. I thought about her grey page-boy's hair, her bright lipstick, her thin arms and her muscular hands and neck, her sporting, no-nonsense talk, and the life she had made for herself. She seemed incongruous; but, in her usual way, how was she fitted together! How neat and workmanlike she was! There was a touch of mystery, too, in her manner of coming and going. She would walk towards you, or away, casually, almost striding; yet you felt that as she moved she had important, even sinister thoughts in her head. She appeared to be weighing schemes which she had no intention of imparting to anyone. Thus when she spoke all was openness and common sense, but when she was seen walking she seemed altogether deeper and more disquieting.

As the day wore on, Nurse Goff came to treat me with less suspicion; she even began to talk. While she shut the window, drew the curtains, and poked the fire after tea, she told me that she was the daughter of a rich farmer in Wiltshire, who had disapproved strongly of her passion to be a dancer, not thinking it a ladylike or respectable career for one of his daughters. And so she had at last decided on nursing, since this was almost the only profession for women held in any esteem by him.

Whenever she could, she went back to her family for Christmas. Then they had great times, eating and drinking and giving parties. There was more than a hint of opulence and gentility in all Nurse Goff's descriptions. One was not allowed to forget that one was talking to someone who had been forbidden by her father to be a dancer. I tried to imagine her in ballet-skirt and blunt-toed dirty satin shoes, with dark hair plastered on her forehead and breath coming in gasps . . . It was difficult. She was so tall, so rigid, so unlike any dancer I had seen.

My attention had strayed; I was now being told about a young man. My room had not been inhabited before me by the bird-loving skeleton-witch of my fancy, but by this young man, who was dark and solid and Nurse Goff's fiancé. She stressed the darkness and solidity, then went on to describe the romantic meeting: how he lay in the bed when she first saw him, how carefully she nursed him, how their conversations began, and how they now spent their free afternoons together. For his birthday she had given him a silver cigarette-case, and at Christmas he was to have gold cuff-links engraved with his initials.

The story of Nurse Goff's love affair unfolded. I listened, even noted details in my mind, but so much talk all day had exhausted me and I had no feeling left. Gradually I drifted from Nurse Goff – only heard her voice as a stream, tinkling far away.

I waited passively for her to go out and leave me alone with the licking, jumping, fire shadows.

XVI

A T ABOUT twelve o'clock on the third day Mark suddenly appeared. He came into the room smiling to himself, breezily holding out his hand, as if we were Victorian merchants about to do a deal. He often made these mystifying artificial entrances. I never completely understood why, usually explaining them to myself simply as 'nervousness'.

He told me now that he had been giving drawing lessons to an admiral's daughter, and that the admiral's wages had paid the expensive fare from London.

'I can come and see you every week while the job lasts,' he said.

The ungrateful thought, 'Do I want to see Mark every week?' flickered for a moment, then was stifled, and we settled down happily to lunch.

In some ways things were as they had been. The huge purple-black shadow of the hospital had gone and we could breathe freely. We had a room and a fire to ourselves. In snugness and privacy we could talk all day, describing plans for the future, recounting bits of gossip, dramatizing amusing little incidents.

Mark looked round my room, then out into the garden where the birds were still picking up stray crumbs. We began to talk about the matron; in a moment he was burlesquing her for me, swelling himself out to suggest her grand, up-jutting bosom, copying her tituppy steps and her tea-cosy conversation with its hint, its prying question underneath. Flourishing his handkerchief, he swept round the room, just as she did with her yellow duster. He was a mimic who could give curiously true impressions of things seen or heard only once. When he started on Nurse Goff, he brought out all the potato quality of her short-sighted eyes. He parodied her unblinking, judging stare, her air of one standing stiff-necked behind stone battlements, limbs encased in armour, face, always and unwaveringly, a 'poker face'.

I watched and listened and laughed; and part of me wondered what was revolting in mimicry. Was it revolting because a human being appeared to turn himself into a mouth-piece, a puppet? – for puppets are always threatening and grim. I wondered and pondered, noting each movement of Mark's.

Presently he came back into his own shell and told me about his new pupil – how pretty and untalented she was, how willing to learn, how full of admiration for him. Then at the end of the description he brought out the plum he had been saving till the last: on the first day that he lunched with the family in their Kensington flat the cook had burst into the room at the end of the meal and given notice.

'But why, cook, do you want to go?' asked the admiral anxiously. 'Don't you like it here? Is there too much to do?'

'No, it isn't that, sir,' said the cook, breathing hard. She seemed to be keeping back something which caused her great agitation.

'Then what is it?' the admiral said.

'I'd rather not tell.' The cook's mouth shut and became ominously pursed, but the admiral was unwise and pressed her.

'Oh, come, cook,' he said; 'you can't leave us without telling us why.'

Then the flood of the cook's indignation was loosed. 'Well, if you must know, there's a couple of young lady lovers next door to me, down below in the servants' quarters, and the walls are that thin I can hear every word, and I don't know what all besides! I don't like it, I can tell you – not a bit!'

There was a terrible silence in the room, then the cook went out with great dignity, and the admiral and his wife were left to deal with the situation. But they were unequal to it. Mark said that the hot, embarrassed atmosphere became almost choking. He wanted to burst into wild guffaws, and was only saved by his pupil, who jumped up hurriedly from the table and whisked him into her own private room. There they both exploded, rolling about in agonies of laughter.

In this way, telling stories and laughing, we passed most of the day.

The light had begun to fade before Mark at last stood up to go. He promised to order an easel and more paints and brushes for me at Winsor & Newton's, then asked if I wanted anything else in London. I shook my head and felt that I was coming to life again. I watched him do up the belt of his navy-blue raincoat, take up his umbrella and dark hat and move towards the door. He seemed effaced, anonymous, concealed. The dark uniform was a protective colouring so that he should pass unnoticed, so that he should see without being seen. 'He is like the secret agent of some scheming eighteenth-century prince,' I thought. 'He ought really to be mixed up in some court intrigue.'

Aloud I said, 'Go out through the french-window, then you won't have to pass the matron's office and she won't be able to spring out on you and start a cross-examination. I can walk into the garden with you.'

'But you oughtn't to go out,' he said.

'Oh yes, why not?' I got out of bed, put on the dressing-gown my aunt had brought me, and walked very slowly down the grass path with Mark.

A night wind blew through the bushes in unaccountable little gusts. I bowed my head and thrust each hand up the opposite sleeve, making a muff, Chinese fashion. Now that Mark was going, talk seemed to flow more and more freely and rewardingly. There was a rush of words, because the time was so short.

The skirts of my dressing-gown blew open. I saw my pyjamas and was filled with an extraordinary and foolish pride. I was going out into the garden in pyjamas, obeying my own whim, and nobody had interfered with me. It was almost a forgotten experience.

As we approached the gate with its stone balls, a small dark blue car drew up, a man got out and walked over the gravel. I turned away at the sight of him, but Mark said, 'That's a doctor, because of the little black bag. He'll wonder what on earth you're doing out here in your pyjamas.'

I said, 'Let him wonder,' and walked with Mark into the road.

'Go back quickly, or you'll get me into trouble,' he said. 'The matron will think that I've enticed you out here, and then she won't let me come again.'

We said good-bye and I watched him walk away. Once he looked round and I waved my hand, but he only jerked his umbrella in an abrupt, stealthy way. He turned the corner and was gone.

As I walked back, along the grass verge, so that there should be no crunch of gravel, a great spring of life seemed to bubble up in me. 'Surely I have been asleep,' I felt, 'blotted out by greyness and unreal horror, and now I'm awakening. Hyacinth bulbs, when spring comes, suddenly find that they are no longer degraded, crackling onions, but stiff green towers, jangling with crisp bells and caught in a trance of scent, heavy and swimming as chloroform. I am like that.' I was not laughing at myself.

This quiet exuberance brimmed over, seeming to flow out through my finger-tips. I made for my garage window with no fear of anything left in me. But just before I reached the summer-house the front-door clicked, and, looking up, I saw the man with the bag coming straight towards me instead of returning to his blue car.

I stood still, my muscles taut for a fight, my mood broken to pieces. What did he want? What was he going to say?

He was tall and dark and dressed in dark clothes. His body seemed elastic but not light. As he came nearer, I saw that he was looking into me with eyes that could not pierce, because they were too brown and soft, too like a stag's eyes. His chin was cleft, his lips square and good; but a harshness from nose to mouth reminded me of Charles the Second's portraits. His expression was too concentrated and searching. He did not conciliate me. I thought of him as an inquisitor; and, smiling with anxiety and annoyance, I lifted my head to confront him and keep him at bay.

'Hullo,' he said, 'I'm coming to see you tomorrow. My partner's going away for a few days.'

I was suddenly conscious of my tangled hair, uncut for weeks. Was it a disagreeable mop to someone so well clipped and trimmed? Did he criticize the crumpled pyjamas and flowered dressing-gown – so obviously chosen by a woman for a man? Was I being quickly slipped into a pigeonhole marked, 'Peculiar – (needs handling)'? This wave of self-consciousness must have been due to the unexpected friendliness of his approach. I had expected grimness, therefore friendliness came as a shock.

He began to ask me about myself and the London hospital. The wind and the gathering darkness were disregarded while he listened to me. At last he said, 'Well, you *have* had a bad time.'

Could it be true? Could he really think that I had had a bad time? No doctor had ever said that to me before. The words seemed to strike out of me a response of pure pleasure.

'I ought to go in,' I said flatly, wanting to be alone with my pleasure.

'Yes, perhaps you ought!' There was a mock threat in his voice and he was smiling, showing his teeth. 'When I saw you at the gate I wondered how you'd got loose. Matron would have fits.'

I began at once to walk towards my window.

'Good-bye,' he said, waving his case at me as he turned away. He took long strides, which reminded me of some cartoon – Johnny Walker, Uncle Sam, or perhaps the Great Big Scissor Man.

I went in, with my arms clutched across my chest now, hugging some valuable thing.

The exuberance was bubbling up in me again. Mark and the whole day had been merged in the last five minutes. I kept saying to myself, 'I wonder why I didn't like the look of him. What was wrong with him? Or is there something wrong with me? Am I suspicious of everybody?'

XVII

I WOKE up in the night and remembered that he was coming to see me. A delightful feeling of security spread over me. It was as if all the problems and difficulties of this new sick life had been halved, because I had found a doctor who appeared to be human.

Then I told myself that I was a fool, that I learnt no lessons from experience. In the morning he would be exactly like all the others – a bright and breezy, free and easy machine. Everything hidden under this disguise.

But the delusion still persisted. I heard his different step in the tiled passage, his different way of opening the door. Then he was smiling at me, making me conscious of his ears. Did the corners of his mouth point to them? What caused the playful monkey-satyr look – the forest look, both wild and amused, of long ago? It went strangely with his sober doctor's clothes.

After his ears and teeth, I was most aware of the extreme whiteness of his cuffs and shirt-front. I don't suppose I had expected dirty linen, but this dull rich whiteness, unspoilt by any stripe, held my attention and I could not help regretting the short life of such freshness. There was a morning feeling about altogether that gave me an ache, a longing to be vigorous again.

He walked up and down the room, asking me more questions; then he sat down on the bed and saw how thin I was. He looked at the colour of my eyelids inside. He said that I should have cream on my porridge every morning, and other things to make me fatter. I remember my surprise as I watched him writing the list down for Matron. To be ordered such things was like being a child again, with someone above you who brooded over your welfare and took all the responsibility. Little attentions after the indifference of hospital struck me as almost too refined, too delicate. This was not true, hard-headed doctoring, but cosseting, coddling. But in spite of my mistrust of it, I liked it, it was just what I needed at that moment. It began to melt my own hard ignoring, my refusal to take thought for my body, that had grown up in the sour atmosphere of the hospital. I saw that I ought to think kindly of my body and respect it, as I used to do before this catastrophe.

I wanted him to stay so much that I began to talk very quickly and animatedly in an attempt to keep him. I did not like my feverishness, but the rest of the day seemed to threaten me. Empty and hollow, it stretched before me without end. I half wished that he had not made me more aware with his interest, his kindness, that I had been left in the shell I had grown.

Of course my eagerness to keep him only reminded him that there were other patients to be visited. He looked at his watch, got up and smilingly disappeared.

There I was, just as I knew I should be, left alone in the bed in the pink-curtained room, with the white blanket of emptiness crowding down to overwhelm me.

I heard the quick animal clip-clopping of Matron's little shoes, then she was bobbing round the room, flicking her eternal ladylike duster, asking me saucily over her shoulder how I liked my new doctor.

It was clear that Dr Farley was a favourite, that I was expected to be enthusiastic, and so something perverse prompted me to say, 'Oh, he's quite nice, I think.'

My voice was tired, far-away, utterly preoccupied with self.

Matron bridled and almost made a cracking noise with the duster; but she found little more to say. My lack of response had chilled her. I was pleased, for I felt I did not want to hear anything she had to tell me.

When my aunt came she, too, talked of him, saying, 'Oh, Dr Farley is a darling.' To me her tone was a little too quiet, too 'religious'. The words seemed to become a ritual phrase, a dogma, so that in imagination I heard them intoned by a thousand voices in some vast cathedral. 'Dr Farley is a darling. Dr Farley is a darling,' over and over again.

Both doctors had suggested that I should practise walking, so I now began to go out every afternoon with Nurse Goff. She would burden me with too many jerseys and scarves, put two grim rubber ferruled sticks in my hands, then take me very slowly along the pavement outside the nursing home.

People turned to look at us, or glanced from the corners of their eyes.

Our slow progress together with my two sticks and Nurse Goff's flying white cap and red-lined cloak made a little spectacle. Nurse Goff glared through her glasses without moving her head to right or to left. She was like an inhuman guardian – a fiery watchdog or steel robot. But I found myself almost enjoying the inquisitiveness, not resenting it. It was as if my nature, determined to find pleasure somewhere, drew it from the stares of the people, although at any other time it would have felt outraged and provoked.

Nothing could change my position; therefore I *must* enjoy being coloured, outlandish – like a rarely seen monkey on a barrel-organ, or an anachronistic church procession in dull commercial streets.

I spoke to myself like this, to heal my wound, and I was successful, for everything pleased me on those walks. I was untroubled. I loved the broad leaves in the gutter, splendid, decaying, rich, like some rare food; and the sound of the feet on the pavement, ringing and yet thick, not hollow. Even the soft padding of the rubber ferrules held a fascination. Sometimes when I looked across the fields to the shining roof of the house where my aunt lived I would see beyond it a sudden glint of cold sunlight on the leathery grey spread of the sea; I felt then for a sparkling moment that anything might happen, that human beings were never really trapped.

My wonder at being out in the world again, walking on my own feet, must have softened Nurse Goff towards me, for one day she went so far as to say, 'Poor lad! People look at you because I'm in my uniform. I'll ask Matron if I can come out in mufti next time.'

I was surprised – she had seemed to notice nothing – and I don't think I was pleased. In many ways it was easier to go out walking with an unyielding pillar, a wire armature draped in cap and cloak. If she came to life for me, I would have to be bright, to talk, to listen, when all the time my thoughts would be far away.

I remembered that Nurse Goff had come to life when she told me about her lover; and she had come to life, too, when I arrived back rather early from the bathroom one day and found her munching.

'I've stolen a chocolate out of the box your aunt brought you,' she said, half laughingly confident, half shame-faced.

But those times had been different; she had been using first my ears to pour her story into, then my chocolates. Now she seemed to be imagining my feelings disinterestedly, and so I was embarrassed.

When we got back to the nursing home, Matron would make a great fuss, asking us how far we had been, exaggerating my improvement under her roof, running to get the jam and scones for tea. She would try to say things to please me. Once it was, 'How nice you look in that grey suit!' But my prejudice was so strong that I could only reply in a gruff voice, 'It isn't grey; it's a sort of greenish tweed.'

'Do you call that green?' she exclaimed, a little shrilly. 'It looks grey to me.'

I was churlishly silent.

She insisted, growing obstinate, hating my dull resistance. It seemed impossible for me to be fair to Matron.

XVIII

IT WAS just as I was about to go for one of those little walks on a Saturday that my aunt arrived with my brother. He had been asked down for the week-end to see me in my new surroundings.

The afternoon was grey and sullen, with the trees weakly swaying against the dull, hopeless sky. We all smiled, but there seemed no link. We were quite divided. And I bitterly regretted the family I had been born into. It was not that they were wrong or that I was wrong. It was the connection that was freakish, invalid, arbitrary.

After the first few words, my aunt left us. 'I know you two will have lots to talk about together,' she said. But when we were alone we seemed to become even more numbed. My brother went to look out of the window. He stood there dejectedly, asking me all over again if I had everything I wanted, if I liked the nursing home, if he could do anything for me in London. But all the time his eyes were fixed rather desperately on the dying stalks of the flowers, the scatter of yellow leaves over the grass and the beds, the holes in the thatch of the summer-house where the birds had nested.

Nurse Goff brought tea in early, and I thought, 'Now something may melt, something may happen; we may be able to talk.'

I looked at my brother's face. The absent smile was still there, the anxiety to please, yet to escape. And when I saw him hurrying through his rock-cake, gulping the hot tea, I knew that nothing could be done. I sat still, just dully waiting for him to go. Even my anger and sorrow at the failure were becoming clouded and submerged.

At last he contrived to get himself out of the chair and to the door; while he was standing there, saying good-bye, the flood of shame and relief and sheer indifference that streamed out of both our bodies seemed to engage in the middle of the room and seethe up into something like a water-spout.

His going drained me of everything. I was washed up on a desert beach where all was changed and made impossible. Writing in my notebook, drawing, reading, dreaming, were as unthinkable, as meaningless as playing Patience. All feeling for myself seemed dead, therefore I was evil, snapping down on every impulse to live, to work, demolishing every suggestion that might have helped to break the spell.

I saw all at once that visits, either pleasant or painful, were beginning to leave me with this sensation of power gone, of lack and dislocation. It was the sensation of the prisoner growing in me. I felt that the room, the house, the garden and the strip of road outside were as poisoning as iron-spiked walls. I must get out and away from them. I must go down to the front and see my aunt and brother again; for although we had only just parted and our meeting had come to nothing, I had a sudden longing to be with them, to stay with the people who had known me all my life. If I could do that, the rat that was gnawing me inside might stop. It seemed the only possible thing to do.

I told myself violently, 'You can do it; it isn't far. You've bloody got to.'

This last phrase I said over and over again. It suddenly leapt into my mind to stimulate me. It must have been remembered from some book. The strangeness of using 'bloody' without 'well' had made me store the sentence away, and now I played with it, always pronouncing the 'bloody' in what I imagined was a rich uncouth north-country accent.

It gave me great energy and turned my thoughts inexplicably but inevitably to Clare and to religion. Perhaps she was right; perhaps if I put all my trust in what was called God I would be able to do anything. All hate and fear and limitation might fall away, and I would see cardboard horrors overturned and blown along ridiculously by a great rushing Wind.

This was the beginning of an ecstatic mood that had come upon me perhaps twice before in my illness and certainly several times in my childhood. But this last state was made strange and rather terrible by a disillusionment which shot through the exaltation, so that the two emotions, woven together and yet striving against each other, were formed into a dizzying, splintering pattern.

At one moment I was telling myself not to dare to believe in such absurdities, and the next I was carried up and licked round by flames of shrill vitality that promised with their shooting and flashing to destroy for ever the spongy, tripe-like substance threatening me.

122

I put on gloves and coat, took up only one of the sticks, opened the ponderous french-window and walked as quickly as I could through the garden.

Matron was at her desk in the window of her 'office'; she looked up as I passed, but nothing could nonplus me. I told myself that her presence there was an advantage. I could call out in a voice that I knew would reassure her, 'I'm just going out alone to practise walking for a little,' then she would smile and nod her head and worry no more about me. I *knew* it.

There was a bridge over the railway outside the nursing home. I crossed it now and looked down into the deep cutting. Far below me the steel rails, like never-ending stilettos, seemed to pierce into the grey, veined, bulging heart of the future. They were for me a symbol of sharp tingling excitement, everlasting inquisitiveness and fierceness.

I started to walk down the track which led to the front. On the left was a hedge, on the right a wooden fence and scattered houses with undeveloped gardens, and mournful strips of field still unbought. Rounded stones and edged flints pushed through the flattened, silky mud of the track, and there were deep puddles.

About half-way down I clutched the fence and leant against it. My body was crying out for stillness and relief, but my mind said contemptuously, 'Go on! Get down! Don't fall to pieces here!'

After a few minutes I was able to force myself on; but now the landscape seemed to be taking on an ugly significance. I imagined that the vacant plots between the raw gardens and houses had probably been left desolate in superstitious fear, because of vile crimes committed there. Perhaps in the moonlight, over and over again, night after night, a little child's atrocious murder would be re-enacted; or there would be ghost figures loping over the ground, arms outstretched greedily, white hair on the palms of the brown-pink hands. Their fingers would be webbed. Yellow fangs, hollow and rotten, would jut from their dripping jaws, and eyes, on fire with hate and lust, would be swimming and swirling as my head was swirling.

I began to see my aunt's house as a goal – a goal like the Cross in that child's prayer book picture, where a woman with streaming hair is shown clinging to the base in utter exhaustion, while storm clouds part, the sun breaks through and one sees the terrible length of her pilgrimage.

When I came out on to the road behind the houses on the cliff, a tram was just passing, and it appeared so grotesque, so strange, that I had to stop and watch. But the elaborate late nineteenth-century shape seemed to lack something. The clanging and snapping and sparking of the tram made me think that it should be some sort of giant mechanical crow; therefore why were there no metal wings flapping by clockwork, no eyes or iron beak in front?

I turned to the right and thought that if only I could reach the garden gate of my aunt's house all would be well. I could sink down then into some bed – not a human bed, I told myself in my confusion, but a flower-bed where the earth would be as soft and enveloping as bran. Hidden in the bran-pie, who could find me? I would be safe waiting there until I had recovered. It would be like the Day of Resurrection – my body springing up out of the ground, transformed, perfect, like a dull rocket that bursts at last. And every horrible thing would be wiped out and the calmest joy would grow and grow and grow.

Now I was close to the house I had gazed at every day on my walks with Nurse Goff, and now I was through the gate with its rose arch; but instead of collapsing into one of the feathery brown borders, I was walking between them soberly, then ringing the front-door bell and asking if my aunt was in.

'Yes, my lady is in, but she is resting,' said the pleasant-skinned maid in a voice so delicate, so sleek that I knew she had been practising, perhaps watching her mouth in the mirror. Her face was creamy and Mongolian and willingly obedient; the idea suddenly came to me that my aunt had been teaching her nice maid to articulate 'My lady' so perfectly, so separately, so peculiarly. Could she have done such a thing? Was it like her, or ridiculously out of character? How amusing it was to imagine her mouthing the plummy words before her pupil.

From maids and mistresses my mind jumped to the mistresses connected with men; and I saw many feathered and jewelled women kept in velvet Second Empire workboxes by curious dandies with large cheroots between their teeth and eau-de-Cologne on their eyebrows. I saw the women as pets – chinchilla Persian kittens on cherry satin cushions – cadmium canary-birds in vermilion lacquer cages. Would the colours and the images never stop forming?

At this moment I was being led past the case in the hall where my aunt kept her collection of five hundred dogs. Some were Chinese jade or amethyst earrings, some were silver and ivory; there were Copenhagen china ones, and glass ones out of Christmas crackers. I immediately added to my list of pets a King Charles spaniel with goldfish eyes, wearing a diamond bracelet as a collar.

Then I was left in the drawing-room doorway and I was looking at my brother sitting by the fire with a book. All was as humdrum as could be. If I walked very slowly, and smiled calmly, perhaps my brother would stop looking so startled; perhaps he would take me for granted and go on with his book. But that was too much to expect. He jumped up, saying, 'How did you get here?'

'Walked,' I answered repressively, feeling that a fuss at that moment would be disastrous to me. Something would happen – I would fall down, be sick, begin to cry, disgrace myself in some way.

My brother came across to me quickly, put me into a deep chair and dragged the low fire stool up for my feet. I felt now that I was sinking into the bran-pie and that before I sank too far I ought to make all the proper remarks.

'I hope Aunt Josie won't stop resting because I've come,' I began, but the words formed rather slowly and painfully, and a lump like a potato seemed to fill my mouth, blocking all further attempts at polite conversation . . .

My brother was standing over me with a glass of sherry which he had brought from a side table. I saw out of the corner of my eye that there were little salt biscuits there, too, and I wished that he would pass me these, but he only insisted that I should drink. The taste reminded me of Sister in the hospital. What was she doing at that moment? What patient had she put into my bed? What were her thoughts as she hurried through the day?

I felt that something important was about to happen. It seemed that all my life was mapped out and that only the thinnest partition cut me off from the plan; the match-boarding was splitting now, and perhaps, if I kept very still, I might soon get a glimpse of things that would come to pass in the future.

But all that happened was that one of the logs on the fire began to hiss and sizzle damply. Baby, the Pekinese, gave her invalid, watery little grunts, and the flame-light flickered on the Thibetan prayer-wheels and copper teapots with bird-headed spouts.

I had come with such pain and labour to a place where emptiness had arrived before me. I was too late, something black and hollow had over-taken me and wriggled through the door first.

'Be quiet, it is ordinary,' I told myself; 'you cannot appreciate the ordi-nary because you are not normal tonight, but one day you will want dull-ness and no help from outside – for only in dullness can your heart and mind grow, and only when other people and events leave you alone will you be able to feel that there is anything inside you at all . . .

'Outside the sea rushes to the cliffs, then sucks away, and in this room fires burn day after day. Whatever has happened to you, you still go on breathing, chugging like an intricate small engine that nothing can stop. Jogtrot rhythm, habit will drag you through almost everything and bring you out on the other side – it does not matter in what condition.'

Here my aunt came downstairs and began to scold me with a severity that was perhaps not so very mock. She shook her head and smiled with fond reproach, but I was aware that she and my brother were anxious that others should have the responsibility of me. When I heard a taxi being ordered, I felt like a present being posted back ungratefully before even the seal had been broken.

'What will Dr Farley say?' my aunt exclaimed with her graceful impa-tient faked concern. I was violently annoyed that he should be dragged in as a bogey; but her words made me aware of the destructiveness of my beha-viour. How he would dislike the pointless little stir that I had made!

They got me up from the warm chair and put me into the taxi alone, telling the man where to take me. As we sped through the dark, I thought of each yard of the way that had cost me so much only a little time before. Now the yards were eaten up and forgotten in a moment. We were flashing past the trams, the entrance of the rough track, the railway bridge; and there was Matron standing in the lighted doorway of the nursing home. Against the orange light, the full dark mass of her was dignified. No details could be seen. Her simplicity alarmed me. She was in the right and I was in the wrong. It was plain that I should be in disgrace.

She said almost nothing to me, but told Nurse Goff to take me away to bed at once.

I lay there in the dark, with the fire banked with ashes to keep it alive through the night. Sometimes a coal moved furtively and I saw for a moment a glowing eye-hole in the pile. My feet were walking still and burning, and my mind still desperate with the problem of reaching my goal. I was so tired that I had travelled far beyond rest. To lie down and be still was a torture, but to move about any more would have been impossible.

I began to long, as I had before, for some special smell, some special music that would fill me, lift me up and carry me away, float me off the rocks of my body and sweep me into some wideness, some vast expanse of blue-grey nothingness.

XIX

MY TEMPERATURE was high in the morning, and there was an ache and tingle, almost delicious, in all my limbs. The ankle that had been broken had swollen up again and turned to rich purple-blue; but my mind was soothed and I lay in the bed contented to do nothing, to eat nothing, only to drink and let the day trickle past me.

Miss Pierce came at her usual time, but only to give me one of her quick workmanlike glances and to say, 'I don't think you're well enough to be done today, we'd better leave it.'

I was sorry, for I would have liked her to rub my legs, even pinch them and slap them, to increase the tingle that seemed to free my thoughts and soothe me.

Dr Farley arrived after Miss Pierce. I could tell that my aunt had been talking to him. He was so careful and confident with me, as if a bird or an angel had given him a special knowledge which he was modestly hiding. He said smilingly, 'What a fool to overdo things like that!' but I could not respond or explain myself, being divided between the vague vain pleasure and the resentment that spring up together when one knows that one has been discussed.

In the evening, when the fever was even higher, a new night nurse came on duty and began at once to tell me of her own illness and to exhort me to use my will as she had used hers. She described the anaemia that had forced her to give up her work for two or three years. At first she could not bring herself to eat the raw liver that was prescribed, but she persevered until she found she could bear it.

'You can make up your mind to *anything*,' she said, 'if you try.' Here she looked at me rather sharply to drive her lesson home. I saw that she was a much older woman than Nurse Goff, and that her face gained an unreal nutcracker severity from the curve and compression of her nose and lips. It was as if a heavy weight on her head had crumpled the features underneath. Her eyes looked out over little sills of wrinkled flesh.

'I was soon quite artful at disguising the flavour,' she was saying; 'I would chop the liver, sprinkle it with tomato ketchup, then sandwich it between pieces of bread and butter. Gradually I began to feel so much better; and now, as you see, I am back at my work again.'

After she had left me, I imagined dark bleeding hunks of liver on a white dish in front of me. I saw them cut up and tossed into some giant mouth; then I followed them down the black throat into the stomach and bowels, where they glistened and churned in a welter of slimy darkness.

I was revolted and fascinated by the liver, so that I would not take my thoughts from it, until a great force seemed to seize on me and spin me backwards. I yielded entirely, giving everything, letting the bed bear me along at a tremendous pace. It was as if we were careering down a mountain side, and I saw stones, gushing streams and trees only when they were passed.

Perhaps it was after midnight when the night nurse came to look at me again. She could not have liked what she saw for she switched on both lights, stuck the thermometer into my mouth and stood over me, frowning as if about to cast some evil spell. Then she took the little glass rod to the light, scowled at it and went out of the room quickly.

I heard the faint tinkle of the telephone bell and felt that she was an alarmist and that she should be stopped from waking Dr Farley. I wished I could hear what she was saying, but only a low murmur came to me. They appeared to talk for some minutes, then she came back to me with a basin in her hands.

'Dr Farley suggests a tepid rub to make you more comfortable and bring your temp. down,' she said, comfortably, no longer anxious; she had his directions now.

I was strangely disappointed. Was this all that was to happen? A sponge in tepid water? Was I no worse than that? How ill would I have to be before I was worth a visit? It would be strange if the patient became a corpse while the nurse was playing about with tepid water . . . Then I was glad that he had been sensible and had not turned out to see me just because a new nurse was uneasy.

She began to put the cool water on my forehead and my wrists. I think she had sprinkled some of her own lavender water on the flannel, for there was a sweet fresh smell. I breathed it in deeply while I listened to another stimulating talk. She insisted on the importance of fighting illness with courage, patience and ingenuity. As I listened, I grew a little resentful. It was clear that she looked on me as a floating wreck to be seized upon and directed by her firm hand. Was I nothing to her but a rag-doll waiting to be stuffed with noble sentiments? Was I supposed to have no qualities until they were plugged into me by her? Still, she was good to me and I liked her for her care. Even the stern lectures shortened the hours till morning, and the morning was all I waited for.

After that night I stayed in bed for two weeks. Mark came as he said he would, bringing the painting things with him. He walked into the room with the easel on his shoulder, and this, together with his lizard's eyes, the drawn, beard-darkened line of his jaw, and his secret air, gave him the appearance of an unpopular saint who was being forced to carry his instrument of torture to the execution place.

He sat with me all day, and I talked, laughed and listened so much that I grew quite numb. I longed to shut my eyes, shut my mouth.

At last there was a lull. It stretched itself out until Mark pushed back his chair, making the legs screech.

'I suppose I ought to be going,' he said. His voice had the aggrieved tone and I knew that he was thinking of the thirteen or fourteen shillings the train journey had cost him; he was thinking, too, of the capriciousness and wickedness of human nature, of the impossibility of finding true understanding or appreciation anywhere.

His eyes were far away as he said good-bye. It was as if he had already travelled beyond me in his search. He forgave me, but dismissed me for my lack of warmth. He would be feeling particularly bitter, because he had told me that the Admiral was beginning to suggest that the lessons with the daughter were unnecessarily long. The invitations to stay to lunch or tea were growing rarer and rarer. Could the father be so absurd as to imagine that he was falling in love with the daughter? All this suspicion and coldness were disgusting.

He would nurse these thoughts on his homeward journey. He had often told me how much pleasure trains gave him, how childishly delighted he was in a fine engine or a long tunnel; but these things would lose their fascination; he would sit in his corner, brooding.

I knew all this, but I could not feel sorry. I felt very little except a greed for stillness and the clear flavour of a pineapple.

This craving for a pineapple grew until I asked Matron to get me one. At first she laughed and said, 'What a curious fancy!' but I persisted and she agreed to choose a good one for me in the town.

She must have bought it and left it on the table in the hall; for one morning, after Dr Farley had been in to see me and had left, I heard him go into the hall, pause a moment, then quickly run back.

I waited, wondering what was about to happen. The door flew open and I saw him holding the great cockaded fruit as if it had been a baby in arms. He was laughing silently and his thick eyebrows curled about like furry caterpillars. All at once he slung the horny, scaly pine on to the foot of my bed, then made an extraordinary face at me and was gone.

I sat straight up in bed, too surprised even to smile at first, seeing only his wild grimace again and the pineapple sailing towards me. Then I began to laugh and touch the scales of the cone, following their pattern with my finger. Every time I ate a slice of that pineapple, his fantastic face was re-created for me and the swelling shape of the fruit in the air. The picture, like something seen in a dream, was haunting, and its absurdity never ceased to appeal to me.

Dr Farley also brought me his gramophone. When he came in, bending over the black box and hurrying forward as if it were hot and he wanted to set it down, I thought that it might be some new medical contrivance, or perhaps another joke. I was not prepared for anything like a gramophone.

He told me that he only had Handel and Tchaikovsky records, the Alcina suite and, I think, the Swan Lake music. He seemed a little ashamed of liking the last composer, as if some smug silly person had told him that he ought not to care much for such music. I was sorry to see his uncertainty; it shook my confidence a little. I wanted someone who was sure of everything he said and did.

When I first had the records, I used to play them every day, so I soon came to know the music well. Sometimes, when no one was about, I would get out of bed and move about the room rhythmically, using my arms and my body much more than my legs. I think the movements of this dance must have been like the swaying of an insect working its way out of a cocoon, or like the waving of the arms of a fly while the spider winds it round and round with fine threads.

At the end of my two weeks in bed Dr Farley asked me to go out with him in his car. The thought of the ride delighted me so much that even Nurse Goff noticed a difference and said, 'You're very lively all of a sudden. What's up?' I don't think she was pleased. She either thought that doctors should waste no spare time on patients or that it was unseemly of me to show excitement at the prospect of escaping from her and Matron for an hour or two.

I was ready and waiting at the window as soon as lunch was finished. When I heard the small blue car drive up and saw the tip of its radiator round the corner of the house, I unwound my scarf and unbuttoned my coat in sheer agitation, or was it so that I should have something to do when Dr Farley appeared?

He was in unprofessional light rough clothes and was smoking a cigarette; the effect was so different that for a moment I felt towards him as I might towards a boisterous stranger who had burst into my room by mistake. When he clapped his hands heartily and told me to wrap myself up, because it was cold, the idea came to me that I ought really to be a dog, and that he should be fastening on my collar before taking me out for a walk. I looked straight at him, but not into his eyes, to try to accustom myself to the familiar face rising out of the new clothes. Their paleness seemed to give him a naked, uncovered look, and to make the head harsher and more gypsy.

We went out through the garden and got into the car. Just at first the rather cramped position made my legs tingle so much that I thought I might not be able to stand it. I said nothing, but Dr Farley must have been conscious of my difficulty, for he said, 'I think you'll soon get used to it.' And almost at once I found that I had forgotten my legs and that I was living through my eyes, taking into me all the sights of the town.

He took me to a lonely bay where crazy beach huts huddled together miserably. We got out of the car and walked down a half-made road until we saw a patch of sea between miniature cliffs. We passed through the gap and found ourselves on the beach with the sea spread out before us. We were alone on the cold autumn beach; only ourselves walking close to the waves.

Thick white shells dotted the beach, and when I bent down to them I saw that they were nearly all broken. The jagged edges had been washed as smooth as ground porcelain, and through large holes in the sides one could see the voluted spines twisting and flowing upwards like lovely spiral staircases. The holes suggested ruined windows, so it was easy for me to see the beach changed suddenly into a desert waste where derelict white villas crumbled into ruin.

Dr Farley took me slowly towards the chalk headland that bit into the sea. I remember its flatness and squareness. It looked like a huge white axe-blade hacking into silvery bark, and it sharpened in me the painful longing to feel *more*, discover *more*, shape *more* than I ever could.

How slowly I walked! My legs were hung with chains and I dragged the prisoner's iron ball behind me. I tried to breathe deeply and give no hints of gasping or panting, but he noticed and took my arm and I was almost bitter at so much watchfulness and understanding. To feel near me the heart and flesh and bones of someone else made a secrecy spring up, a self-protection and sense of complete isolation. He would feel now every uncertainty of my body, every jerk or slowness, and I would be aware of his much greater strength as he helped me forward; but the very closeness of our bodies cut our minds apart; left them as separate as the sides of a deep ravine. We were two caskets walking close together on the beach with all our secrets locked away and never to be mingled. The sides of the caskets could bump against each other, but that only made the division between the contents more sharp and striking. I looked out from my eyes as from the slits in a castle wall.

When Dr Farley paused for a moment, I bent down to gather some of the shells – the skeleton houses, blasted and deserted. I had the impulse to make a picture of them; each one should be a different colour against a background of yellow-ochre beach, with the white arm of the cliff curving round. I would try to put little people in the shells, tramps, or ghosts rising out of ruins at nightfall.

The wind blew on our backs as Dr Farley led me back to the car. Once I looked over my shoulder and saw the sea curling at me, pawing me, wanting me to run back to float out on it and disappear. But I could not be in communication with the sea when Dr Farley had hold of my arm and was smoothly helping on each step I took. I had to flow with him – no time to wait and ponder there alone.

Cold moment on the beach, curving stones under my feet, curling clouds sweeping down low, threatening my head with your sailing grey stomachs; nothing could make me forget you.

We went back to his house and I stood in the dark little hall and looked through the door on the left, where I saw shiny magazines laid out on a mahogany table. All was utterly still and untouched, like a tomb-chamber. But we did not go into the patients' waiting-room. Dr Farley opened a door on the right and I felt a very different atmosphere. The light in the room was already fading, but I could see the shelves of brightly backed books on either side of the fireplace, the leather sofa with brown velvet cushions, the dark thickness of the carpet, the large desk in the bay-window. The room seemed like a brown casserole, a baked dish, warm and comforting and heavy. It gave me a slight feeling of sadness.

'What a lot of new books!' I said, because the crisp red and blue and yellow covers were the most striking things in the room. Then trying to give my remark a little point, I added, 'Most people only have old ones.'

He stood and looked at the books in a strange musing way. 'And one day these will all be old too,' he said flatly; 'one can feel them getting old as they sit on the shelves.' He was not entirely talking to me; he seemed to be reminding himself of old age and decay and all the years to come, when he would be dead.

At the sound of his voice a squat Aberdeen terrier struggled out of its basket and came towards us on uncertain legs. The tail, like a hairy little sausage, waved and then dropped, as if exhausted by the effort. Dr Farley bent down, scolded the dog gently and put it back in its basket. I saw close to the basket a tray partly covered by a cloth, but with jars, cotton wool and shining instruments showing at the edge. It all looked so professional. I saw the dog at once as a peculiar little hairy patient in a miniature bed. It was as if a child were playing at doctors with its pet.

'We're afraid he won't get over it,' Dr Farley said in a grave voice, withholding fact, only making the bare statement.

I was startled, for I had felt certain that the dog would soon be playing and gobbling its food and imploring to be taken for a walk. I looked at it with new eyes, but I still could not feel that it would die, and I was glad of my ignorance and sorry that Dr Farley knew too much.

A small girl maid brought in tea and put the tray on the low bench before the fire. I sank down into a corner of the soft brown sofa and Dr Farley began to pour out. He looked under the lid of the silver scone dish and asked me if I liked dripping toast or hated it. 'We often have it,' he said, 'because I like it so much.' He seemed to expect me to take sides, and I saw at once that there was something both disgusting and delicious about it. I remembered myself as a child out to tea first tasting the strange dark brown stuff, savouring the welcome richness of it; then later at school feeling nothing but a dislike for the heavy animal flavour. But now dripping toast seemed the perfect thing after the cold autumn sea, the grey beach and the broken shells – I felt them in my pocket, knocking together like muffled porcelain bells.

'I love it,' I said with too greedy a determination to enjoy everything – as if there were not time, as if I must exaggerate and emphasize each detail to extract the very last drop of pleasure.

We were silent as we ate the toast. It was not quite a barren constraint, but rather, I felt, a time when thoughts were churning, clearing themselves of a hundred little confusions.

The dog was persuaded to lap a little tea from the slop-bowl, then Dr Farley got up and walked about the room in a way which would ordinarily have made me very uncomfortable and restless; but I was prepared to watch him with interest, as I would have watched a rare animal at the zoo.

At last he stopped prowling and settled at the other end of the sofa, cocking his legs up so that I had a view, first of shoes, socks, legs, trousers, then of face looking small, far away and twinkling, like the sun in a mountain cleft.

He began to ask me what I wanted to do. Now that I was getting better, had I many plans for my future? Was I ambitious?

Faced suddenly with these questions that for all these months had been sleeping undisturbed, hidden under the immediate violent bodily questions, I was thrown into confusion and fell back on the extraordinary expedient of pretending that I had no ambition, since my aunt had unexpectedly told me only a few days before that when I was twenty-one I would probably inherit a little money from my mother.

It was his turn to be surprised. He was displeased, too; perhaps by my pretended indifference, perhaps because it might be possible for me not to earn a living. I only know that there was resentment behind his 'You're one of the lucky ones, then; but don't you want to do *anything?*'

What could I say? How could I tell him of all the things I wanted to do – things I was ashamed of because I wanted them so weakly, so confusedly, yet so persistently? The cloudy beckoning things had been knocked to pieces by the sudden violence of the accident. They had lost all their worth and fascination at first, but now they were growing again. The ghosts were losing their greyness and were trying to draw me from the dulled muted life of bed; but I rebelled, still wanting to be left in my nothingness, not wanting anyone to talk to me of plans and futures.

'You are gifted,' Dr Farley said, wanting, I suppose, to strike some response out of me.

I wondered, without any humour or lightness, why he should think so. Was it gifted to have an easel and brushes and paints? Or to keep notebooks under the pillow? If so, there were a great many gifted people in the country. The very thought of so much messy foozling disgusted me. Which part of me displayed my gifts? My face, hands, behind, feet, hair? I did not feel gifted. I felt bereft, fleeced, defaced.

But his interest in me, his desire for me to prove myself in some way, could not leave me quite cold and dead. Something began to stir in me, to gain a little confidence and warm itself in his encouragement. I might be driven against my will, pushed into making efforts that I did not want to make, but still, a part of me felt glad.

I was divided in this way, half grateful and half alarmed, when I heard the front door open. A moment afterwards Mrs Farley came into the room with her hands full of parcels. She had just come back from shopping. She was smiling and arching her long neck towards me, for we had not met before. I looked chiefly at her fine, thick tawny hair. As we stood talking, I swayed a little; Dr Farley noticed it.

'Time for you to go back,' he said, going to fetch my overcoat. While my fingers were busy with the buttons, he tied my scarf over my ears in a ludicrous way; I felt foolish and pleased, but I was glad Mrs Farley had put down her parcels and gone over to the dog; for it was unlikely that she would find much to laugh at in the situation. She knelt beside the basket and appeared to be washing out the dog's mouth with some lotion.

When I said good-bye she looked up and showed her teeth in a smile, but her eyes quickly returned to the dog.

As we drove back to the nursing home I thought of her there on the floor, tending the dog. I thought of the books on the shelves, the dripping toast, our walk on the seashore; and it seemed an afternoon apart, something quite separate, some different life I had strayed into.

XX

WHEN I started to paint the broken shells which I had brought back from the beach, I found that I wanted to make them very large and the jagged ridges very white. Their harsh bright shapes seemed about to jump off the canvas and close in upon me. They threatened as they floated just above the surface of the yellow sand. I had not dared to put the people in the shells, so the picture was gaunt and empty and, to another person, uninteresting; but I took great pleasure in it, because it was the first thing I had done since my accident. The rich surface of the paint and the sky, like streaked liquorice, pleased me, and when Mark came I wanted him to admire the picture; but he only looked at it and then said something flattering, which showed me very clearly what he thought of it. I turned it away to protect it from him and started at once to think of another picture. I had seen that morning the usual golden 'specimen' in a slender beaker on the window-sill, with the sun pouring through it, and the ham-pink curtains hanging down on each side. Behind were waving bushes with small shiny leaves. It seemed almost a perfect window picture and I decided to begin on it as soon as Mark left me. But he stayed all day, and so it was not until after breakfast the next morning that I got to work.

For some reason I was taken on that day to a different bathroom. I had to go through the hall and up the main staircase. When I reached the landing I was surprised to see a collection of minute champagne bottles outside one of the doors. Never having seen such small ones before, I bent down to read a label and finger the silver paper at the neck. I heard faint uncomfortable noises behind the door, painful breathing, sighs that turned into groans. I wondered if some drunkard was being restricted to these tiny bottles in an attempt to break his habit. When I was back in my room, I asked Nurse Goff about the bottles and she said with some complacency and no reluctance, 'A lady is dying in there. She can take nothing but a sip of champagne now and then. Her husband comes to see her every day. We can do nothing more.'

This startled me, and I could not get the woman and her teaspoons of champagne out of my mind. I thought of her as I squeezed the paints on to my palette and set my easel in place; so that now her miserable condition is mixed in my mind with creamy paint and hog's hair bristles.

Dr Farley, when he came and saw what I was painting, said, 'What a subject! You are disgusting.' He started to laugh at me good-naturedly. I was jarred a little, seeing myself and the picture through his eyes, and I waited to be alone again with no difficulty, no exclamations or amusement.

Before he left, he asked me if I would like to go for another drive. On the next fine afternoon he took me with him to the home for orphan children on the Front. While he paid his visit, I waited in the car with the dog, which, in spite of his fears, had now almost recovered. I patted it as I gazed at the bleak seats of involved and flowering cast-iron. Rooted as they were in the tarred road, cut off from one another by gaunt lamp-posts, they had an extraordinarily desolate air. Only two people passed – a woman in full, heavy skirts wheeling a child in one of those long spinal carriages of basket work. It was three o'clock in some gritty cinder town, and the waves swarming up the beach were like the khaki fungus that grows in flowing tiers on rotten tree-stumps.

Dr Farley came out of the home smiling, as if all the boys had made him feel admired and waited for. I saw at once how delightful he would seem in a grim dormitory – really a golden person, warm and true all through, something that a child longed for, protection from matron, master or other orphans. His understanding and acceptance would enslave the boys, so that they talked of him until their keepers grew tired of the name. I thought of this charm, left behind in the home.

We drove along the esplanade until it ended and we came to bare fields. Dr Farley drove on to the spongy grass and then let the dog loose. We started to walk towards the cliffs, talking all the time about my future, what I should do, what I should avoid. There was some discomfort in the conversation for me and I looked at my feet. Dr Farley looked down, too, sometimes kicking a tuft of grass or thrusting his hands down into his pockets with a jerk, as if new thoughts had come which were not to be mentioned until they had been sifted. Because of our lowered heads neither of us noticed that the Aberdeen had begun to chase another dog; but as soon as Dr Farley heard its snarls and barks, he started to run and call out angrily. He ran so awkwardly in his blue suit and soft black hat that I could hardly bear to watch him. It was as if he felt ridiculous and impotent in pursuit of the small black dog. He lurched, hunching his shoulders grotesquely; he who had long legs and should have run so well. For the moment I could only feel sorry and wish that he would stop running. I hated myself for criticizing so pettily; but it *was* so, I had to accept the fact that he, like everyone else, could be made to look foolish by self-consciousness.

I went back to the nursing home filled with this sense of the absurdity of everything on the earth. Nothing was fixed and sure. We all melted into ridiculousness in the end.

The next time I went out, I went alone. I must have taken a bus into the town, for I know I found myself there fairly fresh and untired. This was a very different expedition from that first nightmare visit to my aunt's. I was now in a reawakened mood. Everything interested me. I saw enticing-looking chocolates in a shop window – truffles, like rusty little cannon-balls because they were dipped in bitter red cocoa powder, fondant sausages rolled in chocolate beads as small and glittering as fishes' eggs, flat discs of peppermint cream, and dominoes of coated butterscotch. I went in and bought myself a little bagful, then I walked down the narrow lane between the Royal Albion Hotel and the shop which showed in one corner of its window small boxes decorated with many different shells, and bottles filled with delicate coloured sands in wavy layers and patterns.

I stopped to look at the shells; the pink ones delicate and papery as a mouse's ears, the pointed iridescent ones, and the voluted ones that presented themselves to me as purple, cruelly twisted nipples. All the shells stared back at me, coldly repulsing my interest, so I moved on to the glass pavilion on the edge of the cliff.

It was a damp, weighted, early November day with almost warm mist blowing in from the sea, and when I reached the pavilion I found someone already sheltering there from the watery vapour. He was pressed close against one of the glass partitions with his head sunk down between his hunched shoulders, and because he wore a furry sandy coat, he looked like a round bear. As soon as he heard me, he looked up and smiled half-heartedly. His eyes seemed weak; they were watering a little, but he had fresh pink-brown cheeks and these for some reason wiped out my first impression of weeping. The toy-bear coat, so tightly belted, and the sporty cock of his soft brown hat also made grief seem impossible. I settled in another corner of the pavilion, as I had intended to do, and did not feel bound to pass on.

At first he blinked at me once or twice, but said nothing, and, feeling that he wanted to talk, I was uneasy, waiting for the words to come.

'What a day!' he said at last, rolling his eyes up, as if nothing else could be expected from such a heaven. The tone told me nothing. The jaunty words were parrot words and I made a parrot reply; then I looked down at my chocolates and wondered whether to offer them or not. I was held back by the old convention, suddenly remembered and exaggerated, that men do not eat sweets. I decided to compromise by holding out the chocolates, smilingly, as if I too thought them rather nonsense.

I was pleased to see that the man looked at them quite greedily; but instead of choosing one at once, he left his hand hovering in the air above them and moved his jaw from side to side to show his indecision. As soon as he had taken one, he seemed to remember that he too had something to offer; after slapping all his pockets, he brought out his cigarette case and flicked it open for me.

'I don't smoke, thank you,' I said between munches of my chocolate, thinking it strange of him to expect me to both eat and smoke at the same time. But the man did not think it strange, he sat there, looking out to sea, a cigarette in one hand and a chocolate in the other, puffing and chewing by turns. I waited for him to bite at the cigarette or suck at the chocolate, but he made no mistake and the rhythm flowed smoothly. Soon he was telling me that he was staying at a convalescent home, had been there for nearly a fortnight, and all he had found to do was to go for walks in the half empty streets or along the wintry cliffs.

As soon as I heard that he, too, had been ill, my interest was quickened. I could not look at him as the person, far away from me, that I had known a moment before. Although it was plain that many, many convalescents and doomed people must have roamed the streets of the town alone year after year, to meet another like this in the mist had for me the attraction of an adventure. I was waiting for some promise, some hidden pattern to be unfolded. I wanted to believe that there was some reason for the meeting, so I listened carefully to all he said.

I don't remember what was wrong with him, because I shut my mind to any gruesome details, but I know that his firm in London, or the club he belonged to, was giving him this holiday and that there was another patient, an old man, in his convalescent home who went about muttering, leaning on gates, singing to the sheep and cows, and complaining that, like a horse in blinkers, he could only see straight in front.

These irrelevant details remain, and the picture of the man's fresh face and watering eyes, the willing smile, which could only keep out the unhappy searching blankness for a few moments at a time. He seemed so lost there, huddled in his corner; streams of aching dullness flowed out of him and seeped into me. I thought of us both walking in the streets, standing on the cliffs, looking in shop windows, staring at the sea, lost in the town with our invalidism. I was blasted by his indifference and made to feel as empty myself. We who should have been strong and vital and at our most flourishing were like two chimney-cowls jerking and swirling round absurdly in the wind – always shifting, always fixed and isolated.

I was straining for the jumbled puzzle to click into a picture – for every crooked piece to lock suddenly together. I had no pleasure in mystery and wanted everything in the clearest language. What was the man for? What was I for? Why were we being wasted? And why was there all round us the vast overwhelming waste of lamps, streets, trees, houses? Why was that great sea mouthing at the beach? And why was the land so passive and dumb?

I looked at the man, but I could say nothing about the waste, nor could I ask him why he was alive. I saw his eyes flitting from the sea to the cliff railings, then to the cast-iron pillars of the pavilion and so back to the sea again. His head moved a little to the right, then to the left. He had no ease because there seemed nothing in the world for him to feed on; but it would be useless to talk; he would dislike and distrust the exaggeration of speech, and I would be made to feel a fool.

Perhaps I was a fool to question so childishly, to want everything brought down to my simple level. Most foolish of all to expect a chance meeting, or any other incident, to hide some deeper meaning, not to accept it just for itself alone.

'I must go,' I said, jumping up.

The man got up, too.

'Is your place strict about time?' he asked.

I said 'Yes' to get away, and we both stood for a moment close to the railings. Once or twice, through the waves of mist, I caught glimpses of the fawn, rippled beach far below us; I wondered what it would be like to fall over the cliff and thwack down on that sand. I tickled myself with a creeping alarm, whilst the mist eddied round us, clinging, then leaving us bare.

The man's eyes were watering more now; he looked utterly unprotected and raw as he smiled good-bye.

'I might as well be going back, too,' he said with no spirit. We walked together back to the lane leading into the town. There he suddenly came on another inmate of his home, a thin man standing on the corner with his hands sunk deep in his pockets.

They both said 'Hullo'; I was made to shake hands; there was a little sad heartiness, then nothing. We stood in a circle round a balloon of emptiness which was swelling all the time, forcing us farther and farther apart.

The town seemed full of almost useless men moping at street corners.

I left them, slipping quickly into a thick pocket of mist between the houses. There was no pang of broken communication at parting. To be with them had meant a horrible intensification of loneliness. Now I began to eat the chocolates one after another exuberantly. Their delicious taste revived my own life that had been frozen, and I thrust my feet forward, half forgetting the difficulty of walking. The man had been all that was calm, uncomplaining, wretched and damned, and how horrible it had been to meet yet another just as I was escaping from the first!

Their helplessness, which had nearly swallowed me up, now began to make me feel curiously bright and powerful and glistening – almost brassy. I was hard and bright and uncontaminated. I saw their good-natured victims' faces again in my mind's eye, but I passed on now to other sights. I was free from their untragic gloom and would not be impaired by it.

And I thought, as I made my way back to the nursing home, walking more and more slowly with every step, that perhaps after all this was the secret which I was to learn from the encounter in the mist.

There were some birds at night beyond the garden. Behind their hard cymbal clashes or sad flute sounds I used to hear the far-away moping of the sea and then the fitful barking of a dog. I would imagine his cry coming across the fields, the brimming icy ditches and the bare hedges glittering with black drops of water. Perhaps it came from some lonely farm where he was chained up in a cobbled yard. The chain would grate and clink like a ghost's as he ran from side to side, barking and waiting for the answer which never came. At last his tail would curve down through his legs and he would huddle back into the dank straw in his barrel.

I wrote about the night bird cries, the sea sounds and the lonely barking, and I liked what I wrote in flashes; but something was wrong with it. There is always something wrong with writing. So I tore the paper up at last, liking the untouched memory so much better, not wanting it forced into the insincerity of words.

All the noises were uneasy in the night, and I was uneasy, too, waiting for the morning, screening my heart from the thoughts that dashed down from my head to cut into it.

I used to wonder how the other people round me slept. How did the matron sleep? – on her great-breasted front? or on her back? or did her hip dig deep into the mattress? Did she sleep on fears, pressed flat like dried apricots in a jar? or were her dreams of fine men, great magnificence and money? Was Nurse Goff planning even in her sleep the arrangements for her marriage to the man who had had my bed before me? Or was she insisting on her consequence before a room full of sluggish, unresponsive patients?

My thoughts would fly down the road to Dr Farley's squat house. I would see the small maid in a bed with white iron bars like a cot, a grey-white stringy coverlet spread over her. Mrs Farley and Dr Farley would be in the largest front room – his trousers and shift would be very near the bed so that he could grab them; he would be in a light sleep, always listening for the telephone. I hated to think of the lack of real calm. It made all the house seem furtive and vibrating. I saw the dark head on the almost gruesomely white pillow, the swarthy face impossibly changed, smoothed out and scoured by sleep. Even to imagine his face in sleep seemed like a prying and exciting treachery. The planes and hollows were all there defenceless, and his eyelids were like pigeons' eggs, half submerged in rich cream soup. There was a statue's subsmile round his mouth. The temples were damp with sleep, a very fine rime had gathered on his lip. I would feel the warm breath on my face; it was like being a ghost, a spirit spy hovering in the air, experiencing everything. In those long nights I imagined details so clearly that reality in the morning seemed a little smeared and shapeless.

Sometimes the brocaded brooding stillness of the nursing home would be broken and I would hear footsteps in the tiled passage and low voices murmuring directions. A broad crack of light would show underneath my door; there would be the plushy noise of rubber wheels, then the tea-time tinkle of all the surgical instruments on the trolley.

On one of these nights of whispering and hurrying there was a sudden silence, when all the footsteps retreated, although the lights were still burning.

I got out of bed, opened my door and looked out. No one was about, so I crept to the end of the passage and found the theatre door open at last. Always in the daytime it was kept locked. The great frosted lamp glared down on the thin white table; but there were no crimson slops, no brimming kidney dishes, no swabs thrown down anywhere on the floor, no tubes, no pumps, no tweezers and no saws – nothing as I had imagined it after an operation.

The floor was frivolous turquoise-blue crazy-paving mosaic, such as one sees in hotel porches. The harsh white walls and metal fittings seemed stiff from dislike of the flash mosaic; and the mosaic seemed to be vying with the red of blood, insisting shrilly on its power to drown it and turn pools of it to nothing but a sticky black.

I turned from the unrewarding theatre to the large cupboard which also had always been locked. Now the doors were wide open and I saw innumerable bottles and jars and phials. Most of the Latin names were mysterious to me, but suddenly I came upon a little tube of morphine for injection. It gave me the jump and the thrill of some rare discovery in an old clothes shop. Here was a tube that any man would hug to himself. He might never even open it, but he would have all the warmth of it for the rest of his life.

I took it up, then put it down again almost at once, suddenly afraid of being discovered with it in my hands. There was another moment of hovering, but I was too prudent to snatch it and hide it away. I saw too clearly the horrible expression on Matron's face and the trouble for everyone that would follow, so I slipped back into my room feeling that lack of daring had taken something out of my reach for ever. Such a cupboard door would never be open for me again. I would never have another chance of seizing a little tube, which my imagination transformed into a long, long tunnel of perfect sleep and calm, with a door at the end into a landscape of cold rocks and weak sunlight. Here people, quite naked, pale as slugs, sat about in groups on the sharp, whining grass. They were like Puvis de Chavannes people changed and twisted by my own caprices.

After these wakeful nights, I never felt tired; rather I had a stronger sense of unused energy and restlessness. I would long to go somewhere unknown, see some new sight, feel the world filling me; and now that my walking was improving, I was able to gratify this longing a little.

I found that if I turned to the left outside the nursing home, instead of crossing the railway bridge, I came, after some minutes' walk, to a large open space, half rough grass, half cabbage field. The deserted cabbages in their very long rows were turning sulphur yellow, plum purple, and lichen blue, and their dungy smell hung above them in the damp air as if they had been cooked. Perfect rain-drops and dew-drops, like minute witch-balls, balanced on the webbed bloomy leaves; and waves of glistening rooks and floury white gulls would glide down, fold their broad wings as if they were on hinges, then settle to the task of finding worms and insects. In their long lines, with their heads bent, they reminded me of evilly disposed children kept at their desks in some open-air school.

The nearest side of this open space was fringed with semi-detached villas, but beyond them I could see a new church, twentieth-century Romanesque, built carefully of sliced flints, and with a shallow roof of crinkling pantiles.

By walking very deliberately and rhythmically I was able to reach it at last. When I came round to the west end, I found it finished only with boards. It was clear that the nave was to be lengthened when more money had been collected. The surprise of the flimsy walling after the solid, well-packed flints made the building more interesting to me. I wanted to go in at once.

In front of the door I found a screen, a sort of letter-rack, in which little cards with black edges were stuck. I saw the words 'Requiescat in Pace' in Gothic script, then 'Pray for the soul of . . .' There were more women's than men's names – and I suddenly saw the little pieces of pasteboard as desperate visiting-cards from Purgatory; not left in the church entrance by elegant corpses in Broughams and Victorias, but shot straight to the board from another world. They seemed crying out for attention, as though the dead people themselves were stretching out their hands, imploring with their eyes for prayers. It was as if Stella Margaret James, George Whitcombe, Norah Holt could stand no more and screamed out to be relieved.

I turned from the calls for help to the holy water stoups. They were still not darkened or polished with hands. The faint gunpowdery smell of new stone hung about them. I dipped my fingers in, then touched my forehead, an inexperienced gesture, perhaps more Hindoo than Christian. I wondered why I now enjoyed copying other people's religious observances. In a Protestant church I was often disappointed that there was so little to be done. But as a child I had hated to do *anything* – even to kneel down had seemed preposterous and indecent.

I stood at the bottom of the church and looked about me. High up in the gloom the solid new beams seemed to be floating. A long, long chain with a crimson lamp at the end hung before the altar. The chain was so long that, as my eyes followed it up, I imagined myself as a minute man, terrified and sweating, climbing from link to link into the darkness. The red lamp would be like a bicycle rear-light dwindling away down a black country road.

I began to walk slowly· round the walls, looking at the Stations of the Cross. They had evidently been brought from an earlier more temporary church, for they were tawdry blue-green oleographs in Oxford frames, perhaps forty or fifty years old.

The church was filling with greyness now. As I stood in front of each brightly coloured picture of humiliation and agony, it seemed to be isolated from everything else, to be the lighted exhibit in some chamber of horrors. I forgot the Passion story and saw each torture scene with new disgusted eyes, as if I were a man from the moon.

In the north and south walls I came upon little recesses. The one in the south wall was still bare, but the north one had evidently just been furnished. The little altar had a new purple cloth stiff with dressing and gold embroidery. The cross and candlesticks were of cold chromium-plate. Perhaps the flower vases had not yet been chosen, for the old bronze chrysanthemums were in jam-jars. I could see their black decaying stalks through the glass. The dead smell of the green water came to me when I moved nearer. I read the engraved plate between the windows and learnt that the chapel had been fitted up in memory of someone. I thought of all the bereaved one's care to make the chapel grand; and it came to me very clearly why corpses and not living beings are honoured. The reason was that the dead were no longer able to object or to disgrace themselves. Once the power to ridicule or to degrade had been taken away from them they could be manipulated; they were ready then for honour and remembrance. Being fixed forever, they could be ornamented without fear. They could never answer back.

At the corner of the chapel and the aisle stood a large plaster statue of the Virgin Mary. She had underclothes, pink marshmallow cheeks, and her rose-bud mouth was melting forever in a honey smile. Gold stars were powdered over her gown, and candles stood before her on a tiered black stand, which looked like the charred skeleton of an elaborate wedding-cake.

I dropped some pennies in the cross-shaped opening of the metal box, then speared four slender candles on the topmost circle. After they were lighted, I passed on to another statue and another.

Soon the church was glimmering with candle points, beetle lighthouses in the sea at dusk. I went to the far end and sat by the west door to admire them. Close to my raw oak chair a silvered radiator was breathing out warm dusty air, releasing the new paint, wood, stone and plaster smells. My solitude and warmth there sent a shiver of true pleasure through me and I decided to come often to the church. I could be comfortable there, yet all alone; and if I fixed my eyes on the red lamp, I could float away on my thoughts and be lost.

The next time I visited the church I noticed to the left of the altar a little door which I had not remembered before. It was open now and I saw that it led into the bell-tower. A coloured rope-end, like a twisted sweet, or a woolly barber's pole, hung down, and behind it were cupboards, perhaps for vestments or song books.

I was about to go through the door, when I heard someone moving about inside. I sat down quickly and stared in front as if I were studying the details of the altar. It was not long before I caught a glimpse of a small figure behind the bell-rope. In the dim light it might have been a boy, a girl, or a dwarf. I could not tell at first; there was something strange about it. It kept its head down. Its chin was holding in place the pile of books it carried. It seemed very intent on its work and did not look once in my direction. When it had passed beyond the space framed in the doorway, I heard more noises of objects being arranged, the rustle of starched cloth, and a low humming. I moved a little nearer to the door and waited for it to reappear again.

This time I saw that it was a boy, perhaps nine or ten years old. He was wearing a curious helmet seemingly padded or covered with dark velvet. It was this helmet which had given him the strange appearance of a dwarf or of some medieval knight, whose limbs had shrunk, but whose visored head had remained as large and threatening as ever.

I wondered if the child were wearing some Roman Catholic priest's head-dress I knew nothing of. Was he amusing himself by dressing up in the empty church?

He must have seen me, sitting so close to the open door, but he only glanced once at me, then away again to his books and vestments. He had the isolated air of one busy on important work, with no time for trifling. I decided that dressing up would seem quite frivolous to him.

I left when I saw him go towards the bell-rope, for I knew that he would be ringing for an evening service, and I had no wish to be near other people.

When I was outside, I heard the single bell ringing in the tower. No worshippers had yet appeared, and as I walked home I thought of the goblin-headed boy alone there, pulling the rope, thinking his thoughts, keeping a stern set expression always on his face.

The next day I told Nurse Goff that I had walked as far as the flint church. I described the boy in the heavy velvet helmet, and as I did so I saw that she already knew about him. She told me that he had been pulling the rope in the church one day, just as I had seen him, when suddenly the bell crashed down through two floors and struck him on the head. He was found senseless on the floor with his skull badly fractured. They thought he would die, but little by little he had recovered; and now he was back ringing the bell again, with only the strange protective helmet to show what had happened to him.

I saw the boy in the dust-smelling new church calmly ringing the bell;

then I heard the great weight of bronze smashing through the floors, and saw the boy again, now lying in his own blood on the white stone. No one came to him. He was quite alone, with his life bleeding away. I pictured the face of the person who found him later.

It was amazing to me that the boy could be back now, ringing this same bell. Did it never terrify him? Did he never feel the weight of it swinging far above him – the bell that had his blood on it? I thought that when its clapper tongue clanged in the hollowness, swelling the tower with its vibrating drone, he must feel terror at its violence. But his face on that afternoon when I first saw him had been smoother than any sea-ground pebble.

XXI

Now there came an invitation to tea from my aunt's mother. She lived in an old house on the other side of the cabbage field and waste place. When I walked to the church, I had looked back and seen it hiding in its dark ilex trees; but it held little for me, since I had known it only once before, when I was six years old. My mother had taken me there. The day had been very hot, and I was dressed in crisp white cotton. We stopped at a toy shop and my mother bought me a decanter and a set of tiny little goblets on a round glass tray. They were painted with red and black dots, and the minute stopper of the decanter was a great delight to me. As soon as we came to an old horse trough, I insisted on filling the decanter, then pouring from it into the thimble goblets. It was the perfect present for that hot day.

I remembered the unexpected trams clanging past us, the people inside looking worn and hollow and sticky. I had seen very few trams before and they still surprised me, especially in this quite small seaside town.

After we reached the house my memory clouded. There had been a long room full of people, then someone opening a cabinet full of snuff-boxes and other treasured things, and taking out, not one of these beautiful objects, but a jagged venomous piece of rusted metal and saying to me comfortably,

'You couldn't remember, but that's shrapnel from the Great War.'

There was a smile on the woman's face. She seemed pleased with the rough starfish of iron. The mysterious new word shrapnel worked its magic on me; I excused the lump its ugliness and began to allow it its resting place in the cabinet . . .

On my way to tea I tried to remember other details of that first visit, but nothing more came back to me until I reached the corner of the garden.

There a grove of ilex trees, rich and glistening like some dark Jewish men, brought back a picture of the brilliant green of wide lawns, and a covered way leading from the road to the front door.

There it was, some way in front of me. When I reached it, I found that the door on the road was set under a plain little Gothic revival porch painted cream colour. The stucco, the pointed arch and the varnished door pleased me; I was glad that I had come. I pulled out the brass bell-knob. It was like the pommel of a sword or an ancient water-closet handle. I waited until someone came and took me down the covered way. It was all of cast-iron work, very pretty in its extravagant thinness. I imagined the garden in rain, dripping on each side, while the path under the spindly colonnade kept dry and dusty.

Outside the oldest part of the house was a narrow verandah under a tin pagoda roof, delicately curved. There were square French doors on the ground floor, but the upper windows had slight Gothic decorations at the head. These and other details, together with the pillars of the verandah, were picked out in black, and perhaps because of this black against the cream stucco, I was reminded a little of the cottage of the ladies of Llangollen.

The air of fantasy quickly died when the front door was opened. It was killed stone dead by the heavy 'butcher's furniture' of rich mahogany. But everything in the room glowed. It was clear that an old lady lived alone, loved her house and saw to it that others loved it too.

My aunt's mother came down the stairs rather dreamily and found me standing at the foot.

'Hullo, my dear,' she said, still as if her thoughts were far away; 'we'll go into the dining-room now and have tea. Yes, you have had a dreadful time; you must tell me all about it. You were only a very little boy when I saw you last.'

The table in the dark dining-room was laden with scones, bread and butter, cakes, biscuits, ginger-bread, honey, and jam. I saw that it was all for me, that I was to be treated as a school-boy, that fiddling drawing-room saucer-balancing had been considered quite unsuitable. I hoped very much that I would be able to eat enough to please.

We sat down and my aunt's mother poured from the lumpish swirling silver teapot. The effort seemed to make her anxious and worried. When the ordeal of filling the cups was over, she turned to me to ask about my dreadful time.

'Has it really been six months!' she exclaimed.

'Almost,' I said.

'But you're getting much better now, aren't you?' she insisted. 'I never thought that you would be looking so well. I was quite surprised when I saw you in the hall.' She paused, then said more slowly, 'You know, I always think that a man will get well if he doesn't drink. Drinking is *such* a pity and so dangerous; it spoils all chances of good recovery. I'm sure you'll be all right if you don't drink. Don't drink!' she said, with a little gesture towards me and a funny wry face, as if the taste of drink were very unpleasant indeed. She shook her head, still with her nostrils broadened and her lips twisted. She might have been saying 'Nasty!' to her child.

I wondered what had happened in the past; what ordeal had made her come to think that men and drink always went together? Had her husband not been 'all right' because of drinking? I knew nothing about him. Or was it her father who had spoilt his own chances of recovery? I only knew that he had been a hard-working baronet, mining coal and making nails in the north. Perhaps my aunt's mother was still troubled over the fate of someone quite different; someone she had only met a few times, but whose miserable career she had followed eagerly and painfully. This more sentimental notion blossomed in me and I saw swiftly melting pictures of flattened straw hats, attenuated rackets, green plush lawn and sagging net. Then there was a ballroom scene with palms, fans on the wall, blue china, swirling couples, and a line of chairs seemingly twisted out of gold and black wire.

I wondered if my pictures of life fifty or sixty years ago were at all true; if my aunt's mother could have recognized the young self and the scenes I was imagining.

'Perhaps she went boating with her drunkard, too,' I thought. 'Perhaps they floated on a lake with duckweed and water lilies all about them. There would be a curious smell each time the punt pole came up dripping from the oozy muddy bed. Perhaps she had a beautiful Japanese sunshade; she might even have had a mandoline tied with ribbons. They might have sung together, while she stroked and plucked the strings.'

My aunt's mother was talking to me now about something else. She had begun while I was far away imagining, and I only came back to hear the words, 'Every morning there was blood in the pot and the wretched nurse-maid had said nothing to me about it. I only discovered by the merest chance.'

I realized that she was telling me about the illnesses of her children when they were little. She told me in her hard bright voice, never bothering to be squeamish or delicate. The mother was now so old that all those feelings had dropped from her. She was like a parrot or other talking bird, quite unabashed by intimacies, swear words, or even blasphemies. The clear words flowed out, never changing colour; I began to think that she, like a bird, was unaware of their meanings.

'And afterwards we'll go into the drawing-room and smoke our cigarettes,' she said, at the end of her stories of illness; 'that will be nice.'

I could see that she looked upon the cigarette as a little ritual. It was taken for granted that I smoked; although at that time I had only had four or five cigarettes in my mouth in my life. I still had the superstitious fear that I neither lighted other people's properly nor smoked my own with ease.

She took me up a few steps into the long room where the sash-windows came down to the ground. We sat down in front of the fire at the far end. I remember that the *Daily Telegraph* was near me and that I looked down at the heading nervously as I struck the match and held it out to her. I watched the position of the cigarette in her mouth and the way she puffed, then copied her. I was suddenly very pleased to be sitting there smoking with her. It was as if she had flattered me, treated me as a man with a great deal of good sense and experience. It was a very rare feeling, and I often wonder why it came. I suppose deep down she accepted me placidly, did not necessarily understand, yet did not question; so this acceptance flowed out to me and I was warmed.

I looked out of the long windows and saw the lawn stretching away in a tight vivid sheet. It was checked at last by the dark ilex trees and the kitchen garden wall.

My aunt's mother saw me gazing and said, 'Shall we go out?'

I took my stick up from the arm of the chair and we both bent down and stepped out of one of the sash-windows.

I thought as we crossed the wide lawns that she, so old, should have had the stick and I the springing step. Later she took my arm, and I wondered whether she did this to help me or because she needed my help. She did it well and I was not to know.

First I was shown the deep air-raid shelter that had been made for the zeppelin raids of the first war. She took me down the narrow dungeon steps, mossy now and damp, with baby ferns sprouting between the cracks. I helped to push back the heavy iron door, and then the smell of the underground room came out to us: earth, slime on concrete, cobwebs and moss and the lack of any human being there.

For a few moments I could see nothing, then my eye made out the walls sloping inwards as I imagined the walls sloped in the tomb chambers of the pyramids. I could see, too, the ends of long benches boring into the darkness like railway lines.

'Whenever we knew they were coming,' my aunt's mother said, 'we would invite as many people as possible into the shelter; then we would have hot coffee and cakes and tell stories till the devilish things had gone away.'

Listening to her there in the underground room, I had the feeling that she was telling me about some very ancient time, long forgotten, a time of glowing life, high excitement and terror. She seemed to be living still in that time. All the new terrors and threats passed over her unheeded. The dungeon was to be gazed at as a relic of heroic times.

We walked to the roses and the vegetables and the greenhouse, talking all the time of shells, explosions, dirigibles and Belgian refugees. My aunt's mother had adopted two little girls for the period of the war. Although they were now grown women with children of their own, they still wrote to her. When we were back in the drawing-room she showed me photographs of them in fluffy white dresses with huge bows in their hair. Their sulky dark eyes stared back at me, their blackish lips pouted. I wondered what they looked like after so many years. Would the sullen glowering look be washed out of their faces, and with it all the promise too?

I was shown again the jagged piece of shrapnel that I remembered as a child. There it lay, looking like a used tooth-paste tube or other piece of trash amongst the cherished snuff-boxes, patch-boxes and vinaigrettes. I learnt that it was treasured because it landed in the garden, at the feet of my aunt's mother's dearest friend.

'What a narrow escape that was!' she said, her eyes glowing; the memory of that time still thrilled in her.

My eyes turned from the cabinet to an old oval mirror with gold balls close to the curved glass.

I admired it and was told that it had come to my aunt's mother from this same friend who was no longer alive.

'But of course,' she added more quietly and firmly, 'she isn't really dead; for we *know* that they still go on.'

Her gaze was far away. She drummed a little on the table. Her mouth was set. I knew that she was about to tell me something, and I waited.

'Mrs Hart was here only yesterday,' she said in the same low firm voice; 'we had a wonderful afternoon. She was able to get through to Malcolm. He's only waiting for me to join him now.'

Here she paused and looked deep into my eyes. She seemed to be wondering if the next remark were suitable for my ears or not. She was heavy with the remark she had not made. She gave an anxious little smile, then let the words tumble out in a rush.

'He ran towards me, picked me up in his arms and said, "Darling little mother!"'

Her voice had thrilled on the last words. She was quivering a little, and her eyes kept swivelling away, as if she were out of countenance. But she felt triumph, too. She might have been saying, 'You don't believe it, but it's true. It *must* be true.'

I remembered that Malcolm was the son who had been killed; and I suddenly understood why we had been visiting dug-outs, talking of shrapnel and zeppelins and refugees, bathing in that old atmosphere. His name had never been mentioned, but he had been in her thoughts all the time. The war conversation had been woven round that thought of him.

I had not known that my aunt's mother was in communication with the dead. Her conviction changed her for me. She seemed madder, less dignified, but more interesting.

She told me of Mrs Hart's weekly visits and of the wonderful messages she was able to bring from Malcolm.

'It is *such* a deep comfort – wonderful!' she said, drawing in a deep breath and becoming dreamy again.

I began to think of the medium, to imagine her looks and her behaviour. I only knew of mediums through books, and so I created a large woman made out of pale lard, sitting in a snug stuffy room on the sea front. Her eyebrows wriggled into each other when she frowned, and she did not smell very nice. She had flat cough-lozenge tins which she fixed to her bread-poultice pudgy knees with rubber bands. She rubbed them together whenever she wanted to make strange crackling noises. Her eyes glittered like Francis Bacon's serpent eyes. I imagined the oil dripping from her mouth as she said, 'And Malcolm sends you a great big hug and a kiss!'

Afterwards, when the teacups tinkled, she would lie back, as if exhausted, with her eyes half closed; but from time to time she would dart quick glances at my aunt's mother, to read from her expression the remark that would please most.

Sometimes she would make difficulties, stop communication with Malcolm; only to reward the disappointed mother at last. There would be salt in some of the messages to be rubbed into the mother for her own and Mrs Hart's good.

I imagined her first as a fraud, and therefore as a wicked woman, taking admiration, money, hospitality, love, and secretly sneering at the simplicity of the giver. But out of her evil grew the delightful food for the mother. The weekly meal kept her heart alive. The mother had felt herself cut off forever, now the huge black door was delicately pushed open a few inches, and the rich messages came through. The mother was very old and she had grey curling hair, like sheep's wool; but she was kissed, cherished, talked to by a ghost. This experience was so precious that she would gladly listen to the medium's heavy breathing that was not quite a snore, gladly pay her all she asked. She would even be persuaded to ignore fiercely any suspicion that she was being exploited.

When I said good-bye and went back to the nursing home, I was still thinking of my aunt's mother and her son. I took off my clothes and pulled on my pyjamas. I was about to put on the dilapidated smoking-jacket that my aunt had lent me, when I suddenly remembered that she had said lightly as she handed it to me on the day after my arrival, 'This is very old, but it will be warm for you when you sit up in bed; it's quilted. It belonged to Malcolm.'

I had thought then very little of Malcolm, but now I held the jacket out, noticed the bald patches in the bottle-green velvet at elbow and wrist, followed the stains down the front, and felt the lumps that had formed in some parts of the diamond quilting. Directly and indirectly, I had been hearing of Malcolm all the afternoon, and now I had his jacket in my hands. I had been wearing it for months without thinking; but now, if I put it on, surely

I should feel something, know something of him! All of him that was left in the world above ground lingered in the coat.

I put it on and lay back in the bed. The lapels rose up to my ears. I ducked my head down into the little area of hot darkness in front of me and breathed there for some moments; but no thoughts of Malcolm were conjured up. The camphor smell only brought to mind a large wardrobe where the jacket hung year after year after year in perpetual night.

XXII

WHAT WAS my life? It was all a scraping together of little incidents, a sucking of them dry before I hurried on in search of one more drop of nectar.

The thought of what I should try to do in the world came as a black face looming nearer and nearer. I could never look into the eyes for more than a moment. I would turn away, saying, 'I am not well enough yet; I can wait.' Yet the waiting was such a burden of waste that I longed to free myself by smashing it in pieces.

With such emptiness inside me I turned fiercely to Dr Farley, until he grew to have all the significance of some model person. I would test others by him and find them unbelievably sham and tawdry. Intolerance seemed to grow with wretchedness. I would apply the test to myself with the same destroying result. Everyone was contemptible, except perhaps Dr Farley.

I say perhaps, because there were those naked moments when even he seemed to lose some of his meaning; then I was sinking into the black bog of nothingness.

But these states would suddenly clear, or rather lift, and I would have the tingling gaiety again, the impatience for every smell and taste and sound. This gaiety that grew from no solid body of content soon grew too heavy, over-toppled itself. I would feel it rising in me, bubbling to a froth. It would be seething in my head, so that, if I had a companion, a cascade of words and laughter would pour out of me. If I were alone, I would put on the Handel records, then the Tchaikovsky, move my arms about, sing songs I could remember, try to write down some fragment of what was buzzing through my head. The nonsense sentences went down into my book, to be held there and to stare back at me on the next day with all their magic gone.

It was on one of these days when gaiety bubbled up in me and I longed to be gone, to be away, somewhere new and unknown, that Matron came in, as usual with her yellow duster for excuse, and told me that the Amateur Dramatic Society were doing their play that night. Dr Farley would be acting, and she was going. Would I like to go with her?

I smiled at her for the first time for many weeks. I felt that she had known of my state of mind in her office and had come to entertain me. I was relieved, too, in some deep way that I should be going to the play with such physical largeness. Her fatness was protective. I wanted very much to see Dr Farley act, but I had been in no crowd for a long time and the thought of the audience at the theatre was disturbing. I had the ill person's conviction that people would be aware of my state, watching for every sign of weakness. I could imagine them comparing me in their minds with what I should have been.

'He should not walk like that,' they would say; 'he should not be so thin, you can see the bones in his face; and his legs are stiff, as if they were turning to stone.'

Then, when I told myself that nobody would look, nobody would know me or be interested, I was caught by the other fear that I should be trapped in their midst, unable to move, until I began to cry or be sick. Then the faces would stare and I would have no mercy, because nothing was known of me. I was supposed to be a well person, I would be judged as such.

When evening came, and Matron, dressed all in black, discreetly lavender-watered and powdered, called for me, I climbed into the taxi after her with excitement.

The town was dark and the lights gleamed on the wet road. I had not been in a night street scene for a long time. I watched the people's faces as they pushed through the theatre doors. The faces changed when they passed from the street into the building. Outside they were more hardened, more scoured and flinty, tragic too from all they had withstood. Inside they grew more cushiony and fluid; they lost the vagrant, hunted look. The look of anxiety melted into the sparkling monkey, or the soft bear look. And people undid belts and buttons, loosened their hair, patted, polished, breathed out their warm breath, like animals penned together in a farmyard.

Matron and I in our seats in the circle gazed down. The music was playing softly and I had bought a programme. Matron was very restrained, never asking me inquisitive questions, never teasing round the edge of me to madden my mind. She just sat still and looked peaceful in her black. The sleepy cow quality of dignity became her, and I liked her much more than before.

The play was a piece in modern dress, but that is all I know. I waited for Dr Farley to come into the sitting-room with its slightly waving, trembling walls. When he came, he looked taller and stiffer and thinner than in real life. He wore a dark suit that I knew, and seeing him in it amid the artificial stage properties, the red bulb glowing in the heart of the 'coal' fire, the waving canvas walls, gave me the feeling that there was something counterfeit about him, too; that it was an image that I saw there, dressed in his clothes.

He had told me that he had begun to act and sing because he was forced thus to overcome embarrassment and build up self-confidence.

I thought of this as I watched him on the stage; and I was anxious, afraid that a wave of self-consciousness might sweep over him. What would I do if he stammered and turned red, forgot his lines or rolled his shoulders uneasily?

But nothing happened, I did not have to turn away or plug my ears. I never forgot who he was; but he was composed and stiff and controlled.

And he smiled as he did in real life – the smile that I distrusted because it seemed so perfect as a smile. It would begin with lowered eyes, shy, pulled-in lips and a swallow in the throat; then the shyness would be drowned by rising exuberance and you would be caught up in his boisterousness, so that your eyes flashed back and you were in complete agreement. It had the wicked quality people are fond of, but none of the malice they fear.

I distrusted it, not because I thought it false, but because I felt it pleased me too much and so falsified my judgement. I told myself that it was a trick of his and that he knew it pleased, just as a child sometimes knows that its childishness is endearing. I waited for him to overdo the smile and repel me. But he never did, or if he did I embraced the extravagance wholeheartedly.

As Matron shepherded me back to the taxi, I wondered about this smile. Did the people in the audience notice the quick snatches of it sandwiched between the dull lumps of dialogue? And if they noticed, had it any of the significance it had for me? Were they drawn to him because of it? Would they remember the evening afterwards as nothing but a dark auditorium, then a quick smile spreading and vanishing? Just as the picture of the Cheshire Cat, grinning, stays with us mysteriously forever, so I thought the picture of Dr Farley, smiling his quite different smile on the stage, would stay with me. The fact that I had seen him framed in the proscenium seemed to fix in my mind. I had realized him, seen him apart from myself. He was like a statue or a marble pillar, something I could contemplate from a distance.

While we drove back in the taxi, I forgot Matron entirely. My thoughts were fixed on Dr Farley; they followed him home, and I saw the squat house with the lights burning and the small maid at the door. The Aberdeen was barking, lifting its square wooden-peg paws. The wife was pouring out tea or some other hot drink.

It was not an ideal picture, not anything that I cared about very much; but it held its own unexplained poignancy for me. The humdrum scene hung before my eyes as if it had been real; I could not blot it out. The lights burned, the dog yapped joyfully, the tea poured, the human beings smiled without ceasing. It was as if they were all enchanted, unable to move until the spell was broken.

As soon as we were out of the taxi I left Matron and went hurriedly to my room. There the silence and emptiness which I so often longed for seemed to drag at me, to pull me down. I was made brutally aware of my own hollowness. The hard light shone down on my head. I stood looking at the heavy clogging folds of the curtains drawn across the great glass door.

Quite suddenly I began to cry, not discreetly so that no one should hear, but with an abandon that called out for hearers. I seemed to want my weeping to sing in all the walls of the nursing home, to vibrate and shake the people in their beds.

Matron came hurrying in still in her coat and gloves. For a moment her poached eyes fixed in a stare that almost shocked me into calmness, then she looked and said, 'Oh there! It's too much! You're overtired. What a nuisance! I'm sending the night nurse in at once.'

She clip-clopped away, complaining to herself, murmuring, 'It's too bad; what a nuisance!'

Before the night nurse had time to break in, I had pulled off my clothes and slipped into bed. She found me looking down at a book, with my face away from her, the corner of my eyes and mouth firm and cool. I could not have cried another drop. I was stiff with dislike of my puffy eyes.

Matron must have spoken to Dr Farley about my behaviour, for on the morning after the play he hurried through the usual health questions, then asked me disconcertingly and suddenly why I had been upset the night before.

'Oh, I don't know,' I said, trying to be cold and lively and unapproachable; 'I suppose the change, all the people. I haven't been out at night for a long time, you know.'

'Is that all that worried you? Just the newness and strangeness after being shut up in this room for so long?'

I waited, wondering how much to say and *what* to say. To explain to myself was difficult and hard; to explain to him preposterous.

'Well,' I said slowly, trying to spin out mild bantering expressions until he left, 'it was rather peculiar to see you on the stage.'

'Why peculiar?' he asked, refusing my banter.

'I don't know; I kept looking at you, wondering about you, watching your smile spreading and shrinking, wondering what it was all for. What did the other people think? Then, when it ended and we were going home, I began to imagine what it was like at your end. I saw it all, the dog, your wife, the lights on, hot drinks.'

He smiled a little uncomfortably, then narrowed his eyes as if to look into me. 'Were you thinking that my life seemed much better than yours at the moment?'

The idea in this bare form seemed quite foreign to me. To be thought envious was humbling.

'No,' I said quickly, 'I don't think it was that at all. We're so different; your life wouldn't really suit me. But sometimes anything will make you want to cry. Why do people feel so sad and burdened when they see beautiful things? That is always being mentioned; it must be quite common.'

As soon as I had added this afterthought about beautiful things, I was afraid he would mistake me and imagine that I meant his life was beautiful. The idea made me squirm. I began to talk faster and faster. 'You don't cry because of things outside, you cry because of things inside. That's why people feel so ashamed and angry and guilty when they see others cry. They can't be inside, however much they try. They are shut out and only see the sticky face. And because they can never be inside, they resent the tears coming out to worry them.'

It was difficult to stop this rigmarole of explanation. I was hemming myself in with my own words, and I wished he would speak to break a way through for me, instead of listening so intently and with such a serious expression.

I know now that this slight talk was unfortunate, for my most desolate time dates from it. Unhappiness seemed to be fixed on me as my part, and I took it up and accepted it. I thought that Dr Farley began to bear me with more anxious care and less easy friendship.

And because his attitude seemed to have changed, even if so very slightly, I began to change. When he had treated me as no trouble, no problem, I felt that I must do nothing to spoil my good record. He had said one morning after seeing me, 'Now I must go and do some work.'

'But haven't you already begun?' I asked.

'Oh, I don't call *this* work!'

The answer, with just the right flick of joking disregard, had delighted me. But now I felt that he might be beginning to class me as 'work'. I thought I noticed a wary, rather harassed frown between his eyes when he thought I was not looking. I kept remembering stories of people who pestered doctors at every hour of the day. There was still the middle-aged woman who called at the doctor's house so often that he had learned to dodge her by darting out of the back door as soon as he heard her voice in the hall. Then there was the girl who, when she thought that her doctor's visits would be coming to an end, heaped a spoonful of sugar into her 'specimen', imagining in her simplicity that this would deceive him into thinking her diabetic. There was the story too of the young man who could not resist looking through the keyhole while his mother undressed. Whenever she left the house he would run to her room and put on all her clothes, down to her stockings and corset. He felt so much guilt that he was for ever wasting his doctor's time with all the details of his eccentricity.

When I first heard these stories, at odd times, in different places, I was amused, a little sad, interested; but now, when I had begun to be eaten by the fear that Dr Farley was watching my behaviour, preparing for the outburst, the unreason, the nuisance of instability, I turned to hating them. I did not want to be added to the list of grotesques. They were with me to haunt me and goad me, finger-posts pointing the wrong way, a way that fascinated and repulsed.

I began now to go out more in the evenings, just before the light faded. I felt freer then, and able to walk in my new stiff way without self-consciousness. And the coming of night was in itself an excitement. I could watch people hurrying home from work, their faces hard against the world until they had had their supper-tea. Then there were less tight, less settled people walking slowly, arms round each other, eyes roving to find some deeper satisfaction that still evaded them. They would linger on the railway bridge, the soft curve of their hams pressed close, as they bent forward, hugging and peering down at the trains. The lovers seemed lost and mournful, and searching. Only the returning workers, concentrated on food and rest, looked as if they had come to terms with life. They had settled, but the terms were bad for them, and they showed it in their shut mouths.

There were the unreal people, too; the women coming from the cinema. They might have been stuffed quails or satin pin-cushions. So often they seemed to have this padded quality. It made me feel that nothing could touch them. They were impregnable. Horror, pity, hatred, fear and love would sink into the soft firm upholstery and be made dumb at once.

It was while I was walking behind two such women, or women imagined to be such by me, that I felt the exaltation and the misery coming upon me again. The night was dark, and rain slashed down sparsely but with sullen force. The flashes of it under the lamps seemed fierce and desperate, like miniature lightning to me. The rain made me want to sing and exult and give up trying. I wanted to sink like a burning ship, with immense guttering of flames. Without thinking, I began to walk faster and faster, until I had overtaken the women. Their heads were close together. They were deep in their hard chatter, intimate and cold. I felt that they had noticed nothing, not even my low humming song. It was rising all the time; the notes seemed to want to leap out of my throat like clear crystal balls trying to escape from the frogs of my gulps and sobs. I was some way past the women when I came to a turning that led to a small waste place. I walked down it, wanting the darkness, the rain, the feel of wet leaves and grass, rubbish about me, old bricks and paper and twisted iron.

I was waiting there and singing, making, I suppose, a noise that could be heard above the wind. I looked down the pathway and saw the pneumatic shapes of the two women at the end under a street lamp. They were hesitating, looking in my direction, clearly wondering whether to investigate or not.

As I watched, the larger, more busted one, approached. She leant forward a little against the wind and I was absurdly reminded of that picture of Captain Oates which is hung somewhere in most boys' schools. The smaller one, hugging the safety of the street lamp, seemed to watch her progress anxiously.

'Are you all right there? Has anything happened? Is there anything we can do?'

The words came to me as little irritating jabs, perfunctory enquiry to be resisted at once. She was hovering, uncertain whether to come nearer or to retreat. I think she was a little afraid.

I muttered, 'Oh, nothing is wrong, thank you,' then turned away abruptly. When I glanced back, I saw that she had returned to her friend and that their heads were together again. Just before they walked out of the pool of light, I saw their lips moving and their eyes turned in my direction for a last glance. I wondered how long my freak of conduct would engross them. Would they still be talking about it over supper? Or would they return at once to their cosy topics? In my uncertainty I was even afraid that they might tell a policeman. What if an officious dark blue uniform should come to probe? I hurriedly left the place and walked back towards the nursing home.

When I was in my room, lying back in bed, calmed by my tiredness, I could hardly believe that I had behaved so foolishly. The remembrance was shaming. I tried to harden myself by saying, 'What does it matter? Make a clown of yourself, be excessive. You no longer care about anything. Why pretend any longer?'

Dr Farley, seeing my growing wretchedness, said, 'This is a very difficult time for you, perhaps the most difficult time of all; and hardly anyone will understand or even know about it. You will just have to work through it by yourself. Recovering is always difficult. Everything is a great effort, and yet you are so restless. I think I know.'

Then, when I said very little, he added, 'But what we haven't really done is to find you some friends. I've often thought that it must be very lonely for you here. I've so little spare time, and there aren't many young people in the town. But now that it is nearly Christmas someone I think you'd like has just come back from Oxford. I'll bring him to see you.'

I looked at him without gratitude not caring very much to be fitted up with a friend, or to be told that I must be lonely. I thought, too, that he might be anxious to find companions for me so that he need not come to see me so often himself. Always now I was having this mistrust of others' motives. I almost enjoyed doubting, being bitter over supposed small treacheries.

'Perhaps he won't want to be brought to see me,' I said dully.

'Oh, I think you will have rather a lot in common. He's interested in all sorts of things – acting especially.'

My heart sank.

'I'm not interested in acting,' I said.

'Well, he might stimulate your interest.'

There was a slight tartness in his tone; I felt that I had succeeded at last in provoking him a little. I wanted to make it quite clear that I was not at all easy to help. The perverse wish to turn faces against me was growing.

The proposed friend came, and, because I was so ready to dislike him, I found him quite surprisingly agreeable. He was tall, with large bones, broad high cheeks and rather long glinting hair. He seemed often to be narrowing his eyes above the ridge of the cheekbones and to be looking far away; this, I thought, gave him a little the appearance of a large athletic sleepy cat. It was this quality that made his face acceptable to me. I would have shrunk from bright button eyes, digging, swivelling about, laughing and seething; from ears cocked, and all darting movements.

When introduced, he seemed to notice very little about me, yet there was a sort of sad consideration. After smiles and jokes, Dr Farley left us together. We were rather silent. Then David, the new friend, suggested that I should go back to tea with him. Still speaking very little, we set out together down the road.

He only lived a few doors away, so we were soon in the front room of the little house, talking to his German mother and her two German school-girl guests.

On a low table in the bow window the Nativity scene was set out – little figures carved in wood and brightly painted: Jesus in his straw-lined crib, Mary, Joseph, the Ox, the Ass, the Wise Men, the Shepherds and the Angel. There were other larger angels too, holding up crowns of red candles and with flowers in their glistening buttercup hair. The figures lacked much; they were crude and unfeeling, as if their maker had carved so many that he no longer thought at all at his work. I had often seen Christ in His crib and the others in churches or in shop windows. I had also seen the angels with red candles before, in Switzerland. But now the group in this private house gave me a new pleasure. They came as an unexpected refreshment. I thought, 'Here is a woman who still likes to play, who takes care of things and brings them out every year. She is sure to have other rituals, too, and all the years gain shape from them. Her life may be grim to me, but it has a rhythm – I want my life to have a rhythm more than anything else on earth.'

In the new atmosphere I forgot the nursing-home room; it seemed to me that I had suddenly taken a step forward out of the tangle and mess, just when it had been most difficult to move. Yet I was wary, knowing now that this sensation of stepping forward had come several times and had always been followed by a sense of utter deadness, or a time of worse confusion.

But for the moment I was happy to be with David's mother and the girls, to have their different faces to look at. The girls were smiling and shy, the mother smiling and set in her religious convictions.

Before we went into the dining-room for tea I looked at some of the old photographs that the girls were pasting into a book for David's mother. Fascinating, dull, pathetic, humorous things! They filled me with a sudden astonishment. I saw past scenes in the life of this unknown family. I was there, ten years ago, in all the profusion and untidiness of a birthday picnic on the Downs. I sat with them on the beach, throwing pebbles into the waves. The photographs forced an intimacy on me, whether I would or no.

After tea one of the girls recited some German poems to us; it was suggested that I, who knew no German, might be pleased just to listen to the flow of lovely sounds.

I let the words pour over me – low, uncoloured, even rising in wild excitement, then dropping to a plaint, only to rise again. Once there was a passage where the girl laughed bitterly, almost tossed her head. She had been ashamed to recite at first, had needed much persuasion and encouragement; but now she was enjoying herself, snatching quick breaths between the phrases, glorifying herself in the poems. Her eyes looked right through the wall of the room; I was reminded suddenly of the epileptic maids in the ward. They had worn almost that same expression. They had held out their arms and declaimed, and I had not understood the sounds they made. Their lips had been wet, and they, too, had appeared to be acting breathlessly.

I was pleased when the girl stopped and came back into herself. She was shamefaced and we praised her awkwardly. There was a silence in the room. I thought I caught a glance between mother and son, one of those glances where the mother is thinking, 'He appears to have no gratitude, no appreciation, only impatience; but I must pretend not to notice, to be smiling and calm; then some warmth may be drawn out of him'; and the son replies, 'Don't look at me long-sufferingly, don't paw, or expect anything. I will *not* feel guilty.'

As if to escape from this glance, David stood up and asked me to look at the books in his bedroom. He climbed up the stairs very slowly, carefully, so that I should not feel slow.

I enjoyed the snug confinement of his bedroom; it reminded me of playing 'houses' under the nursery table. I sat on the end of the bed, he in an arm-chair, and we both almost touched the bookcase with our knees.

He took out a book that had been signed by Walter de la Mare at some poetry reading. I think it was the first autographed book I had ever held; I looked on it as something very precious and rare. I imagined the poet bending over it, spreading the page flat, breathing and thinking, before he wrote.

'Did he say anything when he was writing in the book for you?' I asked.

'Oh, he made a sort of joke, said what a watery name it was, or something like that.'

David did not seem to value the book quite as I did. He was too used to possessing it. He added, 'I had another signed copy, but I gave it away'; and as he spoke I noticed again the vague sadness in his voice and far-away gaze. It was as if he were thinking, 'It is all nothing, it is emptiness.' But there was a streak of anxious striving that cut right through this mournfulness. He made me think of a man tossing and turning before waking up.

The book of poems lying on a pair of rough corduroy trousers was the picture that I took away from the bedroom. We went down again to the others, and after a little more talk I got up to go.

The girls stood about, awkwardly polite; the mother smiled and asked me to come again. David said he would walk back to the nursing home with me. The pleasant afternoon had lost its glow, was dissolving into a set of humdrum actions. There was no place for me there, or in any family. My life must shape itself alone. I knew this and was dumb.

XXIII

THEREFORE IT was to the outcasts and wanderers that I was attracted. I wanted to watch them without being seen. I wanted to know their thoughts without making close contact. I wanted to share without my body being present. Such cold invisible spying was impossible; and so I found myself asked for cigarettes, asked for money, asked what I wanted and what I meant by staring.

They were right to question my fixed gaze. I gave money, I gave cigarettes whenever I remembered to buy any, I gave sympathy, listening to long involved stories; but it wasn't in me really to want to help. Everything seemed too hopeless for help. The word was a mockery. I wanted to listen and look, then to free myself and get away.

I met a woman on the outskirts of the town. She had two children with her and was hurrying along, constantly looking back to catch the glance of any passing motorist. When she noticed me, she slowed her pace and said 'Good afternoon' with careful refinement. She told me that her husband was a barrister, but that everything had gone wrong with him. He had been too interested in politics. Unscrupulous people had cheated him, or not paid the large sums they owed. At last he had taken to drink, so that her life and the children's had been made unbearable. She had had to leave him to try to make a living herself. She hoped later to be able to go back and save him from a drunkard's grave. If only she could get him on his feet again he might fulfil his early promise yet.

She spoke intensely, with a sort of thrill in her voice. The voice was strange, impossible to place. It might have been the accent of some unknown colony. Vowels were thinned and perverted, consonants clipped, or mouthed until one found it difficult to follow her rapid utterances.

Now she was on her way to what might prove to be a very important position; but, of course, if she were late for the interview she would have no chance. If she didn't get this job she would give up hope. She would want to take herself out of this world, and her children also. It was no place for motherless waifs. So could I lend her four and six? That would just cover the bus fare for the three of them. She meant 'lend', not 'give'. She would take my name and address and pay me back for certain as soon as she was earning again.

I fumbled in my pocket and found two half-crowns. I murmured something about not wanting to be paid back.

'Oh, but I must!' she protested fiercely. 'Me, to take money from a stranger and not to pay back! I'd never think of it. You oughtn't to suggest such a thing.'

'I haven't an address, really,' I said.

In my confusion I dropped my eyes and saw her shoes and stockings. They were not the shoes and stockings to wear to an important interview. The heels of the cracked brown shoes were worn right down; one strap was held with a safety-pin. The pinkish-grey stockings had a curious dead chalkiness about them. Below the calf they trembled a little and were empty. She had not enough flesh on her legs to fill them out. I was pierced by the little trembling empty spaces in her stockings. They seemed to spell all sadness and privation to me. Why was she there on her trembling thin legs with her two children? I wanted to know her *real* story; then I longed for her to run and catch her bus, so that I need never look at her legs again. As if she knew my thoughts, she gathered her children to her, gave her coat a little hitch, patted her hat and said, 'You're a brick, you are.'

She turned almost at once. The sluggish children were swivelled round. They stared back at me, but she pulled them on towards the next bus-stop. She walked so quickly that they had to trot. I stood still, my eyes still on her legs. The seam of one stocking twisted, like a thread of smoke from a cigarette. Once one of the worn-down heels made her ankle turn over, but she took little notice. She hopped painfully for a few steps, then hurried on as before.

Another time I found myself in a straggling little street set in market gardens outside the town. I went towards a window crowded with deal washstands, coconut matting and rusty fire-irons. I longed to discover a piece of china, an old tea-caddy, anything that would make my day come alive. The wish to preserve dilapidated objects from the past was strong upon me.

As I searched the unpromising window, I was not aware of an approaching figure until he stood almost beside me. I turned, then, to see a tall young man looking at me earnestly. Perhaps the strangest thing about him was his mixture of dirt and cleanliness. On his feet were squalid old gym shoes with holes at the toe. His trousers were frayed round the bottom and very stained, but above them he wore a heavy sweater with wide school-boy collar. It was pure cream in colour, as if it had just been laundered. It was only afterwards that I realized that one of the arms hung empty at his side.

At first he said nothing, only stared at me as if he wondered what could interest me so much in the shop. Then he said slowly and impressively, 'I'd do anything for a bob, I would.'

The looming greatness of 'anything' set beside the minuteness of a 'bob' startled me for a moment. I had absurd pictures of stupendous acts being performed for a shilling; but I knew that it was not required of me to imagine amazing situations. I was simply being asked for money. I felt in my pocket and found a shilling. As I held it out to him, I thought how shoddy and used it looked, the bright silver covering wearing off, a pinker colour showing underneath, the King's features all rubbed and worn and debased. It was a very obvious symbol of man's life on earth. I suddenly felt all the horror of being old and worn and used.

White Sweater took the shilling gladly. He did not ask or wheedle for any more. He slipped it in his pocket, then stood beside me, his one and only hand clutching his other shoulder so that his arm lay across his chest. It had begun to drizzle a little, but we still stood there, both apparently not wanting to part just yet.

As the rain increased, I looked about me for shelter and saw a little deserted corrugated iron hut not far away.

'I think I'll make for that and stay there till the rain is over,' I said, walking towards it. He followed me and we sat down on the mud by the open door. The rain beat happily on the thin metal roof. I had a feeling of cosiness, almost of peace, in that dirty little place filled with chicken's feathers, dead plants and broken tools. The rain spotted my companion's old gym shoes. I could see his purplish, yellowish big toe-nail through the hole in the canvas; he wore no socks. A clean, soapy smell, masking the staleness of his body, rose up from the damp white sweater.

'A lady give it to me just now,' he said, looking down at it with satisfaction. 'She said it was her son's and he wouldn't need it no more; seems like some sort o' college thing, don't you think?'

I nodded and looked at the sweater approvingly. The man must have thought that I was staring at his empty arm, for he said, 'Ah, I don't expect you'll ever guess how that happened.'

I protested that I had only been taking in the general effect of his new white sweater.

'Well, all the same, I'll tell you how it happened. Me and my father an' mother was coming back from India, my father was a sergeant out there. I was only a nipper and on board ship me and some others was playing about in the corridor outside the cabins. Some silly sod tried moving the great big iron door what they shut when the ship's sinking and they want to cut off the leaking part. He pushed an' he pushed with some other chaps and then the door went slam on me arm. I don't remember much more.'

I felt the iron door shutting on his arm. The horror of him hanging there entrapped haunted me. I could not rid my mind of the picture of crushed bone and mangled flesh.

'It doesn't hurt now?' I asked anxiously, remembering stories of pains that still persisted in legs that had been amputated.

'Aw, no, I just ain't got it, that's all.'

White Sweater paused for a moment and threw a stone at a broken flower-pot out in the rain. 'It don't make it easier to get a job, though,' he added thoughtfully. 'I can go back to my grandma; she'd help me, but I likes it better on the roads. It's not so bad; you have some queer things happen to you. Had a woman ask me the other night to go down on the beach with her.'

'Did you go?' I asked.

'Yus, and, what's more, she give me ten bob.'

There was something droll about his laconic, simple statement. He looked very childlike in his creamy sweater. I wanted to smile at his innocent, unquestioning expression. He must have looked very much the same when the iron door clanged to and trapped his arm. I jerked my head, trying to rid it of the picture which would keep reappearing.

After we had waited for some time and the rain showed no sign of stopping, I stood up and said good-bye.

'So long,' he said, looking up at me from the ground. His legs were pulled up to his chin with his one arm encircling them; the empty sleeve hung down, reminding me curiously of part of a fireman's flattened-out hose. 'P'raps I'll run into you again one day,' he added.

'Umm,' I said, nodding my head.

I turned away and felt the gentle rain on my face. It was both refreshing and uncomfortably cold; I had to get used to it before I could fully enjoy it. Soon my face was streaming and I could feel trickles from my hair wriggling down my warm back. I could see White Sweater in the open doorway of the hut across several fields. I waved before I disappeared and I saw his own arm raised in reply. Because it was his only one, the gesture seemed more valuable. It was a swan's neck stretching up to say good-bye to me.

Matron put on a great air of bustling disapproval when I arrived back with all my clothes wet. She told Nurse Goff to put me to bed at once. I stood in front of the fire in my room and steamed as I rubbed myself with the warm towel. I felt wonderfully cleaned and purified by the rain, as if it had washed me inside as well as out. I lay in bed and thought of Christmas. Mark was coming down to stay in a room on the front, and my aunt had asked us both to lunch. I thought of all the Christmases of my childhood – the sheer delight in presents, food and festive decorations. Surely no one could hate Christmas who remembered this past joyfulness! I supposed it was the change in themselves that people hated, the being so much older, the difficulty of feeling pleased, the anxieties that had come to roost on them, so that they were like naked trees weighed down with black hens.

I wondered if I would hate this Christmas because of the change in me.

When the day came, Mark walked into my room in his stealthy off-hand way and said, 'Here's a present for you.'

I felt awkward, having nothing for him. I unwrapped my parcel and found a book of mid-Victorian book illustrations with a modern limerick written under each one. It was impossible not to laugh when one turned from the intensely dramatic situation to the silly verses underneath. I laughed in spite of myself, for I admired many of the engravings and felt sad that they could be made to look ridiculous. It was strange at that time how afraid I was of people and objects falling off their pedestals. I did not seem to have the strength to accept things as they were. I wanted to believe in only one side.

'What is your room like?' I asked, looking up from the book. 'Is it all right, or haven't you seen it yet?'

'I've just come from there,' Mark said. 'I went to leave my suitcase. It's really rather good. I look out on to the sea. The guest-house itself has an unusual name; it's called Lesbia. You can't miss it because it's written in large gold round-hand right across the front.'

We talked ramblingly in this way, trying to give life to silly remarks, until the taxi came to take us to my aunt's. I kept thinking of the hogskin gloves lined with lamb's wool which I had given to Dr Farley. I had not thought of a present for anyone else. It gave me great pleasure to think that the gloves had swallowed up nearly all my pocket money for the next month. It had been embarrassing when he burst into the room before Mark arrived and thanked me for them. I longed for the time when I should have the right face and manner for every occasion. It seemed that this power must come with age and experience. Then I remembered all the mature people I knew with awkward, floundering ways.

On the way to my aunt's I wondered how she would agree with Mark. Would she find him difficult to entertain? He went so silent when he was with strangers, and his curious artificial sang-froid became so pronounced that it was almost affronting.

I need not have worried. As soon as we were in the long drawing-room overlooking the sea I could tell how charmed Mark was with her. She was indeed doing all she could to please. She was like the aunt of my childhood – a sort of fairy godmother, infinitely gracious and indulgent.

After we had shaken hands with my uncle in the wheelchair, we were both taken up to the tiny glistening Christmas tree and given our presents. This little ceremony in itself was a surprise, a return to much earlier times. I took my long thin parcel to the window-seat and unwrapped the tissue paper. My present was a Brigg's walking stick, very handsome in its newness, with its silver band engraved with my initials and its dark horn handle. Mark had been given a fountain pen. It was clear that he was delighted with this quite unexpected present from someone who had only known him for the last five minutes. His small grey-blue eyes sparkled as he examined it possessively and lovingly. I looked again at my stick. My aunt had thoughtfully supplied it with a rubber ferrule so that I should not slip. I wondered if I could take the ugly thing off without offending her. I decided to wait till we had left the house. Meanwhile, it spoilt my stick for me. I could not look at it without a sense of angry shame or outrage. How did my aunt dare to give me a stick with a hideous rubber ferrule! Did she imagine that I was to hobble and totter for the rest of my life? Even now, if I were careful, I could walk for short distances almost normally.

My aunt took us upstairs to show Mark the rest of the house. In the hall the lavatory door was left wide open, and immediately I knew that my aunt had planned it thus, so that we should know where it was without having to ask. I smiled at her forethought; she had forgotten nothing. She was leading us now along the upper landing, talking to Mark while I walked behind. I made some remark, I think about an old embroidery picture which I liked, she turned her head, threw me an answer rather casually and went on at once with her conversation with Mark. I knew another thing then. I knew that the charm and the graciousness were specially for the new acquaintance, that I need not imagine that very much attention was to be paid to myself. To become suddenly aware of such discrimination makes pride swell and resentment simmer. After the first shock, one is determined to show no pique, but simply to appear bored and rather impatient to be gone.

But in spite of this unresponsive manner which I at once assumed, I became really embarrassed and sorry for my aunt when she took us into the little boudoir study room where she kept all the drawings that had been done of herself. Pastels and charcoal drawings lined the walls. They were all, without exception, inept and vulgar. Most of them had been done many years ago. They showed a young woman with enormous eyes, a swan neck and golden tendrils of hair. All of them, even the later ones, were quite unrecognizable as portraits of my aunt. Mark stood in front of them uncomfortably, until my aunt, to break the tension, said smilingly, 'Well, what do you think of all these portraits of me?'

Mark hesitated. I knew that he was incapable of saying the easy graceful thing. His tactlessness sprang from some deep lack of feeling for others.

'Of course they'd be very nice,' he said at last, 'if they were at all like you.'

He laughed nervously, then reddened as he saw the dismay on my aunt's face. She laughed, too, to cover up her wound. 'Oh, don't you think any of them are like me then?'

'Well, not very; I mean they're awfully nice. Perhaps they were more like you some years ago.'

Mark, stumbling over his words, making matters worse with each addition, stood shamefaced in the middle of the room with all his jauntiness gone. My aunt caressed her rings as though she did not care. I turned away, pretending to be very interested in a comic hunting scene of the Edwardian era.

A gong boomed downstairs. My aunt said brightly, 'Lunch is ready; let's go down.'

I followed her with relief. My uncle was wheeled into the dining-room. We all admired the decoration of the table. Tiny salmon-pink crackers tied with silver ribbon were grouped round a bowl of tinsel roses and fanciful flowers made out of feathers, also dyed salmon-pink. It was all very delicate and fleeting, just the sort of thing my aunt loved to arrange. I remembered other parties and other colour schemes; they stretched back, back, until I was a tiny child.

We started with smoked salmon. It was an old conceit of my aunt's to carry the predominant colour of her party decorations into the food itself. I squeezed my pig of lemon over the sliver of salmon, watched it grow paler, then put a piece in my mouth and ate it with brown bread and butter. I thought how delightful it would be to have a large plate of smoked salmon before me and to be alone, so that I could savour it to the full and think my thoughts. I did not want to pass on to turkey and plum pudding; and talking was difficult. My uncle had retreated into that world of clayey silence which invalids often inhabit. It is as if they have withdrawn from the world, found no resources in themselves, and so lapsed into a kind of mournful muteness. My aunt, I think, was still suffering from Mark's ineptitudes. Never again would she be able to feel quite so complacent about her portraits of herself; but she was trying hard to regain the feeling and manner of the charming hostess. Mark ate carefully and was silent. He only seemed able to talk freely when alone with one other person. Even the smallest group made him shut his mouth and look on with guarded eyes. The two glasses of champagne which we were each allowed made no difference. I was glad when we reached the fruit and the sweets.

After the meal, I went up to the thing I liked best in the house, the picture over the sideboard in the manner of Frith. It had been painted in mid-Victorian times for a member of my aunt's family. The scene depicted the departure of the bride and bridegroom after the wedding breakfast. All the richness of the drawing-room was there, the heavy crimson curtains, the gilt consoles, the enormous mirrors, the glittering gasolier. A group of children in wonderfully fantastic clothes played with a great collie dog on a carpet patterned with roses larger than the children's heads. In the centre of the picture the sorrowful parents were saying good-bye to their daughter. She looked very beautiful in her dress of grey watered-silk. Her bonnet was a wonder of tiny flowers and bows. She was about to weep. Her lace handkerchief was already in her hand. Out of the long windows the sun poured down on the lawns and the vivid, rigid carpet-bedding.

As I gazed at the abundance of the scene, the richness piled on richness, I became suddenly aware of the poverty of our refined little luncheon. The food had been good, but what of the human beings? We had all been dried up or dammed up, four *things* performing the ceremony of eating because it was one o'clock. Then I thought, 'But the artist, of course, would romanticize his scene. There was probably in reality a costive heaviness in the air; those children would have been quarrelling; that collie would have smelled; the bride's father would have been thinking of his kidney disease, or his money; the bride herself would have suffered from the tightness of her stays and the fear of the spot that was threatening to appear on her chin.'

In the drawing-room the wireless was switched on so that we should hear the King's speech. We drank our coffee in a sort of reverent silence, afraid even that our spoons might make a distracting tinkle.

Suddenly my uncle began to cry, quite quietly, but obviously. There was no attempt at concealment. The fat tears rolled down his fat cheeks, disappearing under his chin. He did not look like a great baby; he looked much more disquieting. He looked like an elderly man crying hopelessly at the end of his days, after a full and busy and successful life.

Of course we were all supposed to notice nothing. My aunt gazed into the distance with eyes that were kept rigidly dreamy and wistful. Mark twiddled his new pen with an almost ridiculous nonchalance, and I pretended to be engrossed in the truisms the King was carefully repeating. But even through my confusion I could feel that it was a natural time to cry.

The sacredness of the day, the hushed expectancy, the waiting, then the quiet voice speaking so slowly, all went to make some strong tension. Indeed I wondered why we weren't all crying to relieve the strain.

Soon after the end of the speech I felt it best to catch Mark's eye. I was afraid of what my uncle might do next, afraid, not on his account, but on my aunt's. Mark, I thought, stood up rather reluctantly; my aunt, too, seemed divided about our going. Half of her appeared to want our company, half wished for solitude and privacy.

She said good-bye to Mark with flattering attention, fixing him with her eyes as if she approved of all she saw. The episode of the portraits was to be forgotten. He was again the talented young stranger whom she wished to charm. I even came in for the fag-end of her sweetness. It was as if she grouped me now with Mark as a sort of appendage.

I went out into the hall, feeling impatient with all tricks and wiles. I carried my new stick, and that made me angry, too. As we passed through the tiled entrance lobby, I looked idly at the umbrella-stand and suddenly noticed a stick with a horn handle like my own. I pulled it out. Yes, it was exactly like my present in every detail, except that it had a *gold* band instead of a silver one. On the gold band were my uncle's initials. As I stared at them a sort of cold hatred possessed me. I was without humour or light-ness. 'How unutterably mean,' I thought, 'to give a present with a silver band, when one considers that gold is the thing for one's husband.' It was almost as if my aunt had said harshly, in the manner of one of the Ugly Sisters, 'There! take that. It's quite good enough for you.'

I tried to smile, angry with myself now for taking everything so seriously, for being so easily ruffled. I told myself how petty it was to be forever brooding over slights. It was self-important, pompous, pathetic.

But I could not rid myself so easily of all my resentment.

When we were out of the front door, the wind from the sea did more than all my thoughts to freshen me. I let it blow through my open coat and under my raised arms. Mark went up to the edge of the cliff and I followed him. We were just outside the windows of my aunt's house, and I won-dered if she was watching us.

'How delightful your aunt is!' Mark said feelingly. 'I've never known anyone quite like her. To give me a fountain-pen, and a good one at that, when she's never set eyes on me before!'

I paused, half from compunction, half from pleasure at the thought of poisoning his mind against her and puncturing his self-satisfaction. I ended up by compromising and being rather mild and colourless.

'I'm afraid it's all rather on the surface,' I said; 'but the fact that she even bothers to switch on her charm is, I suppose, a sort of compliment.'

Mark looked at me sharply, as if searching my expression for some guidance.

'Why are you so carping?' he asked.

There was a complaint in his voice. He disliked me for threatening his illusion.

'One can never be certain of her next mood, and so one takes nothing seriously.'

I leant on the balustrade at the cliff's edge and stared out to sea. Suddenly an idea came to me. Twiddling my stick round, I pulled off the rubber ferrule and squashed it in my hand for a moment or two. I put a finger in the hole and wore it like an enormous blunt thimble. I thought of it, too, as a miniature elephant's foot, round, clubbed and stumpy. Mark watched me as I lifted my hand. I threw it as far out to sea as I could.

'Why on earth did you do that?' Mark asked in consternation. 'Your aunt might have seen; we're still so near her house.'

'Yes, aren't we,' I agreed. 'Let's get farther away.'

We walked slowly along the esplanade, enjoying the wind and sea before returning to the nursing home. I used my new stick, pleased to feel the bite of the metal ferrule on the hard road. Once or twice it skidded a little and that pleased me more.

Soon afterwards I lost my stick, leaving it by mistake on the top of a bus. I was sorry to lose it and even went to the bus depot to make enquiries. But perhaps this was the fate which had been ordained for it from the first.

XXIV

CHRISTMAS HAD been a point at which I gazed but would not look beyond, a full-stop to the year and my catastrophe. Now that I was past it, a great plain spread out before me, threateningly featureless. Was I to live indefinitely in the nursing home? It would seem so, if Matron and my brother had their way; but Dr Farley always spoke as if I should soon be out in the world, learning new things, working towards some wonderful but undefined goal. His almost extravagant encouragement added to my restlessness. I knew it for what it was – talk to stimulate the invalid – and discounted some of it; nevertheless it inflamed my own impatience, making me furious when Matron came in, shaking her head and saying, 'You ought to be extremely careful for the next year at least.' She pottered about the room, not even dusting, but peering at books, hairbrushes and flowers, setting them to rights, as she would put it, by moving them half an inch, or regimenting them into lines. It was clear that she was gathering courage to say something more to me.

'I'm not going to tell you what might happen if you're not careful, it's not suitable for you to hear; but things would be *very* serious indeed.'

After her speech her bosom seemed to swell. She was a mother full of solicitude, a prophetess talking to a fool, a bird of ill omen ashamed suddenly of its threat. I picked on this wavering guilt with savage pleasure.

'What an awful thing to hold over my head! Dr Farley has never hinted at anything; but, of course, I don't know what *you're* hinting at. That makes it all the worse.'

Matron was a little uneasy at so bald an attack.

'I'm not saying anything against Dr Farley; he's a very clever doctor and a very nice man, but it isn't easy, even for a doctor, to understand all the intricacies of nursing. To do that you've got to go through with the whole business from the beginning. I've done that and I know how careful one has to be in cases of your sort.'

I looked at her, fascinated because she had tried to frighten me, because at last someone in authority had said something dark and forbidding and solemn. Of course she was only attempting to keep me in her nursing home, but I was perversely grateful even for such mock high seriousness. How depressing the indifference or the heartiness of the hospital doctors had been; and Dr Farley's careful minimizing of all the difficulties of my condition also depressed me sometimes. I was made to feel drab, as if I had been suffering from nothing more interesting than a cold in the nose. If I could not be well, I should really prefer to be told grizzly stories; they at least drove away some of the greyness of my new life.

I was grateful, too, because at last I had a real cause for complaint. In the past my opposition to Matron had often seemed petty and excessive; now that she had tried to terrify me for her own ends I could disapprove of her wholeheartedly.

There would be a certain meanness in repeating her threat to Dr Farley. It would be very like sneaking to one of the masters about a big boy's misdemeanour, but I did not doubt that I should do it sooner or later. I wanted to watch his face as I told him, and I wanted to know what exactly she had meant by her threat.

I told him as we drove towards the neighbouring town on the coast where he had a patient to see. I had not been out with him for some time. The experience seemed new again, and a little disconcerting.

'What utter nonsense!' he exclaimed after he had heard me.

'But what did she mean?' I asked.

'Absolutely nothing. You must take no notice of anything she said.'

He emphasized each word, banging it into me with such force that I began to feel that there must have been some truth in Matron's threat; otherwise would he expend so much energy in trying to wipe out her words? I wished he would treat the incident a little more lightly. His anger with Matron made me feel that I was a poor thing in need of protection against an ogress; whereas at that moment I felt Matron ought really to have protection against me.

'Why do you think she came in and said it?' I asked.

'I suppose she guessed that you were getting restless and would soon want to leave her home.'

'That's what I imagined.' I paused a moment, uncertain of his answer to my next question. 'Do you think I could leave soon?'

'Yes, I do, but what then? Have you decided on your next move?'

'No, I haven't decided anything. I suppose I could go and stay at my grandfather's.'

'But that would only be marking time.'

'Yes, I know.'

We had reached the outskirts of the town. Paltry bungalows and shops and traffic roundabouts made it difficult to be fond of human beings. Self-disgust spread out to include all others. The world was a shoddy place. In this unpromising setting Dr Farley began to confide in me. He spaced his words out at first, as if between each one he doubted my discretion anew.

'You mustn't tell Matron or anyone else at the moment, but I'm leaving; I'm going to another practice. Everything's fixed up at last; we shall move in about three weeks.'

His words shocked and startled me. My first thoughts were for myself left alone in the nursing home with Matron and Nurse Goff. Dr Farley had seemed so settled, so permanent. What could I rely on now?

'Have you suddenly decided to go?' I asked, wanting to know his reasons without questioning.

'No, I've been thinking about it for a long time, but it's only just been arranged.'

He drove on in silence for a moment. 'You see, I haven't really got enough to do here, and most of my patients are old; you're my only young one at the moment. I want a different sort of place, where I can be more useful.'

It was almost as if he were making excuses to me or to himself. I had never thought of his days as lacking work before. He had always seemed so busy, and I had been grateful for any spare moments he chose to waste on me. There would be other reasons – questions of pay and partnership that he did not care to discuss. My mind began to accept his going. After the first desolate feeling, so strong now that it was he who was leaving and not myself, I found myself drawing a sort of exhilaration from the thought of the change. Already a scheme was forming.

'You know you said you thought I could soon leave the nursing home,' I said carefully.

'Yes.'

'Well, couldn't I find a cottage or a flat near your new practice? Then you could keep an eye on me and I wouldn't have to start again with yet another doctor; I should hate that. To get out of that nursing home and have a little place of my own would be a great step forward for me.'

Dr Farley was thinking. I waited, feeling that his silence could only mean one thing. How surprised I was, then, when he said, 'That is rather an idea; but don't discuss it yet with anyone. Wait till I'm in the new place. If you talk about it now you might make trouble for me here. It might even be possible for you to come and stay with us for a time.'

Could he really mean that last light sentence? For the past month or more I had imagined that he treated me with a vague uneasiness, as if his belief in my good sense and stability were slowly draining away. But could this be so, now that he was suggesting my living in his house? Would he have anyone whom he considered unaccountable or troublesome?

He parked the car outside a bank and went across the road to his patient's house. I was in a glow of pleasure. I almost looked forward to returning to the nursing home, where I would cosset my secret and the knowledge that I had been invited to live somewhere else. Matron would look at me, poke and prod, but get nothing for her pains. My quiet self-sufficiency would drive her to distraction. Then one day I would suddenly be gone – she would not even know where.

I watched people going into the bank and others coming out. It was impossible to tell anything from their faces, so I thought of the dirty notes and coins in their pockets and bags. The notes and coins were like children put out to nurse in the bank, then taken back to be employed, enjoyed or married. Or the bank was a little local temple, where the people went in to leave their offerings or break off pieces of love for their own use.

I was pleased that the car window was between me and the crack and crash of the town. I was still unaccustomed to the headlong traffic, the jostle of crowded pavements. Even the wind off the sea was different in the town. It swung signs violently, so that it was easy to imagine the boards or the metal plates falling like guillotines on the heads below. It buffeted people round corners, slapping their faces or shoving them from behind. There was even a threat in the way it rattled the cords against an absurd little flagpole in a front garden. The faces so near to me, haggard and pale, roughened and red, children's faces with that india-rubber ugliness only seen in children, voices shouting raucously against the wind and the traffic, mouths so wide open that one saw the ruined teeth; why did I seize on the sights and the sounds that troubled me? I seemed to have lost the happy trick of disregarding them.

I was pleased when Dr Farley returned to me. He was smiling, but in that nervous fashion which is a cloak for uncomfortable thoughts rather than a sign of any satisfaction. He was still in the patient's bedroom, weighing the problems of illness; but to make a show of being with me in the car he began to talk animatedly, jumping from one thing to another until he reached the unexpected subject of drug addiction. He described some of the fantastic wiles victims resort to when deprived of their poison. I listened only carelessly, wondering why I was not more interested. My thoughts seemed unable to leave the bright picture of my walking out of the nursing home and going to a new place. I left it vague, refusing to imagine myself living in Dr Farley's house. The idea was too unreal, too far away, and, although I hated to think this last thought, perhaps not utterly desirable. I should be so aware of myself, so aware of others' awareness. The atmosphere would be taut as a drum for me. And all the time, however successful the arrangement might seem on the surface, I would know that I was not in the right place, that I was adapting myself wastefully.

But all this was buried under my new hope and excitement; just to write it down has given it too much importance. It was only the slightest of misgivings.

Any buoyancy of mood was always commented upon either by Nurse Goff or by Matron, so, to save myself from the irritation of 'You look perky,' or 'What's got into you?' I determined to show nothing. I saw to it that my face was solemn, even a little sulky, as I passed through the hall to my room. There, sitting by the fire, I was assailed by all the faces of the people who had come to see me since first I was in hospital. They must have started to form as I gazed into the red coals and thought, for the thousandth time, 'Why do people talk about *faces in the fire*? What do they mean?' I was thinking of faces, and there was the fire, and so they formed: Cora's face, Betsy's face, Mark's, the rather mad face of the sleek man who said he had been sent by my dead mother to heal and to rescue me. This brought me to Clare with a shock. I had turned away from the thought of her for weeks, even for months. Now her face welled up at me. Because she had been so good coming to see me week after week in London, I felt a sort of guilt at not being able to believe that she could help me any more. It was as if I had allowed her to do what she could, let her bring me down to the sea in the ambulance, then had gained other interests and forgotten all about her. The truth was that Dr Farley's unexpected friendliness had made me much less dependent on the kindness of earlier friends. Now that I looked at it coldly, from a distance, Christian Science suddenly assumed all the forms of a burlesque madness. There was the jargon of *mortal mind, error, passing on,* and a hundred other set phrases. Christian Scientists juggled them about until they became as jaded as the little pieces of gristle that people put out on the sides of their plates after desperate chewing. I never doubted that they were right in stressing love; but again the word was used so mercilessly that it became monstrous, unmeaning, a swelling sound in the ears, a senseless flapping of the tongue. I wanted my love to be much less mauled and mechanical. And what was one to make of 'Divine Mind always has met and always will meet every human need'? If one didn't take it literally it was of no use to anyone on this earth, and if one did take it literally it was merely silly and cruel. But why was I carping at words and phrases? Every religious sect had its own irritating language. I was nothing to do with religious sects, never had been. There was no need to get hot and angry because I could not agree with Clare who had been good to me. I must not feel burdened with gratitude, for that would make me harder and more unsympathetic than ever; and yet I could not forget that it was I who had asked her to come and see me on that terrible first day in hospital. That craving to be healed magically and at once came back to me. I saw it now as the desperation of the person who has never really been ill before. I was no longer in the mood to believe in any miracle, but at first I had tried to force myself to believe anything but the gruesome truth.

I saw all at once that sooner or later the grateful person must show ingratitude in order to regain his integrity. To bite the hand that feeds you is unnecessary, but at least you must stop kissing it. If you don't, everything will become slimed over with your mawkish thanks and you will secretly begin to hate. This came to me as a blazing truth, because I had discovered it for myself in the middle of my confused, unhappy thinking. I felt freed already. The mysterious exalted mood was creeping over me. I jumped up to get my notepaper. I must write to Clare at once, thank her whole-heartedly – a thing I had never done before in so many words – then explain gently that I could no longer share her beliefs. The letter might offend and annoy; it would probably be more considerate not to write at all, but I had to be done with my uncomfortable feelings. I had to get out of my false position.

I opened the glass doors and went out into the dark garden, walking as quickly as I could. I wanted the letter in the pillar-box; only then would I feel that I had done all there was to be done. The grey road, the little grey houses packed tightly on each side, the grey pollarded trees, like giant brussels sprouts on lanky stalks, all brought on an extravagant sadness. I could never be sorry enough for Clare. If only one *could* change the world and oneself merely by taking thought! But I greedily embraced the never-ending sadness of human life. At that moment I wanted to be overwhelmed by it. Nothing else but the sadness of destruction seemed real. I would sink down, be its victim, fall asleep in it. How can I describe the deep vibrating pleasure I felt? Perhaps it was a little like the moment just before a child bursts into tears. He knows he is going to cry, he does nothing about it, he has no shame, he wants to be drowned, to be swallowed up for ever in his own unhappiness.

When I came back into myself again, a little suspicious at such an outflow of feeling, I went back to the other faces I was thinking of before I came to Clare's. I seemed to date everything now from last June; it was as if I had been born again when I woke up to the horror of the green screens round me in the hospital. Of course I often thought of things that had happened to me before then; but these scenes were always docketed 'Old Life'. The New Life, because it was so different, because it had been forced on me, and because it was painful, had taken on the aspect of a pilgrimage or special journey. I looked for significance in every tiny thing. The people who looked after me and the people who visited me were not seen in the old way. I no longer accepted their common humanity as the chief thing about them. I had become much more aware of their vices and virtues. They lost some of their roundness, the most extreme cases became almost flat; and they all wore labels round their necks. Thus one person would be Hard, another Cruel, another Lively, another Serene.

Now, as their faces swam towards me in imagination, I felt that they were embodiments of my good and bad qualities come to visit me and haunt me. Even the presents friends had brought me took on a new significance. It was easy to see what chocolates symbolized, but what could one make at first of balls of wool? sketch books? or bottles of sherry? Interpretations came pouring in. The ball of wool that I had wound and unwound all one night had been a symbol of my journey – on, on, on through the darkness – having to begin all over again, just when the end had been reached. The bottles of sherry were inspiration, hope, vitality. The sketch book was each day's pure whiteness before one sullied it with stupid actions or words.

My game of finding meanings grew and grew, overtoppled itself and collapsed in absurdity. An allegory suddenly seemed an old conceit, cumbrous and puffed up. I was left with all the scattered faces, the presents, the kind acts and the cruel. The accident, and all that had happened to me since, was so much trash in the dust-bin, and I, turned scavenger, was picking over the pitiful rags, the filth, and broken pots, trying desperately to find a use for them, to relate them to each other.

My mood had changed so completely that I found it best to stop picking and to look over the past with an animal indifference. Surely that was the way to look at things – to eat them up with your eyes for what they were, then to pass on, but never to chain them together in a silly pattern. The idea of a pattern was only satisfying if it was to be utterly unknowable and mysterious to human beings.

It was very late now: the night nurse had been in long ago to bank the fire and open the window. I lay on my bed quite content to be awake still. I could just see the chromium arm and handle of the gramophone glimmering near me on the table. Divorced from their black suitcase, seemingly floating in the darkness, they looked like a sorcerer's magic instruments. I fixed my eyes on them and experienced the utter silence of the house. To be awake in the sleeping house gave me power. It was right that I should watch. I was no longer part of the nursing home; it seemed incongruous that I should still be there.

XXV

IN THE days that followed Matron's anxiety grew with my secret schemes. Although I said nothing and tried to show nothing, she could tell that my eyes were fixed beyond the nursing home. She prolonged her morning visits now, hesitating by the fire or with her hand on the door, reluctant to go without learning anything. In spite of my antagonism I suddenly felt more for her; understood her fears. Running a nursing home was an expensive and precarious business. She hated to lose me, because, through the months, she had come to look on me as a sort of fixture, someone whose bill was paid with gratifying regularity. It was clear that she had hoped to have me for another year at least. But knowing her fears, even feeling for her a little, did not change my attitude at all. I was against her because I had to be. A wicked pleasure crept into my voice as I gave the frustrating answer, the maddeningly unrevealing 'Yes' or 'No' to some leading question. She almost gave up asking me questions, contenting herself with remarks spoken to the air. One day she paused by the dressing-table, gazed into the mirror and said, 'Of course, we can all see how fond you are of Dr Farley. I think you'd do anything *he* said. You don't seem to trust us in the same way.'

An angry flush mounted to my cheeks. Surely this was an outrage! She was trying to turn what she chose to call my 'fondness' into an absurd schoolboy hero worship, only too obvious to everyone. I was too angry to answer sensibly or tellingly.

'*You all* see a very great deal,' I muttered with scathing emphasis.

'Oh, have I said anything wrong? I didn't mean to. I think it's so nice for you to have at least one person here you like and trust. You seem to me to have been such a lonely boy. Except for your brother and your aunt, you've had no family to come and see you. Having a family makes *such* a difference.'

This new Matron, troubled by my 'loneliness', pitying me because I had no family, pleased that at least I had one person I was 'fond' of, seemed quite unbearable. Her impertinence was as enormous as her body. What would she dare to say next? I longed for her to lose her sympathy and become the self-seeking busybody again. Even an inquisitive question about money or ancestry would have been welcome – anything but this dreadful cupboard love. And yet, deep down, a little unproud part of me was pleased to have her remarks. It wanted to push through the freezing silence of the rest of me and ask for more. It was the little part that feeds on enormities, that is tempted to listen at keyholes to hear ill of itself. It treasures up all personal allusions from insults to extravagant praise, and perhaps the insults are the most prized.

But the stronger part of me was saying, 'You're quite mistaken; I'm not lonely at all. I'd hate to be surrounded by a family.'

My voice had hardened until even I was shocked by its ugliness. Matron blinked at me irresolutely, then left the room with an aggrieved air, as if to say, 'All that sympathy and understanding for nothing. It's too bad.'

I think it was the very next morning, or the morning after that, when she came in looking really excited.

'I've had quite a shock. I've just heard Dr Farley's leaving the neighbourhood. It all seems very sudden to me; but I believe you've known for quite a time and haven't said a word. You are a funny boy, keeping it all to yourself like that.'

This 'boy' business was beginning to annoy. It only seemed to date from her conversation on my loneliness and need of a family. She would vary it soon, go one worse and call me a *lad*. I felt sure of it.

I was still very wary with her, suspecting that her information came from some not very reliable backstairs source, and that she was waiting for me to confirm it and fill it out. I appeared to take no interest in Dr Farley's departure. My only answer was an uncouth and apathetic grunt.

'Everybody knows now,' said Matron brightly, hoping perhaps to loosen my tongue. 'We all wonder why he's kept it such a secret till the last moment. There doesn't seem much point, since we had to know sooner or later.'

'Perhaps he didn't want people to talk about it and ask a lot of questions. It's easier to do things if nobody else knows what you're doing.'

Matron looked at me sharply. She seemed to take this last sentence as a dark hint of my own intentions.

'Now surely you're not going to be the next one to say he's going,' she exclaimed with real agitation. 'I've told you you're not nearly fit enough to leave us yet. I don't like to think what you'd be like without expert attention.'

I did not answer. I was thinking how quick anxiety made even the dullest person. Matron took my silence for a confirmation of her fears. She looked at me with deep reproach.

'We've done all we possibly could for you, I'm sure – tried to make you comfortable and happy; but I suppose you're tired of being here now. You want a change, even if you suffer for it and undo most of our good work.'

A long intake of breath swelled the bosom until I was made to feel that Matron, like a true Christian, was damming up all just resentments so that no harsh word should pass.

'I must leave the nursing home one day,' I said gently, catching the Christian mannerism.

'Yes, of course, but why spoil the ship for a ha'porth of tar?'

Hackneyed images and proverbs have always had the power to jump suddenly alive for me. There is a click and I see the needle in the bottle of hay, the stupid one crying over the spilt milk, the stitch in time saving nine. So now I was vividly aware of myself as an old hulk, leaky and stinking, swarming with rats and covered with barnacles. I saw the crooked shipwrights pretending to repair me but spoiling me, all for a ha'porth of tar. I was not pleased with Matron for presenting me with this picture. I wanted to say something sarcastic about the ha'porth, but it was too late; she would not connect it with her fees, and in any case one can only feel pleasure in thinking smart remarks, never in hearing the flash words issuing from one's mouth. The atmosphere seems never to be quite right for repartee, so that even the great wit's performances sound a little shaming when read aloud.

That afternoon, as I was passing through the hall to go for a walk by myself, I heard Matron in earnest conversation on the telephone. The door of her 'office' was shut and I could hear no words distinctly, but the thought suddenly came that she was discussing me. I dismissed it as an egoistic suspicion. How often as a child had I felt that people were talking me over, or planning unpleasant things for me, when really their thoughts were far away on their own concerns! But this time I think I must have been right, for at the week-end the telephone rang for me. I went into the dark polished alcove off the hall and sat down without touching the receiver. Nurse Goff had just said, 'Someone for you on the phone,' so I had no idea who was at the other end of the line. I steeled myself to hear Clare's voice. Was it an absurd, excessive letter that I wrote on that evening when I tried to explain my state of mind to her? It must have been; I had felt so exalted and freed. After these fears, it was a relief to hear my brother's voice tingling in my ear; but I soon realized that this was to be no easy casual gossip.

'Matron tells me you're thinking of leaving,' he said suddenly. 'You can't do that yet; you're not nearly well enough.'

'Dr Farley thinks I am,' I answered, a dogged, truculent note already creeping into my voice.

It was not long before we were arguing violently. Because my plans were so unformed I could explain very little. I could only repeat stubbornly that I was going and that I would probably try to find a flat or a cottage near Dr Farley's new practice.

'But you can't go house-hunting in your state of health,' my brother exclaimed; 'besides, you're not of age yet. Nobody would take any notice of your signature on a lease, or on anything else for that matter.'

'I expect I shall be able to manage the details,' I said grimly, though at that moment I had no idea how I would manage even the first step. I had under my own control no more than five pounds, probably less. But these problems were trivialities. All that mattered was to defy the forces of oppression. The real joy of persecution possessed me. I would fight Matron, my brother and any other tyrants who tried to keep me tied up in a nursing home indefinitely. What enraged me most was that both my brother and Matron seemed to discount Dr Farley's words. They might think that I per-verted or exaggerated them, but the explanation that commended itself to me was that they both disregarded them for their own ends – Matron because she wanted to keep me in her home, my brother because he liked to feel that I was safe and settled and because he did not want the worry of a change.

At the height of my anger something, perhaps a soothing note in my brother's voice, sent a cold little thought through me: Did you always behave in this excitable way? He evidently does not think so, for he is treating you as an invalid. But are you much changed by the accident? You think not; how do you appear to other people?

This thought, so far from sobering me, made me speak louder and louder in an attempt to drown it.

'I've decided to go and I'm going,' I shouted. Matron in her office must have heard every word.

'Do be sensible,' my brother pleaded, trying, unsuccessfully, not to sound exasperated.

'This call from London must be costing a lot,' I said, conscious of the folly, not only of quarrelling, but of paying for the privilege.

'What the hell does that matter? I'm paying for the call, not you.'

My brother had the power to make me feel petty, spinsterishly careful, really rather contemptible in my concern for pennies and shillings.

'I was only wanting to bring all this absurdity to an end,' I said. 'You can't stop me from going, so why jabber any more?'

Jabber did sound suitably pathetic and ineffectual, but wasn't there a better word, if only I could think of it? I searched in my mind, but nothing came, so I took the final reprisal and replaced the receiver. I held it down firmly, as if afraid that it would jump off its stand and begin answering me back again. I imagined a murderer holding a baby's head under the black water of a midnight pool. It gave me pleasure to silence my elder brother, to treat him like a baby and hold his head under the water. If he rang again, the tinkles would be like bubbles coming up to the surface to be laughed at demoniacally.

The quarrel had exhilarated me. I left the alcove with my arms across my chest, as if I would hug my brimming energy to me. My only regret was that there was nothing I could do yet. It was much too early to pack. Dr Farley had not even left the town, and it was agreed that I should remain for at least another fortnight after his departure. When he had settled into his new house, he was to write to me, describing the situation and helping me to arrange matters. I thought of him in his cramped little house. I imagined him leaning over a chaotic pile of papers, trying to sort them into some sort of order. He would not be very good at this sort of thing; he would alternate between a ruthless determination to destroy everything and a hankering after useless preservation. Next he would turn to his wardrobe and find that his wife or the little maid had packed almost all his socks and shirts. There would be something a little humiliating in this discovery. I was glad I had no person with the right to touch my clothes.

Thinking of Dr Farley reminded me of my brother's disregard of his opinion over the question of my leaving the nursing home. In a moment I became furiously angry again. I wanted to put my anger on paper. I began a letter to him there and then. It was full of all my resentments, disappointments, despairing moments since I found myself in that old infirmary ward. I blamed him for not moving me at once, blamed him for hiding behind what the doctors said, blamed him for leaving me to languish in the other hospital until I roused myself at last and insisted on being moved. There was no end to my blame. Where he had not been neglectful he had been perfunctory. I, who had had to depend on him for all the arrangements which might have made me a little more comfortable, had been cheated of all true attention. I would have fared no worse if I had been an orphan with no relation or protector in the world. I went on to stress what I thought of at that moment as the 'abominable conditions' of some modern English hospitals – the noise, the cruelty, the indifference, the uneatable food, the petty tyranny. If this was enlightenment and reform, what must eighteenth-century Bedlam have been like? Of course my pen was running away with me, but surely vehemence did not always overreach its mark! Surely sometimes it struck home, wiping the complacence off a face as if by magic! Or was it always a mistake to overstate one's case? Would my brother just smile sceptically, think, 'Poor ass! he seems rather unbalanced at the moment'? Although I realized quite clearly that the letter gave my brother the chance to think this, I hardly cared. I wanted him to have it.

Even the injustices in it seemed just to me. My brother was the scapegoat who must bear all the transgressions of the doctors and nurses to whom he had abandoned me.

It was strange, after this furious letter, to receive one morning one of my aunt's rare notes. My brother, very wisely, had not answered, since nothing he could say would have seemed right; I wondered now if he had told my aunt about my letter and if she was taking me to task for my abuse and ingratitude. But as soon as I saw the beginning of the note, I realized that she knew nothing of our quarrel or my state of mind. The note was simply a suggestion that, now that I was so much better, I should buy my brother a present, 'perhaps, a really good gold watch', as a token of my indebtedness. 'He has been so very good to you and has taken such infinite pains over your comfort and welfare.' My aunt ended by telling me to think over her suggestion, and then, when I had decided on what sort of present to give, to let her know so that she could buy something 'really nice' for me the next time she went up to London.

The letter was so extraordinarily ill-timed, so blind to the real situation, that it reminded me of some creaking contrivance in an old play. I felt that I should give a deep stage laugh and say, with heavy irony, 'How droll! How very droll!'

I let the note flutter down to the breakfast-tray like an enormous blue snowflake. There was indeed some true humour in the timing of it, but it was of the quiet, bubbling, malicious sort. I would write to my aunt and tell her of my real feelings. I would explain that a present of 'a really good gold watch' was as far from my thoughts as anything could be. I wished I could be there to see her head jerk back, to see the confusion spreading as she read. The solemn thought came to me that nearly all advice must always seem impertinent and ludicrous, just because of this impossibility of knowing another's mind.

XXVI

D R FARLEY was going. The day had arrived at last. He had been in to say good-bye. The meeting had been a little embarrassing and hearty. Perhaps there had been too many smiles, too vigorous a handshake at the end; and he had left me with a schoolboy phrase which I still heard in my head, 'You needn't worry, I shan't let you down.' Why had he said it? Had I ever suspected that he would? Was I alone in thinking such protestations sinister? Would not most people take his remark simply as a reassurance of continued friendship? He had heard of my quarrel with my brother, knew that Matron was unwilling to let me go, and so he wished to tell me that I could be sure of him at least. That was all he meant. There was nothing more to it. And yet I could not quite rid myself of the idea that no man ever says, 'You can depend on me,' unless the thought of desertion has already entered his head. But what was 'desertion' in this case? Was I afraid that Dr Farley would have no more time for me? Would leave me to flounder alone with strange doctors and all the difficulties of returning to the outside world? I supposed that was what I meant. I could use the word 'desertion' to myself, cloudily; but to say it, or to envisage it spelt on the air, made it seem silly and extravagant.

The town was suddenly changed, as if some important landmark had been pulled down. The bicycles, the cars, the busy shoppers passed by, noticing nothing; but I could see the scarred site, the rubble dust blown about by the wind. Another picture came to me. I realized that, for me, Dr Farley had been a pea in a pod at the centre of the town.

As evening drew on, the wish to see the pod, the squat house, grew. I knew that there was nothing to see but an ugly little roughcast house with all its windows black and blind; but still the desire grew. It was useless to tell myself that I could make the dull journey very much better in imagination. Some compulsion was upon me and I felt I had to go.

It would be easy to slip out just as I was in my pyjamas and dressing-gown. If I stopped to dress, I would be tired before I had begun. I looked down at the civic robe which I had brought with me from my London room. I did not often wear it as a dressing-gown, but tonight I had put it on, perhaps because its crimson damask, gold braid and violet satin lining had suddenly caught my eye anew when I swung open the door of the wardrobe. The idea of going out in it amused me a little, but it did not seem so very strange. It was night; I did not expect to pass many people; I would soon be there and back again.

The grass in the garden soaked my thin slippers almost at once, and I was soon to discover that their looseness added seriously to my difficulties in walking, but I refused to take any notice. I would force myself down to the bottom of the gentle incline, see the house I had come out to see. I thought of my walking the year before. One day I had travelled thirty-five miles along the downs, dipping down at last into Midhurst, almost too tired to scramble up the stairs to my hotel bedroom. But how glorious it had been to be able to get so tired! To wake up the next morning deliciously achy! To indulge oneself by only walking a gentle eleven miles that day!

A lighted bus passed me and I thought, 'If only I could jump on that!' Then I remembered my crimson robe, and the fact that I had brought no money. I pushed my feet on. There was a damp, gritty film on the pavement. I hated the feel of it through my thin soles.

The little house was waiting for me; its senseless decoration of false beams jumping out from the whiteness of the gable. What could be more debased than those hooded, cramped windows? That hideous scatter of shingle over its whole surface? Yet for a moment my whole being seemed to play about it. It was a giant's skull, thrust up through the ground to stare and wink and goggle at me. It was a soiled box, filled with the ghosts of sights and sounds and smells. Its impassivity exasperated me. Waves of an ugly melancholy came out from it. It would impose its common joyless-ness, its dwarfish meanness.

I turned away, angry to have come all this way for a caprice. The house had done its work and I was very sad, so sad that my dragging steps seemed right and proper. The homeward journey was uphill, if one could call so gradual a slope 'uphill'; but it made a difference to me. People had passed, no doubt even stared at me, but I had drawn into myself and noticed very little. Now, at the worst moment of my journey, I heard a rasping catcall. I was under the weak glare of a street lamp; it illumined the crimson of my robe, catching gold threads in the braid. My head was down, and I was thinking of the sickness and despair of all street lamps, so at first I did not connect the catcall with myself. Then I heard murmuring, a man's and a woman's voice. They were on the other side of the street, but I refused to look at them. The man raised his voice and I heard quite clearly, 'What's 'e think 'e is? 'is 'oliness the Pope, or something?'

The woman gave a little giggle. I still betrayed no sign of being conscious of them. I knew that they longed for me to turn, to show alarm and confusion on my face. All at once I heard their footsteps pause. Out of the corner of my eye I thought I saw the man bend down and grope for something in the gutter. The next moment a stone hit the heavy folds at the back of my robe. I was not hurt, only consumed with a violence of hate that quite transformed me. My sadness and exhaustion were swallowed up. My one thought was, 'Go on! Go on! show nothing, not even a quiver. Only kill him in your heart over and over again. Kill all that contemptible male affectation of being bold and intolerant and humorous. Do not forget the humour – the great-hearted cockney richness of "'is 'oliness the Pope" with all the aitches almost self-consciously dropped in grand old music-hall style. Do not forget that manly catcall, either.' How long had he practised to make it quite so dashing and devil-may-care? My hate stripped him down to his pitiful grey underpants, then turned away from his secret dirts, the yellow-green pustules hiding coyly under the whiskers on his narrow chest, the unwashed staleness of groin and armpit, the black rot digging ever deeper in his broken teeth. How right that he should have his woman there to admire and applaud! To gaze on him with wonder.

I should have been grateful to the man for throwing the stone, for it got me home. Its flight seemed to continue in me, sweeping me on mercilessly. It would have been useless for my body to cry halt. It gave me strength, too, to suppress the night nurse when she came in and saw the soaking slippers by my bed.

'You've never been out in your night things! That grand robe and all!' she began, but my face silenced her exclamations. She was pugnaciously northern, and she probably already looked on me as almost foreign, and therefore unaccountable. Nevertheless she told Matron what she had seen. I had a visit after my bath the next morning.

'Well,' Matron said ominously, 'what about your escapade last night?'

'What do you mean?' I asked in mock surprise.

'Nurse Horrocks tells me she came in here last night, found your slippers dripping wet and you in your red gown lying on the bed dead beat.'

'Dead beat' was rather an unusual expression for any but a sporting woman to use, I thought irrelevantly. I had sparred so much with Matron that there was hardly any heart left in the game. I waited for her next remark.

'What's going to happen if you go on like this?' she asked, opening her eyes wide. 'Wandering about in your pyjamas! Why, you might be taken up by the police. Anyone might give you in charge for a madman or –'

'Or what?' I asked sharply.

'Or – or somebody not responsible for his own actions.'

'Isn't that more or less the same thing?'

'Not quite,' said Matron professionally. 'But I tell you, you really ought to be careful. You can't go on playing fast and loose with us if you want to be treated as normal.'

'I shan't trouble you much longer, Matron,' I said in my politest voice. 'I shall be leaving very soon now.'

'Where are you going? Does your brother know?' She was like an angry bird, pecking at crumbs that she was afraid were not worth eating.

'Oh yes, he knows.' I almost sang my words.

'But where are you going? You haven't answered the first part yet.'

'I haven't quite decided yet, but, since you are so pressing, I think I shall try to find a little flat or cottage of my own.'

'At least you couldn't worry us all then. Nobody would have the responsibility of you. But how can you live alone in *your* condition?'

My condition seemed to be flung at me as something discreditable that I had made for myself.

'Perhaps I shall find someone to cook and keep house,' I said with an attempt at poisonous sweetness.

I was not to know how soon my words would come true; but first there was the visit of Dr Farley's senior partner, the doctor who had come to see me on my first evening at the nursing home. As soon as I saw his smiling abstracted face and wire-wool hair again I was transported to that crowded day when he had talked about the Church of England, told me of his new poem on Ethiopia, then, after the hastiest of examinations, had disappeared before there was any time for details and tiresome health questions. Now Matron had caught him on his way in and poured poison in his ear, for he began at once to say, 'What's this I hear about your wandering about half dressed?'

His smile broadened, his gaze focused on an even more distant peak. 'Don't be a fool,' he added with dreamy indifference, the smile still fixed as if it were screwed into position. Was he planning a new poem, this time on Egypt or Arabia? Perhaps he was thinking of the next religious conference at Canterbury or London or York. Quite suddenly he seemed to become more aware of me. He looked into my eyes and said, 'Would you like any bromide?'

Nothing had led up to the question, so it hung in the air, sounding madder and madder with every passing moment. It was like an absurd invitation to partake of a little light refreshment: 'A cup of tea? A little whisky? Some nice bromide? Yes? No?'

'But it's only for dogs who have fits,' I said, keeping up the air of fantasy, but also voicing a belief of my childhood.

'Oh no, it's for humans, too,' he reassured me. He seemed to want me to be really brave and try some. I would find that it was quite nice, yes, really and truly nice.

I began to feel angry; if this was what came of going out into the street in pyjamas, I must certainly never do it again.

'I don't think I'll have any now,' I said firmly. I wanted to add, 'I don't quite *fancy* it at the moment.' The word 'fancy' had just the right touch of cosy vulgarity and dottiness; but I couldn't bring it out. His age inhibited me, and I was frightened of something in his eyes. Perhaps it was the lack of all wish to understand. I had seen it before in the eyes of other people preoccupied with the affairs of their different churches. It was a kind of beaming hardness that appeared to be matter for self-congratulation.

Before he left he turned to me again and said, 'You're quite sure you won't have any? No? All right. Well' – he raised his hand, the sunny smile swelled, he seemed to disappear behind it – 'as I said before – don't be a fool!'

He had paused, popped the 'Don't be a fool' out roguishly, bobbishly, so that the underlying hardness was thrown into even higher relief. I felt buffeted by his complacence. To recover from its effects I walked up and down the room, as I might have done if I had banged into a wall. I realized for the first time that Dr Farley had not been mentioned once. It seemed strange. Perhaps he was in disgrace for daring to leave his senior partner. I imagined that it would not be difficult to displease that benign face. I wished for Dr Farley as one might wish for the comfort of one's own things in the dreariness of a strange bedroom at night. Listening to a poetaster's modest disclaimers of all merit, hearing of church matters, receiving kind suggestions of bromide, these seemed a poor exchange for Dr Farley's interest. Then, as I continued to think of Dr Farley, it began to be clear that something had revived in me the moment he had left. At first it had hardly breathed, being smothered under my sadness and agitation, but now I could feel it springing up. It was an old joy in being free from the strain of friendship. It lifted its head almost guiltily; for had I ever been burdened with kindness? Hadn't I rather accepted every crumb greedily and waited for more?

Relief was still very far from being my sensation. I felt lost at his going and eager to follow; but just for the moment I would try to recapture my old self-sufficiency. I would play with the idea of living alone like a hermit for ever.

My contentment grew with each day. It seemed that I had not been so untroubled for months. It was wonderful to be able to disregard doctor, matron, masseuse, nurse, and any stray visitor, with perfect good nature. No one about me meant anything to me, and so I could smile and be pleasant and nothing was drained away. I had a store of strength which nobody could pilfer. Although I waited with impatience to hear from Dr Farley, at the same time a voice kept saying, 'But wouldn't it be easier to stay here? To find a little place in the town or just outside? Wouldn't it be better to try to arrange everything for yourself than to go to a strange town where you know no one but Dr Farley? You don't want to have to depend on anyone.'

I was lying on the bed after lunch, my thoughts sharply divided in this way, when Nurse Goff came in and said, 'A visitor to see you – a Miss Wilberforce.'

'But I don't know a Miss Wilberforce,' I exclaimed, sitting up hurriedly and running my fingers through my tousled hair. Already I could hear footsteps in the passage. I steeled myself for some mysterious visitor. Excitement was growing. The ordinary explanations – a mistake – a friend of my aunt's unknown to me – were swept aside.

Someone in a fur cape and a little felt hat was standing in the doorway smiling enigmatically. To my tense, expectant eyes she looked like some embodiment of Winter. For completeness she should have worn skates and carried a muff. It was a moment before I realized that it was Miss Hellier who stood before me. We had not met since Clare and I called at her house to collect some of my things on our journey down to the coast. Her unfamiliar clothes, the strange name announced by Nurse Goff, had entirely bewildered me.

'Why do you think I was told that a Miss Wilberforce had come to see me?' I asked exuberantly, wanting to show my pleasure as well as my surprise.

'I gave her that name – you see, it was my great aunt's.' Again the sphinx's smile. 'I wanted to make you wonder who it could be.'

I had almost forgotten this inconsequent side of her nature. In the hospital, in the first days and weeks, when she brought me chicken essence and biscuits and sweets, the atmosphere had been too grim for tricks and games. She had been uncoloured then, just as an anxious person bringing titbits. But now I remembered earlier caprices. Once I had come back from the art school to find her dressed up in a suit of mine. It was Christmas-time and she wanted to give the other people in the house a surprise at dinner. Another time I came down very late from my room. I was lazy; I wanted to read and enjoy my breakfast slowly, instead of hurrying off to draw a plaster-cast or a plate of vegetables. Usually at this time Miss Hellier would have been busily making the beds, sucking the dirt out of the carpets with her deafening vacuum-cleaner, polishing the floors; but today she was reclining on the floor by the fire, her head against the seat of the arm-chair, a pile of books at her side. She looked up from her desultory reading and said, 'I don't think I shall do any work this morning; I don't feel like it. The rooms can just go hang.'

Such queenly indolence put my own paltry slackness to shame. I decided at once not to go near the art school till the afternoon . . .

I came back to the present and settled Miss Hellier in a chair by the fire.

She took off the fur cape and lost her mysteriousness. Her cheeks began to glow.

'Did you suddenly decide to come all this way to see me?' I asked, guessing that this also was a sudden whim.

'Yes, just like that. When I woke up this morning I had no idea I'd be coming, but I *am* glad I did. It's fine to see you looking so much better.'

'Let's go out to tea,' I said, jumping up restlessly. 'We can look at the antique shops and you might like a glimpse of the sea. We can get a bus just outside.'

I wanted to get away from the nursing home, to have a little outing with a friend in the old, almost forgotten way.

Over the tea-cups and soda bread talk began to flow freely. Miss Hellier buttered a chunky slice, stopped with it half-way to her mouth and said, 'My brother thinks I'm no good at all at running a guest house. He says I ought to be much more economical; but I don't want to be mingy and scraping, so he says I can go. You see, it's mostly his money that's sunk in the house.' She took a large bite and started to munch contentedly.

'But what's going to happen? What are you going to do?' I asked, quite taken aback by her lack of perturbation.

'I don't know; I haven't given it much thought. I've told him I'll be out by the end of the month when the new manageress arrives.' More munching of soda bread; this time with a dressing of blackcurrant jam. Miss Hellier had once told me that she was already twenty-two in the year when I was born; but now, as I glanced up quickly from my plate, I caught an expression of a little girl of nine. It was not only that she was eating her bread and jam with placid enjoyment. Her whole nature seemed becalmed as a child's often is. The short-sighted brown eyes gazed out unenquiringly. Any unusual happening, I felt, would be accepted without question, much as a child accepts the extraordinary tastes and antics of grown-ups. It would be difficult even to frighten her.

Thoughts began to race through my head. Since she was free and had no other plans, why shouldn't she come and keep house for me? Would she like that? Would I? I saw us both in a dark little country cottage, the sort I would never choose. Outside it was raining; drops came down the enormous chimney and hissed in the fire of green twigs. Through the streaming window-pane I could just make out a huddle of grey sheep under some wind-bitten trees. The clock in the kitchen struck three. I looked at Miss Hellier and smiled. She had passed the test. I had almost smelt the cosiness of that dreary afternoon. Aloud I said: 'I'm leaving the nursing home very soon now. If I can find a little cottage or a flat, would you like to come and look after me?'

The brown eyes turned slowly in my direction, but they fixed on some point far beyond, through the wall, through the street, out to sea.

'Of course, there is nothing I should like better in the world,' Miss Hellier said. Her expression did not change, unless a little disdain gathered round her mouth to protect her against the generosity of her words.

I was startled by their strength. They had really been meant. They put a burden on me to be something more than I was. I tried to make things lighter.

'Oh, good; you do like the idea? Then I'm going to begin looking for somewhere at once.'

Matron *would* be pleased to hear that I had already found someone to live with me. I enjoyed the thought of telling her in the morning. This first success, this willing sliding of Miss Hellier into one of the gaps in my scheme gave me great encouragement. I began to feel that it would not be so very extraordinary if I had my own way. Matron and my brother had made me imagine that I was fighting against great odds, perhaps rather ridiculously. Now, with Miss Hellier, everything became saner and tamer and much more possible. The one great objection, that I could not look after myself, had been swept away.

Over little coffee cakes and orange iced biscuits we began to discuss details.

'I can bring my own bed and the nice old table you found for me last year,' Miss Hellier said. 'I might even manage some pots and pans; but I mustn't take too much, or my brother will make a fuss.'

The excitement of planning and contriving was upon us. We sat over our empty cups until the whorish-looking waitress in her incongruously demure smock of flowered cretonne advanced on us threateningly and said, 'We are closing now.' She flapped down the bill with vicious relish. It might have been a *lettre de cachet* consigning us both to the Bastille for life.

Out in the street we pressed our noses to the window of a small antique shop which was still open. A bulky man pottered about under a naked electric light bulb. His head looked like a boulder balanced precariously on the top of a mountain. It was sad and ineffectual and a little trembling. I turned from him to his wares and saw amongst some rubbish on a five-shilling tray a little oval enamel box extremely badly broken. A large chip out of the lid broke the engraved inscription in half, showing the purple-brown copper underneath. Just because it was so broken it called to me. I said to Miss Hellier, 'Let's look round quickly before he closes.'

When I had the little box in my hands and was enjoying the refinements of its curve, its delicate eighteenth-century hinge and thumb-piece, I was a little nonplussed by the warmth of its inscription. The flowing script spelt out this couplet: *Accept this trifle from a friend, Whose love for thee will never end.* The triangular chip obliterated most of *never* and part of *for thee.* Somehow this tempered the lavishness of the sentiment and made me less shy at the thought of giving the box to Miss Hellier. On opening it I saw that the tiny mirror inside the lid had been cracked across and across. Some of the old silvering had withered, and one could see through to the minute space between the flat glass and the curve of the lid. Flakes and grains of silver fluttered about in this space like mysterious imprisoned insects. The dilapidation of the box was poignant. I had to rescue it from its degradation on the five-shilling tray.

Miss Hellier blinked when I asked her if she would like to have it. The idea seemed to take a moment to reach her consciousness; then she said, 'Oh yes, I *should!*' I handed her the little package. We were walking down a narrow alley to catch one glimpse of the sea before she went back to London. 'I like so much what's written on the top,' she added in her most unruffled, most detached voice. I felt angry with the words printed so long ago on the enamel. They should have had no power to please or to confuse any more; yet here they were, falsifying the spirit of my little present, pricking us both, if even so very slightly, with self-consciousness.

I left Miss Hellier at the corner near the station. My bus was approaching and our good-byes were hurried. She smiled up at me on the step and then waved. At that moment I think both of us felt a deep satisfaction. That morning neither of us had known what we were going to do; now we both had a plan to work out together.

I watched her cross the road and disappear into the mouth of the station. She was taking her happiness back to London. No one would guess what was hidden under that fur cape and snug felt hat. No one on the bus could guess what I was taking back to the nursing home.

Only afterwards did I realize that I had not told Miss Hellier where I intended to look for a place to live. Unconsciously I had been leaving the way open to stay, or to go to Dr Farley; and she in her dreamy acceptance had never questioned me. It was clear now that I could live alone with her.

XXVII

D R FARLEY'S letter, when it came, was a disappointment. It could hardly have been anything else; I had been waiting so long for it, expecting so much from it, just because it was my only source of outside help. He touched on the business of settling into the new house, told me that the other part of the town was the pleasanter. If I wanted to come, I should certainly look there and not in his section which was newer and grimmer and nearer the shunting yard. He went on to describe the loveliness of the surrounding country. I sighed when I came to this part. There was no renewed suggestion that I should live in his house. It was strange how we had both dismissed this idea almost as soon as he had mentioned it. Without a word on either side the suggestion had been allowed to melt into nothing; but I wished he had revived it in his letter. I felt that he should have done so. It seemed to me that I had the right to pass it over, not to take it very seriously, but that he, as the originator of the scheme, should at least repeat it if only to show that he meant it. 'But perhaps he didn't mean it,' I thought; 'perhaps it was just one of those things that people say weakly to please.'

I folded the letter again and slipped it back into the envelope. Instead of tearing it open I had slit it carefully with my scissors. The neat, workman-like writing stared back at me. I read the time on the postmark and tried to imagine the mid-Kent market-town with its squalid railway junction, its polluted river, and huddle of old houses along the high street. All the ground floors would be ruined with plate-glass windows and art lettering in chromium, jade green, or scarlet. The noise of heavy traffic would never cease. I tried to make the town as spoilt and degraded as possible, so that, if I should ever go there, I should not be too disillusioned. In the same way I told myself that Dr Farley's letter was dull and unhelpful and full of padding on the beauties of nature. If I stressed its defects strongly enough, I might then begin to feel that, after all, it was not quite so valueless and unworthy of being kept; for, from the first, in spite of my disappointment, I had determined not to tear it up.

Its very flatness made me practical and bustling all at once. 'Not much help there,' I told myself briskly, copying the manner of my preparatory school matron and the even earlier example of a Kindergarten mistress. I decided to go into the town at once and find an estate agent's office. I was filled with the extravagant hopes and fears that come when one decides to do a new thing. 'What are house agents like?' I wondered. 'Will they be rude if they think I am too young and have no money? Will they try to take advantage of my inexperience? Perhaps they will be easy. Perhaps they will find me just what I am looking for at just the right rent.'

I sat in the little office on a high bent-wood chair. All round me were the framed advertisements of building societies. They had such solid religious names; I might almost have been in a missionary's bedroom hung with illuminated Bible texts in Oxford frames. The clerk had gone into a back room to look for 'more particulars of properties that might suit you, sir'. There was no hint of irony in his politeness, but I felt that he was playing with me; or was it that I was playing with him? Something was wrong. My brother had added to the nervousness of inexperience by telling me that I could not yet sign a lease, 'or anything else for that matter', in my own name. Perhaps the clerk would suddenly ask me how old I was. My face would flush red as I hesitated, and he would show me the door. His lips would be tight. He might even mutter something about his time being wasted.

I looked at the two keys before me on the counter; both had dirty linen labels attached to them. A picture of orphans travelling by train with the address of their destination round their necks came to me. I called out as lightly as I could, 'Don't bother to find me anything else at the moment. I'll go to these two addresses first.'

I wanted to hurry out of the office before the clerk could reappear and ask any awkward questions, but I made myself wait and smile at him as he stood in the doorway. Then I was free, out in the street with the two keys jangling in my hand. They made a pleasant noise. I saw myself as a scarecrow hung with tinkling bits of glass in the middle of a lonely field.

I climbed on a bus, deciding to visit the house before the flat. We passed through the town and came to a district on the outskirts that I have never seen. New little houses, coupled together in twos, crawled up the side of a steep hill. The road was still rough and unmade. There was something monstrous about the long avenue of coupled pink brick boxes. I felt that I was climbing up between gigantic naked Siamese twins with eyes all over their bodies. I climbed slowly and patiently, telling myself that I should come to something better over the brow of the hill; but I knew really that I should not. I was only forcing myself to see what I had come out to see.

When at last I stood still outside the right address, my head reeled and I swayed a little. I sat down where I was on the pavement and stared at the bow window and steps up to the front door. It was the very place for a murder; it had the newness, the trashiness, the dinky lattice panes and the sundial in the garden. Its cramped minuteness would breed rage and terror as a trap does.

This notion was first only an idle fancy, but as I approached the house it grew in strength until I felt a little shiver of fear run through me. The sun and the rain and the sea wind had withered the beef-blood paint on the front door. I turned the key in the lock, but the wood was warped and I had to push hard before the door moved. It opened suddenly with a crack. I stood in the narrow hall with my eyes fixed on the cupboard under the stairs. I doubt if I could have looked inside. I pictured a human trunk, dressed in nothing but a ragged singlet, with great, crude, butcher's wounds where the head, the arms, the legs had been hacked off.

Walking as softly as I could, I passed into the front room. The boards were naked except for a sticky surround of dark stain. Soot had fallen down the chimney and lay about in little lumps. The words 'devil's-dung' came to me. I knew vaguely that they applied to some other substance, but they suited these droppings of soot. I was transported to the little blind well behind my bed in hospital where black mossy cushions had collected on every ridge. The varnished picture-rail held my gaze. My eyes followed it round and round the room unable to escape from its tyranny. I wondered numbly why I lingered in the fearful atmosphere. One glance had told me that the house was impossible, and yet I felt compelled to savour the meanness of each room. I spared myself only from opening the cupboards. There were several in the kitchen-scullery. I turned from them to the cracked concrete floor and the grease stains on the wall round the gas-stove. The air was still tainted with the faintest smells of meat-fat, onions and cabbage water. There was a view from this back window, a fine expanse of flimsy roofs and tousled gardens dipping down, then mounting to merge into the green country beyond. 'If I go upstairs,' I thought, 'I shall see even more'; but one glance through the open bathroom door drove me to the front of the house again. I had seen the red-brown stain from the dripping tap, and the ghastly stillness of the water-closet chain.

In the best bedroom misty autumn crocuses sprouted at each corner of the wall-paper. Last summer's flies lay on the window-sill, their tiny legs pointing straight up to heaven as if they had died praying. Below me the cement sundial emerged from the rank matted grass and pointed its metal claw at my face. Now was the time to leave, rapidly and silently, before any evil befell me. A superstitious fear took hold of me, driving out the melodrama of dismembered bodies, butchers' knives and blood stains on the floor. In contrast to my new imaginings these almost made me smile. There would always be some saving touch of burlesque about such violence.

With every step I wished myself down the stairs and out in the street. I could not run, I could only concentrate my whole being on this thought. My head and eyes were rigid, my hand stiff on the banisters. What safety there was seemed to depend on disturbing the air as little as possible. I longed to be on wheels so that I could glide swiftly without a movement of my own.

I had carelessly left the key in the front door and I entirely forgot it until I looked back and saw the crumpled label hanging down, like the tiny grey ghost of a criminal fluttering from a gibbet. I retraced my steps and snatched it out of the lock impatiently. I was already angry with myself for horrific imaginings, for teasing thoughts out to their end with such silly persistence. It was almost as if I could no longer leave slight hopes and fears and pleasures alone. I had to build them up until their swollen shapes suddenly confronted me in all their absurdity.

I became very matter-of-fact. My anger turned against the clerk for sending me to such an unsuitable house. It had none of the things I had wanted. But then, what had I asked for? Just a very small house or flat, 'the plainer the better'. By this I had meant him to understand that I was not fond of tarry beams or anything too quaintly Tudor. He must have imagined that the pink brick semi-detached box would be perfect for me. Already my thoughts fixed on the flat. Whatever it was like, it could be no worse than the house. In spite of my tiredness I decided that I must see it before going back to the nursing home. In the shaking bus I held myself taut; it was as if I were afraid of being disintegrated by the vibration. I floated above the sights and noises of the town in an almost pleasant daze.

It was fortunate that the flat was on the front, only a short distance from the bus-stop. A sharp wind from the sea swirled between the buildings, refreshing and heartening me. I was back in the part of the town that I knew. The tall, ill-kept, grey stuccoed houses were as sullen as children's nurses who will not let their charges see their true protectiveness. I was glad when the label on my key led me up to one of these. In spite of the cold, the front door was open. I saw the coloured tiles in the hall, and then I heard the humming, wiry tinkle of a distant piano. The notes swam down the stairs, then drowned; but not before a tiny watery echo had been woken in each tile – or so it seemed to me. Walking over the squeaking, chirruping tiles I reached the stairs and climbed to the first floor, where I found that my key fitted into the lock of a new partition. I was in a black little contrived lobby. The biggest door was to my right. I pushed it open and found myself in the old drawing-room of the house. A great bay-window filled it with cold light from the sea. Someone, perhaps as long ago as King Edward's reign, had made the walls grand with a thick paper imitating silvery watered-silk and satin ribbon. The white overmantel was a cluster of minute balconies, balustrades, and arched recesses filled with looking-glass. The thinnest film of greenish-grey lay over all the sparkling surfaces of silver and white, so that I was reminded of pale lichen on a roof. It was easy to imagine myself living in the lichen-coloured room looking out to sea. I could even accept the tortured overmantel. Paleness and the patina of dust and age had robbed ugliness of its punch.

There was little more to the flat, a smaller, darker back room, a doll's kitchen and bathroom with match-boarding between.

'We could live here,' I thought; 'it would be easy for Miss Hellier, and I have grown to like eating and sleeping, writing, painting, reading all in the same room. I would like to watch the hopeless sea. Even that far-away piano dropping its sad notes doesn't seem threatening today. Perhaps in the summer I shall be maddened by the crowds on the esplanade, maddened by wirelesses and other noises, but why think of that now? I have to decide, not find rather fanciful reasons for not deciding.'

I was about to go back to the agent and tell him at once that I would have the flat. The fear came to me that at that very moment someone else was planning to take it over my head. Hurriedly glancing round the old drawing-room for the last time, I placed my few pieces of furniture in the most suitable places, put myself on the rug by the fire with all my things about me. But there was something wrong. I tried to think what it was. Had I not achieved my plan?

It came to me almost with the shock of discovery! 'But how could you ever be happy here, in the hands of strange doctors who will treat you as so much meat and bone, no longer in the best condition? How will you bear their impatient eyes which seem to blame you for having had so troublesome a misfortune? What could have deceived you into thinking that you wanted to stay here, alone in this town? It has all been a pretence, a device to cheat yourself. From the very first you have intended to be within reach of Dr Farley. He is the only friend who can be of any help to you. You do not like to think that you depend on anyone, that you even have need of anything outside yourself; but what are you alone at this moment? – a fluttering rag, a hollow stone, a scurry of brittle leaves, something paltry and used up.'

The sudden need for reassurance was so great that I did not even begin to ask myself what I meant by 'help'. I dared not question Dr Farley's power of giving it. I must stop doubting or my last drops of strength would trickle away. Like an enormous candle-snuffer the conviction that I must leave the town came down on me. I let it shut me in, glad at last to be cut off from every other sight, I would hold to my decision blindly. Blindness and darkness were my friends.

XXVIII

I BEGAN to look up the times of trains. I had already written to Dr Farley to say that I should be coming for the day. Miss Hellier was meeting me at his house and we would hunt together for a cottage or a flat. To make these dull arrangements calmed me. Ordinarily I would have found excuses for not telephoning Miss Hellier; I might not even have written to Dr Farley, and certainly I would have consulted no time-table; but now each tedious little action added to my sense of purpose. It was another brick for my new life. As yet I hardly knew what I was building. I only took pleasure in making small decisions and holding to them stubbornly. Matron, when she saw my set expression, seemed to surrender her last hopes of keeping me.

'You oughtn't to travel alone,' she said lugubriously, with all her old insistence gone. 'Someone should certainly go with you.'

I waited for her to suggest herself or Nurse Goff; but she had not even the heart for this pretence. She knew that I would take no notice of her. Ever since my return from the silvery flat on the esplanade she had seemed curiously impotent. My sudden obstinate determination had the effect of draining form and colour from her; and my brother, far away at the end of a telephone wire in London, retained no more reality than a ghostly, half-remembered figure in some story. I wondered why I had ever thought either of them formidable. To plan my own future seemed easy, simplicity itself. It need cost me nothing more than the price of a railway ticket to Dr Farley.

Yet when at last I stood on the platform waiting for the train, Matron's words returned to add to my disquiet. 'She is quite right,' I thought; 'I am not really fit to go alone. The thought of the long day frightens me. I must find a compartment to myself, then I can lie down on the seat, and if I am suddenly taken ill no one will know; I could even die there quite quietly.' I saw myself falling to sleep on the dingy tapestry and not waking up again. I held to the peaceful thought. 'Be still,' I told myself. 'Speed through the fields and woods. Feel the wind on your face. Be dead.'

At Ashford I had to change trains. I was used to my journey now. By keeping my face quite rigid I had induced a sort of artificial calm. 'Inscrutable, sphinx-like, poker face. Imperturbable, stoical, Egyptian mummy.' A chain of words, all holding some suggestion of immobility, flowed out of me. I walked to the rhythm of my incantation. Noise and crowds and squalor had little power to touch me. I felt protected by my discipline.

The new train bore me through a deep cutting in some hill. I looked up and saw scrubby gorse bushes far away at the top of the neatly sliced banks. As I looked, they seemed to stretch up jerkily to the sky. The earth was mounting and soaring all round me. I felt exhilarated by the illusion. If inert things were not chained down, how could not I rise and flow!

I thought of the train as a jointed steel worm. I was a tiny insect in the worm's stomach. The worm was devouring its way into the heart of the land. We had left the bent trees, the whistling grass, the flat fields with chalky dykes. Everything was growing richer; but it was a winter richness of scrubbed silver boughs, glowing rain-washed bricks and hedges clean as skeletons. I remembered Dr Farley's letter with its praises of the country-side. I thought of him looking at the fields and the woods and saying with great heaviness of heart, 'Yes, it is beautiful.' Why would his eyes be uneasy? Why would he be weighed down with a sense of futility? Perhaps I was quite wrong. Perhaps I was giving him feelings that he had never experienced; but I could not rid myself of the mournful picture of him.

I looked out of the window, knowing that I had almost reached my destination. We were in a shallow valley. The low hills round about were no more than bulging sides to a misshapen saucer. Smoke and mist hovered in the saucer melting the buildings of the town together. Only a church spire, a small factory chimney and a green gasometer pierced through the wispy pancake. The inexorable, inhuman rails were bearing me under that pancake. They were shining stilettos stabbing into the future. This thought that had come to me first on the bridge outside the nursing home returned now with vividness. I was a drop of blood about to fall from the tips of the daggers.

I had expected that I would have to find my way to Dr Farley's house alone, so I looked at the crowd on the platform with only the shallowest interest. I refused to be caught by a look or a movement that would disturb my calm. But something familiar suddenly jumped out from the strange faces and hats – a narrow little collar of astrakhan and a black cap to match. Miss Hellier was there, waiting for me, worried because she could not see me. I had never watched her unobserved before. She looked different, more vulnerable, as if her dreaminess were breaking up. For the first time I noticed that her dark brown, unpenetrating eyes bore a curious surface like-ness to Dr Farley's. It was a little bewildering that similar eyes should belong to such different characters. I puzzled a moment before accepting them and warming to her wholeheartedly.

It was good to see her face gladden when she caught sight of me. The tension in me lessened; I was with a friend, and so my behaviour no longer mattered half so much. If I walked very slowly, if I had to sit down on a public bench, her presence was a barricade between me and the world. We could joke about my state, even feel snug about it in some mysterious way. Her smile turned her cheeks into two little pin-cushions, mauvish because of the cold. I thought it absurd that I had no name but Miss Hellier for her. It seemed as impossibly formal as Dr Farley; yet Christian names would have seemed too coy. I was condemned to call them nothing to their faces. As if she knew that my thoughts had strayed to Dr Farley, Miss Hellier said: 'Isn't Dr Farley nice! I've just come from there. I caught an early train from London and found the house quite easily; then I thought I'd come down to meet you. I knew there wouldn't be long to wait. Dr Farley's very busy, of course; but we've both been asked back to tea. I said we'd do our house-hunting first.'

To have made any plans for the day was unlike Miss Hellier. I guessed that Dr Farley or his wife had put forward a few gentle suggestions. I was quick to feel that we were not altogether welcome – much too quick, I told myself, trying to retain my precarious calm.

'Well, let's go down the high street at once and find an agent,' I said briskly.

As soon as we were out of the station I began to remember parts of the town. I had never stopped in it, but the friend who had taken me out on half-terms at my preparatory school had often driven me through it to her converted oast-house under the North Downs. These exciting, miserable journeys came back to me. I was torn again between joy in the day before me and despair at the thought of returning at night. The roast chicken, the bread sauce, the tiny sausages and bacon stuck in my throat again, and I could hardly get through the trifle. The dingy black beams crowded down on my head. The rain beat against the cottage window in its deep embrasure of rough stone. I hugged the racing minutes to me desperately . . .

Miss Hellier was saying, 'There's an agent on each side of the road; which do you like best, "Roberts and Holden", or "Clement Lyly and Son"?'

'Clement Lyly's more peculiar,' I said, as if this were reason enough for choosing him. I was still absent, away in my world of eight or nine years ago. I let Miss Hellier do the work. Clement Lyly and his office held nothing new for me now; I had already braved a house agent.

Miss Hellier was vague; those soft brown eyes left the man's face, travelled round the walls and came to rest on me.

'What do you think we want?' she asked. 'A sort of little country cottage near the town would be best, wouldn't it?'

I agreed, adding something about a small garden and a quiet position. I felt that I should soon be talking the language of the orders to view. 'All main services', 'desirable', 'secluded', 'well-stocked kitchen garden' crouched on my lips, ready to spring.

We were only given one address in the country and we decided to go there first. The agent explained that we could catch a bus to the 'delightful old world village' in a few minutes' time. If we missed it, there would be a wait of over an hour. Gathering up our papers we hurried out into the street. He came to his doorway and encouraged us by smiling and pointing to the plainly marked halt. It came to me that finding a house was a silly, fretting business instead of the adventure I had imagined.

I tried to enjoy the short bus ride, but already my body was beginning to tire and I had little hope that Catherine Cottage would be better than its name. I saw 'Catherine' as one of those vaguely Early Victorian women, depicted on tea-cosies or calendars, the sort in lace pantalets and a sunbonnet. She would carry a posturing little basket tied with a bow. Her sloppy untruth contaminated me. I could see her peeping winsomely out of the diamond panes.

This distressing picture was so vivid that my spirits rose extravagantly when I looked across a pleasant village green and saw a little tile-hung house amongst apple trees. There seemed to be nothing fancy about it; indeed dullness rather than affectation would have been its fault, if one were looking for perfection. But I was determined not to be over critical. I longed to settle somewhere soon, to stop this searching and uncertainty. I refused to take any notice of the walk across the green; 'It's nothing,' I told myself obstinately. Even Miss Hellier caught some of my hope.

'Oh, it's nice!' she said with sudden animation. 'I really think it might do for us, Pusky, don't you?'

All my thoughts were fixed on walking, so I hardly noticed the odd name until she put her hand up to her mouth and added, 'How absurd of me! I've called you by one of the pet names I used for my cats. I hope you don't mind.' She gave a tinkling little laugh, artificial and yet childlike because spontaneous. I still did not quite take in the situation. Dimly I felt that I was going to be called Pusky for evermore. I wondered if I minded. Would it sound very ridiculous to other people? Then I started to worry about the spelling; should it have one 's' or two? The question churned over and over, until, in despair, I chose one 's'. It was written on the air before my eyes, I solemnly made myself prefer it to the, perhaps, more correct two.

We were on the rough little path between the apple trees. Overgrown herbaceous borders reminded me of a beggar's matted hair. Hard patches of earth underneath were scabs on his scalp. I went up to the old green rain-water butt and leant against it, resting my legs a little by putting my elbows on the lid and supporting my head. For a moment I kept my eyes almost shut, then curiosity won over tiredness and I opened them wide. From my position, with my head on one side, I could see straight into one of the rooms; a window in another wall lighted objects within – great imitation leather easy chairs grouped on either side of a brick fireplace, with a stained oak tea-trolley between. The bulging chairs seemed to fill the room, leaving only a narrow passage round the walls.

It was an instant before I realized what was wrong, then I exclaimed to myself, 'But it's not supposed to be furnished. Why are these ugly things here?' We had been told to ask for the key at the next cottage, but now, with this furniture blocking the interior, there seemed to be no point in going for it. I could even see parts of a thick dirty fawn carpet and the rising sun in fretwork on the front of the wireless box. I thought clearly enough,

'These things are probably only stored here. If they do go with the house, one could ask the owner to take them away.' But even as I thought, another part of me felt that the task would be impossible. Before I could get rid of them it was as if I myself would have to carry them on my own back.

Miss Hellier came round the corner from the back of the house where she had been peering into the kitchen and the old wash-house.

'It isn't bad,' she said. 'But there are all sorts of things about – pots and pans and a kitchen table.'

'Yes,' I said dejectedly; 'you should see the chairs in this room. Is that stuff called –? It looks as if it ought to be. I suppose the agent made a mistake and this place is really to be let furnished; I haven't read through the order to view yet.'

I opened the sheet of pink paper in my hand.

'But we know the rent's quite reasonable,' said Miss Hellier. 'Why not weed out the worst things, put them in the wash-house or get the owner to store them, then keep the useful ones. Between us we haven't much, you know, for a whole house, however small. You've only enough for your own room, and I can't bring a lot; my brother wouldn't let me.'

How practical Miss Hellier was being today! And how useless her suggestion seemed! A sense of powerlessness had seized on me, turning even the simplest decision or arrangement into something far beyond my strength.

'It looks so hideous inside,' I said weakly; 'and, whenever I'm ill, it would be so far for Dr Farley to come.'

I brightened a little, feeling that here was a real excuse for not taking the place.

'But you're not going to be ill; you're going to get better and better and better.'

Miss Hellier's eyes were gazing into the sky, as if she would pierce the clouds to discover the faint daytime moon. I was impatient now with her dreaminess. How easy to tell *someone else* that he would get better and better and better!

'Well, I don't think it's any good, but you get the key if you want to look upstairs.'

I was decisive, cold, unhelpful. Miss Hellier wavered for a moment, made uncertain by my withdrawal, then she said, 'I can see you're quite set against the place, so there isn't any sense in going for the key.' She was a little disappointed, a little relieved, swayed by me and yet grumbling at my lack of interest.

With one last look I turned away and began to walk down the path. I was thinking of that stained oak furniture and those dirty, cosy carpets and curtains, filling the house to the very attics. They watched and waited, watched and waited, preserving a suffocating calm. Each object held its breath, magnetizing the dust, charming every mote into settling; not even a tremor, a tickle, a wriggle of the skin through endless days and nights. I wondered again how furnishings were able to express this patient, silent, guardian quality. I had always known of it, and how many thousands of other people knew it, too? Yet always in an empty house the transformation of the deserted tables and chairs into dumb, enduring sentinels was surprising, rather magical.

It was gratifying that Miss Hellier took little steps and almost seemed to trot beside me, in spite of my slowness. Sometimes she paused, looked backwards or sideways, then skipped to catch me up; this probably caused the illusion.

'Let's buy something at the village shop, then have a sort of winter picnic on the green or even in the church,' I said, longing to sit down and be refreshed.

'Oh! But I've brought biscuits and cheese and chocolate with me in my bag,' explained Miss Hellier.

'You've thought of everything. Shall we climb up to the church then? It isn't far, and we might get cold on the green.'

Miss Hellier seemed a little doubtful.

'I never think it's wrong to eat in churches, do you?' I asked. 'That is, of course, if you don't drop crumbs. I rather enjoy munching in the semi-darkness; it soothes me.'

'God wouldn't mind,' said Miss Hellier certainly; 'but what about the vicar?'

We compromised by sitting in the church porch, close to the propped-up bier. Parish notices, fixed with rusty drawing-pins, fluttered near us. I felt a thread of my tweed catch in the beetle-eaten oak bench. The bulging, flaking plaster wall left its mark on our backs. Miss Hellier spread out digestive biscuits, pink processed cheese and a chocolate nut bar on her knees.

Each foodstuff sat on its wrapping of grease-proof paper, offering up itself to our hunger. I lay back in a corner, tucked my feet up on the bench and ate as I gazed out over the tombstones to the green and the hills beyond. Our strange refuge, the cold air made the tastes delicious. I knew that a glimpse of weather-tiling through the trees was Catherine's Cottage, a glimpse of white was the corner of the cricket pavilion. It seemed foolish to give up this pleasant scene just because of some leatherette chairs and a dirty carpet. I knew that I was afraid to make a decision, and tamely I upbraided myself; yet still I waited for something to push me in the right direction. I refused to be entirely responsible for the step I wished to take. Quite suddenly I wished for Dr Farley; he could advise me. If he thought Catherine's Cottage would do well, I would settle there and stifle all my misgivings. The unreason of letting another decide about things that I could only decide for myself appealed to me. If the arrangement turned out badly, I need not put all the blame on myself. I should be happier, freer, because blame would be lessened altogether; for in my inconsistency I knew that Dr Farley could not really be expected to make the right choice for me, therefore I would not seriously be able to blame him for making a mistake.

When my thinking reached its cloudiest, muddiest depths, an obstinate little voice broke through and said, 'You are stupid about this situation and think you want outside help because it doesn't interest you enough. Just be obstinate like me and say, No, no, no, till you get what you want.' This gave me some sort of peace and, although the moment before I had wanted to go straight back to ask Dr Farley's opinion, I was now content to see Miss Hellier wander off into the churchyard and lose herself behind some trees.

It was long before she returned, or rather before I heard her voice again. I had gone to read an altar tombstone under the tower and was bending over it when 'Pusky' came floating down to me from the sky. I looked up and saw Miss Hellier leaning over the battlements. Her smiling pink face was isolated, far away, like a wax face on a pole above a model of old London Bridge. The smile broadened and she looked like a well-fed pink cat waving a forepaw complacently.

'You're the one who should be called Pusky,' I said, but I spoke half to myself and my voice did not carry. Surprisingly her words came down to me with booming emphasis: 'I found a little door and I've been climbing, climbing for the last ten minutes I should think.' She seemed delighted with herself for finding the door and climbing the tower; it had been a little adventure which would make her remember the day. Suddenly the pleased expression dropped from her face. 'The bus,' she exclaimed; 'it's just coming in. We must catch it, or we'll have to wait another hour.'

Leaving her to race down the stairs and catch me up, I thrust the remains of the picnic into my pocket and made for the green. The bus stood placidly enough at the side of the road, with one or two people gossiping at the door, but the driver had not left his seat, and so I hurried, afraid that at any moment he would start the engine. I heard the patter of Miss Hellier's feet behind me.

'We'll do it, we'll do it,' she called gaily, filled with some sporting feeling; but I was too strained to respond to her girl-guide exuberance. I reached the bus, sank down in a back seat and clung on to my discomfort. It was as if I had to take hold of it, accept it, before it would even begin to melt away. To have ignored it by talking or looking out of the window would have made it grow harder and harder and more nagging.

The bus left us at the end of Dr Farley's road and Miss Hellier led the way.

'There it is,' she said brightly; 'that house on the corner, just by the pillar-box.'

I looked up the wide, bald road. This indeed was the ugliest part of the town. The ugliness lay not so much in the mid-nineteenth-century houses themselves as in their general air of being uncherished. The gardens were rough, the window-frames dulled and withered; but perhaps the saddest thing of all about the street was that no house was really neglected; all were respectable. I saw the large brass plate of a secretarial college, the smaller ones of a woman doctor and a solicitor. These gave me such a feeling of busy joylessness that my tiredness seemed to double itself and I wondered if I had energy enough to reach the corner where the pillar-box stood. The visit that had occupied my thoughts for weeks now suddenly lost nearly all its glow. The thought came back to me that Dr Farley would not be truly pleased to see me, that his wife would dispense a duty tea to weary house-hunters. Well, I would be just that, I told myself vindictively; I would be a weary, dusty house-hunter noticing nothing, showing no spark of interest. I would drink my tea and smile rapidly from time to time. It would have been difficult for me to point out who was to suffer most from this behaviour; I merely nursed a vague resentful wish to add to the dreariness which I felt was waiting for me.

In spite of my self-communings I could see that the road was very gradually changing its character. Not only were the houses a little later in date but their condition was improving by degrees, until Dr Farley's on the corner stood out in all the brilliance of new white paint and tightly clipped hedges. His house was certainly the queen of the street; it even outshone the newly roughcast public house which bristled hideously a little farther up the hill. Some of my assumed apathy fell from me and I stood still, taking in its details for several moments – the cast-iron verandah, the curious cement dressings round the windows, the ornamental spikes along the roof. Miss Hellier waited at my side, not breaking in on my thoughts but showing in some way that she expected me to cross the road and ring the bell.

I had expected the little girl maid to open the door to us, but instead a bulky old woman peered out, breathing heavily. It seemed to be difficult for her to see or to understand us properly; this, however, did not prevent her from letting us into the hall and leaving us there. I heard a movement behind a door on the left and Mrs Farley came out to our help. She led us back with her into a long, narrow room, where the walls were putty yellow. The discreetly glossy paint rose to the ceiling, covering the elaborate plaster cornice, thus giving the room loftiness and a rather suspect dignity. Opposite the fireplace was a reproduction of a seascape in a silvered frame, and all the coloured books that I remembered were now in low cream shelves, making a sort of cosy barricade along two outer walls. The dog's basket was in the bow-window; but even this seemed changed into something fresher and more ambitious. Mrs Farley was still busy with household tasks; as soon as we were seated she picked up a long piece of soft brown felt and started to stitch.

'The trouble with polished floors,' she said regretfully, 'is that they need such a lot of living up to, so I've decided to make felt surrounds to the carpets in some of the rooms.'

Miss Hellier, who was, I supposed, expected to give some suitably domestic reply to this remark, said nothing. She was far away, smiling her tabby-cat's smile and making a little clicking, picking noise with her fingers. I tried to fill the gap by saying, 'But isn't felt more difficult to keep clean than bare wood?'

'Not really; you see, you only have to run the vacuum-cleaner over it, whereas boards have to be waxed and polished constantly.'

I found myself worrying about all the dust and mud and other dirt that a floor-covering would collect, just in one day. I felt that no cleaner, however good, would rid it entirely of this accumulation. Our fashion of smothering floors in wool and not taking our shoes off in the house struck me at that moment as particularly disgusting. I knew that Mrs Farley's floors, or indeed any other floors, were not my present concern; but I found it impossible to get them out of my mind, perhaps because I was afraid that there would then be nothing else to think or talk about.

'Did you see anything you liked?' Mrs Farley asked, turning the conversation to her guests' interests.

'We only went to one place,' said Miss Hellier, suddenly coming to life. She spoke as if we had been vaguely to blame for visiting no more. She seemed to be continuing a reverie aloud.

'It was called Catherine's Cottage and it was quite pretty with apple trees and a water-butt; but Pusky set himself against it because it was full of bulgy chairs and things. I told him we might need some of them and the rest could easily be stored, but he wouldn't listen. He always has his own ideas and you can't move them.'

She gave her unrelated laugh, which might so easily have sounded a little mad to a stranger. I looked quickly at Mrs Farley, but her face was blank, as if she were refusing to show surprise at the laugh, the odd nickname, or even at the curious understanding which seemed to exist so unexpectedly between Miss Hellier and myself.

'Dick will be in any moment now,' she said brightly; 'then we'll have tea. This new practice keeps him so terribly busy that I very rarely see him in the day-time, except at lunch; but he'll make a point of being back this afternoon because he knows you're here.'

'I do hope we aren't interfering with his work,' I said, hardly knowing myself if I intended sarcasm or sincerity. The Aberdeen scratched to be let in, and Miss Hellier, as soon as she saw him, clasped her hands in delight.

'What a lovely boy!' she exclaimed, bending down at once to play. She began to treat him like a doll, trying to sit him up, hugging him round the stomach unfeelingly, cradling him in her arms as if she would rock him to sleep.

I felt able to lean back and rest a little. Mrs Farley's use of her husband's Christian name made my thoughts return to that subject. Miss Hellier had already called me 'Pusky' in front of another person – she would soon almost forget my real, unridiculous name; but could I ever bring myself to say Keziah? Why was it that she had such a name, so full, as it seemed to me, of Old Testament thunder? My mind flashed back to her father, who had been at Croom's Hill when I first went to live there. He was dead now, but his image returned to me vividly. I saw the square goatee, the old camel-hair dressing-gown and the curious little cap that he wore indoors. His nose curved down, as if trying to reach the out-jutting beard. He was tiny, with deepest little sparrow's eyes, now darting shrewdly, now alarmed, now crazily intent, like any other enthusiast's eyes. I would see him going down to the old basement kitchen which was his living-room. It had broad stone flags, a table round a central pillar, curving shelves round a deep bow, and, against the opposite wall, a still earlier dresser, with legs like crude Tuscan columns. He would go to a corner of this bluntly elegant old kitchen and begin to unwrap some tall broad object. He would seem to be unswathing the mummy of an enormously fat person. Old blankets and ragged shawls fell to the stone floor; there was a glint of gold, then the whole shape of a sphinx crowned a magnificent harp. He would sit down at the great instrument and pretend to be tuning it. The frown of an expert would cross his face as he bent his ear to one of the vibrating strings. All at once, without warning, such a caterwauling and twanging, such a howling and yowling and whining of plucked strings broke out that, to a stranger listening, the most likely explanation would have been some gruesome accident in the basement. But no; it was only old Mr Hellier accompanying his own impassioned improvisations. He had no need of training in the art of playing harp or singing. What did it matter if all the strings were tightened or loosened capriciously? If his voice cracked and screeched and rasped? All that mattered was that he should create wild hymns for the God of the Plymouth Brethren. It was easy to see now why Miss Hellier was called Keziah.

I remembered other incidents. Once, on my way down to breakfast, I had met him on the stairs. As I made to pass I was aware that his little body tingled with excitement. Suddenly he jumped in front of me and said: 'Rejoice! Rejoice! Today you *must* rejoice.' Without an instant's hesitation

I heard myself replying, 'Oh, but I *do*.' I passed on, wondering where the words had come from; there had seemed to be no time for thought.

I was still saying to myself, 'Rejoice! Rejoice! Today you must rejoice,' when voices in the hall drew me back to my present surroundings. I knew that Dr Farley had arrived, but in the tense moment before he came into the room I felt more anxiety than pleasure. It had suddenly become an ordeal to be brought face to face again with the person I had been think-ing of for so long. To keep my mind from him I turned to Mrs Farley. Had she noticed my abstraction? What did she make of Miss Hellier's romp with the dog?

The door handle moved, and the next moment he was standing in the opening with the look of the street and of work and hurry still about him. It was as if he had come into the room by mistake, only to find one more obstruction to his plans waiting for him there. I watched him quickly drown the look in smiles. I felt almost cruel towards him. 'That's right, smile. Damn well smile,' I ground out to myself. To encourage him I assumed my widest grin. Miss Hellier simpered sweetly from the edge of her chair. Her quaint, genteel politeness always came as a surprise. She usually only showed this side of her nature to strangers at tea time. For the first few moments the air seemed to thicken about the three of us, fixing our metal-lic expressions, stiffening movements of hand and head, until we were as unreal as puppets; only Mrs Farley continued to sew unconcernedly.

Tea was brought in and matters mended a little. I held my cup so that the steam rose up into my eyes, soothing them, melting the outlines of things. The hot tea in my throat was a comfort that *had* to be enjoyed, just because it was so fleeting. Miss Hellier, still perched on the edge of her chair, had, nevertheless, relaxed in some way; I could see that her limbs were more supple. I knew how she loved tea. She seemed to prefer it stewed; some-times I had seen her collect all the tea-leaves of the day and reboil them in a saucepan for her night-cap.

Dr Farley stood with his back to the glowing electric panel inset between the bookshelves. From my low seat near him I had to look up at a sharp angle; but I was used to his standing. It occurred to me that I had only seen him sitting in his car, and on the sofa when he first asked me to tea. The remembrance of that happy earlier tea brought home to me the fullness of my present disappointment. Why had the day already taken on the colour of failure? Miss Hellier had been helpful and gay; the only house we had seen, if only I would admit it, was better than could have been expected. It was clear that my depression really dated from the moment when Miss Hellier told me that we were not to visit Dr Farley until tea time. After the effort of my journey I had expected some much warmer response. It was useless for me to tell myself that he had a great deal of work to do, that it was good of him even to spare time to come home for tea; I could not rid myself of the sense of having been passed over. And now, even when we were together, there was this absurd tea-party constraint. For an unreasoning instant I almost blamed him for the presence of his wife and Miss Hellier. Things should have been managed, I thought, smoulderingly, so that we could have had at least a few minutes alone in which to talk of what I was to do.

My impatience grew; I wished that Dr Farley and his wife would treat Miss Hellier with less wary politeness and show some real attention. It irritated me that they appeared to dismiss her from their minds before even discovering one of the vagaries of her character. Their lack of awareness was an affront. Were they really as uninterested as their faces made them out to be? And if so, what were we doing here, eating and drinking and trying to make small talk? An impulse to jump up and leave the house was killed at once by timidity, or common sense. I watched Dr Farley bend down to take another sandwich off the tray. His sense of strain, and the forced smiles that followed, had given place to his clowning, friendly schoolboy's manner. He made a funny face, opening his mouth wide, then cramming in the whole sandwich at once. I had to acknowledge that he had the art of being ridiculous without embarrassing others. Turning to his wife he said between munches, 'I wonder if these sandwiches are all right. Didn't you say this morning that there was something funny about the sardine and tomato paste?'

His wife looked up with icy seriousness.

'I said there was something funny about the jar; in other words, it was a jar of a different shape. There is, of course, nothing wrong with the paste.'

'Oh!' said Dr Farley, still sustaining his role of comic booby, but obviously dashed by the scorn in her voice. His jaws came together and the distortion gradually left the rest of his face, but his eyes were fixed on her, as though he saw her across a wide gulf of unshared feeling. For that moment at least she treated him as the simpleton he had pretended to be; and he was quite unprotected against her hard, feminine assurance. I wanted to call out, 'Don't be so dumb, so male, so slow.' How could I help him against her? For she was so strong, and I could not bear him to look small. If, just for this once, he could be given the quality I disliked so much, a quick maliciousness! In wishing to help the weak, the heart is so much engaged that the head is usually left free to go off and side with the enemy; so, now, I found myself thinking, 'She is right; it was fatuous of him to misunderstand her words and complain, however playfully, about the sandwiches.' But thinking this in no way made me forgive her flash of scorn; rather I held it against her that she had seized on a real chance for displaying it. I wanted to go now, ordinarily, not impulsively with sensation and clamour. There was nothing else to stay for; Dr Farley wanted to forget his little discomfiture and get back to work; Mrs Farley wanted to go on with her sewing undistracted. I held out one of the house agent's orders.

'Have you any idea where this house is in the town?'

Dr Farley looked at the address and seized the opportunity at once.

'How odd! My first call after tea is just near there; I'll take you along with me and drop you.' He looked at his watch rather too emphatically. 'Well, much as I'd like to, I can't laze here any longer; I've left things rather late as it is.'

He made a business of straightening his tie and brushing invisible crumbs off his waistcoat. There was a moment in which I thought, 'You're not very good at escaping'; then the rest of us stood up and Mrs Farley held out her hand as if she had really enjoyed having us to tea; or did she look happier because we were going? It hardly seemed to matter any more. There was a wry sort of pleasure to be got out of exaggerating the deadness of the afternoon.

Miss Hellier climbed into the back of the car and I sat beside Dr Farley. I was intensely conscious of my first ride with him, when my legs had tingled so. The little blue car had brought some of the atmosphere of the sea to this inland town, but the car, and the air it imprisoned, seemed shabby here as if they were survivals from another time that had not worn well. It was suddenly brought home to me that, since his surroundings were so changed, I ought to accept some change in Dr Farley himself; but why did I not accept it? Why did I feel that his change was towards me in particular? He had seemed wary, anxious, preoccupied, as if wondering how best to withdraw his friendship. He had tried to begin the process as smoothly and imperceptibly as possible. 'But he isn't much good at escaping,' I thought again bitterly. I tried to correct my feelings. 'This is all silly egotism,' I told myself severely. 'He is overworked in this new job; he has not even a quarter of the spare time he used to have. How can you expect him to think of your visit as the one important moment of the day, when all morning he has been running from one patient to another? And how absurd to expect him to be at his best over tea with Miss Hellier and his wife! You yourself were probably painfully vapid. Don't add to his difficulties now by being aggrieved. He needs all the help he can get.' Another rush of feeling, such as I had experienced when Mrs Farley answered him bitingly, swept over me; I only wanted to be of use, to protect him from annoyances and troubles of every kind.

The car was slowing down in a gently sloping avenue of planes. The houses behind the trees looked clean and smug and tasteless. We were clearly in the newer, more residential part of the town.

'We must be very near it now,' said Dr Farley, recalling me abruptly to the business of house-hunting. I looked across the road and saw 'Kam-o-yen' in white lettering on the gate of an unexceptionable bungalow. Its walls and roof were of a reddish-brown. Its windows were plain metal casements.

'That's the place,' I said indifferently. 'Why do you think it's called "Kam-o-yen"? What can it mean?'

Dr Farley stopped the car. With the ready enthusiasm of the person who has not to think of living in the house, he turned to us both and exclaimed, 'It looks all right to me; it's small and neat. It'll probably suit you down to the ground.'

I was reluctant to get out of the car. My legs were very tired. I longed for Miss Hellier to inspect the house first, then give me her opinion. If she would do this, I could sit for a few more minutes and talk to Dr Farley alone. But the suggestion was not made. Dr Farley seemed to be wondering why I was not all eagerness to see the house.